Just Wait For Me

A Highland Gardens Novel
The 4th tale in the series.

Dawn Marie Hamilton

In memory of Lisa

ACKNOWLEDGMENTS

So many individuals helped bring this book to fruition. Too many to mention here, but you know who you are, and I hope know you have my heartfelt thanks.

Thank you to Cindy Davis for editorial guidance and thank you to Cathy MacRae and Cate Parke for critiques. Thank you to the very supportive Kimberley Court and Debbie McCreary. Words cannot convey how important you all are to me.

Thank you to Frank, my husband, best friend, and personal hero.

And most importantly, thank you to the readers of the Highland Gardens series.

.

PROLOGUE

9 September, 1513
Near the village of Branxton in northern England

The king is dead.

Anguish tore from her halfling soul with a fae scream that reverberated over the field of devastation like rolling thunder. Silence ensued. Men frozen in fear.

Caitrina dropped to her knees beside the redheaded warrior and ran gentle fingers along the bloodied curve of his handsome face. Damn Oonagh! Damn the Fae Queen! She'd refused to allow Caitrina to intervene in the politics of the mortals and prevent this tragedy.

Now, the king lay dead, fatally wounded by an arrow and a bill. Be damned the English and their nasty weapon—the bill, a staff mounted with a hooked chopping blade and pointed projections. The Scots hadn't stood a chance against the onslaught on the slippery, hilly terrain with their cumbersome pikes.

Heartbroken, she cradled the man to her breast. Such greatness lost. Tears spilled unchecked onto his precious face. Too late. Even the magic tears of a *Sithichean* princess

1

couldn't revive the king.

"Caitrina! Let us be away from here." The *brùnaidh*, the Maclachlan Clan brownie, fussed at her back. "We must remove Stephen from the field before the English learn he lives and plunge a bill into his chest."

She ignored the wee man. How would the Scots forge forward without their beloved king—with only a *bairn* and the sister of the despised English monarch to guide them?

"If we lose Stephen you will never regain your rightful place."

Aye. She must deal with Oonagh and the stupid matchmaking challenge. Caitrina released James from her embrace and eased him to the ground. "Sleep in peace, oh, greatest king."

The metallic tang of blood fouled the air. She rose and moved through the death and destruction. Oonagh had tricked her. Led her to believe after three matches she'd be free to return and live in *Tir-nan-Og*, the beloved faerie paradise, land o' heart's desire. But Oonagh had refused to reveal which match was the third and final. The one that would free Caitrina from servitude to the Fae Queen.

Caitrina and Munn had expended considerable energy on a third match only to learn Archibald and Isobell were the wrong couple. Therefore, one match remained to perform.

"Needs be we hurry!" Munn sidestepped one of the petrified English knights.

They found Stephen's prone form not far from that of his king. Caitrina rolled him over and took stock of his injuries. Thanks be to Danu, the blond warrior would live. She cloaked the three of them in fae mist and whisked them away on the fetid breeze to the healing caves of the Gray Women.

The battlefield returned to morbid activity—an agony of pain.

CHAPTER ONE

Present day
Greenbrier River Trail, West Virginia

"Rattlesnake!"

Jillian pedaled as fast as she could past autumn-tinted trees, to catch up to her brother, *the rat*. Why must he always speed ahead, leaving her in the dust?

"Kyle O'Donnell, did you hear me? I said...no, I screamed...*rattlesnake*."

As she rode the dusty mountain bike alongside, he slowed. "You overreact."

"Do not. There was a rattlesnake on the trail. What if the nasty snake bit me, and you were so far ahead you didn't know? The poison would surge through my system before help arrived."

Kyle chuckled. "That snake was more afraid of you than you of it. Relax."

Sure. The repulsive reptile hastily slithered away, but she wanted to make a point. "Why do you always dart ahead?"

"Because you're a slowpoke." He gave her a toothy grin. "Always wait for you to catch up. Don't I?"

Jillian gnashed her teeth. Why must he be so difficult?

After all, Kyle was the one who begged her to come on this stupid cycling trip. The least he could do was ride at her pace.

Who would have thought at twenty-eight, and as a co-owner of *Foxgloves*, a successful garden business, she still chased after her thirty-year-old sibling? She'd only agreed to join Kyle because she'd needed to get away. Away from all the happy-happy between Finn and Elspeth.

"Come on, the tunnel isn't far. Let's race." Her brother sped ahead again.

Jillian sighed and took her sweet time to catch up. Fifteen minutes later, she crossed the weathered train trestle and arrived at the spot where Kyle waited sporting an exasperated expression.

"Took you long enough."

Oh, how she wanted to kick him. Instead, she blew a kiss.

He brushed strands of annoyingly perfect sun-bleached blond hair out of disgustingly gorgeous chocolate eyes and laughed. "Let's take a break before we ride through the tunnel."

So not fair. He got all the good looks and all their parent's attention. Pah-lease. She was pathetic. Really. She needed to get over the past.

He studied her through narrowed eyes. "What's wrong with you lately?"

"Nothing." She shrugged a shoulder. "It's just…this trip is boring."

"Like teaching strangers how to put multiple plants into one big pot isn't?"

"It's container gardening. It's my job. It's creative." And a hell of a lot better than her help desk job had been.

"And this is your vacation, which you seem to need. Try chilling out."

Right. Easy for him to say.

While they munched trail mix, Jillian covertly glanced into the entrance of the abandoned train tunnel. Dim and ominous. Water trickled from fissures in the stone walls and ceiling. A damp breeze wafting from within brought a musty odor that drilled into her nostrils and sent a chill over her spine.

"Must we go through there? Couldn't we return to the last campsite? Enjoy the afternoon in the sun?"

"Don't you want to see what's on the other side?"

She stared into the dank tunnel. "Not really."

"Don't be a spoil sport. We haven't ridden enough miles today. I promise, after we go through the tunnel, we'll only ride another five. I heard there is a nice campground near a quaint town. Can you say *restaurant*?"

Jillian didn't want to go any farther, but there was no use arguing. She'd never get Kyle to turn back. They would ride all the way to the southern end of the trail as planned.

She righted her bike and walked toward the gloomy entrance. Clouds stole across the sun making it difficult to see anything within. Jillian shivered. The hairs on her arms stood on end. Something didn't feel right about this place.

"Ready?" Kyle asked.

"No."

"Come on, Jilly. It'll be fun."

A couple on a silver tandem bicycle rode from the tunnel, waving as they passed. Sunshine reappeared from the clouds.

"See? It's safe," Kyle said.

"All right. But I'm walking my bike through. Just wait for me on the other side."

Kyle pedaled off, popped a wheelie, and entered the odious opening. Jillian pulled a headlamp out of her pack, secured it over her baseball cap, and flicked it on. Inhaling deeply, she slowly walked her bike into the dark.

The beam of light bounced off brick walls and earthen floor. In the far distance, hazy sunlight indicated the other end of the tunnel. Okay, she could do this. There was nothing here to fear. She proceeded carefully, taking shallow breaths. About a quarter of the way through, rough rock replaced brick on the walls. A blast of super-cold air hit her side.

What the—

She shined the light into what appeared to be a deep well. Narrow and foreboding. She kicked a stone in and didn't hear it land. Suddenly, something pressed against her back. A hand? Her pulse spiked. Whoa! A dizzy sensation swamped her. She stumbled. Lost hold of the bike. Fell—or was she being pulled?

She tumbled into the mysterious opening. Falling forward, her body became weightless as she plummeted down...down...down...into a black void. A horrible buzzing assaulted her ears. She screamed, but no sound passed suddenly parched lips.

This shouldn't be happening. A piercing white light appeared, drawing her to it. What was there? Who was there? The light intensified. She closed burning eyes. No relief. Pain burst behind heavy lids, making her head throb relentlessly. Bile burned her throat. Just when the agony became too much to endure, the cruel light exploded into a zillion vibrant colors.

Fireworks in a July sky. Her mind blanked.

Panting, Jillian crouched, tips of fingers pressed against the ground for balance. The nauseous sensation gradually subsided and she attempted to stand. Vertigo forced her to her knees, and her stomach lurched again.

Breathe, Jillian. Breathe.

She inhaled deep breaths, trying to calm down. The queasiness finally passed and she sat against the rough trunk of a tree. Exhaustion tempted her to curl up and sleep. But she needed to hurry and catch up with...who? Yeah, yeah— Kyle.

Where was he? Where was she?

Jillian didn't recognize the surroundings. The towering evergreens were larger than any she'd seen before, heavy needles blocking a majority of the late afternoon light. The dense forest wasn't like any they'd cycled through on this trip.

She started to shake. This was no time to come unglued. She inhaled a deep, calming breath. Think, Jillian, analyze the situation. *How did you get here?* Her last memory was entering the train tunnel and falling. Had someone shoved her? She'd thought she felt the pressure of a hand on her back as she'd stumbled forward.

Strange. Who would have pushed her? They'd only seen the couple on the tandem, riding the other way. No other cyclists or hikers.

Why had Kyle deserted her? Why hadn't he returned? Shouted for her? Tried to find her?

Frowning, she removed one of the water bottles attached to her pack, took a long swig, and assessed the height of the sun. Would be dark soon. How much time had passed while she couldn't think straight? She scanned the area. Great. Her bike was missing and there was no sign of a trail.

Shit! Her cell phone was in one of the panniers on the bike. Not that it mattered. The damn device hadn't gotten a signal in a couple of days.

Nerves taut, she swallowed hard. There would be no submitting to fear. If she started walking, surely she'd come across a road or some such thing. *Right?*

Jillian trudged along until taking another step became next to impossible. Her feet hurt. Bike shoes were little protection against the rough, rocky terrain. The setting sun painted the sky shades of crimson, and she was lost. Completely and utterly lost, but she refused to panic. Hiking and camping was nothing new. There must be a safe place nearby to settle in for the night. Tomorrow, certainly, she'd find some sign of civilization.

Cripes. West Virginia seemed even more remote than she realized.

On a scree-covered slope, she spotted a protected area under an overhanging ledge. She scrambled up the incline, slipping and sliding, scraping knees and hands. Fleece cover-ups, a wind jacket, and a space blanket were in her pack. Pulling out the silver cloth, she laid it on the ground. She slipped into the fleece and zipped the jacket snug as the sun disappeared over the horizon. Jillian worried her lip. Already the temperature was dropping.

Wanting to save the batteries in the headlamp, she turned it off and ate a power bar in the dark. She wrapped the blanket tight, and used the pack as a pillow. "Hummmm. Hummm. Humm." When humming didn't ease the jitters, she made up silly stories as a distraction. An exceptionally sharp stone dug into her hip. "Ouch." She squirmed, trying to find a more comfortable position. Finally, exhaustion took hold and, despite the chill, she slept.

Thunder from a passing storm jolted her awake. The feeling someone watched skittered over raw nerves. She blinked, trying to adjust her vision to the dark. *Hu...hu-hooooo* an owl called from a distance. Other nighttime forest sounds heightened growing anxiety. She expected to see glowing animal eyes. *Were there wolves in West Virginia?* But no, it seemed she was alone.

Nervous and stiff, it took a while to fall asleep again only to startle awake before dawn. The storm had passed and a bright silver moon slid in and out of clouds creating shifting shadows. An odd disfiguration of bark on a nearby tree caught Jillian's attention. The scarred wood appeared as a young boy's face.

Staring hard at the tree, she smiled as the face changed in the moon's unpredictable light. Two distinctly different faces appeared within the rough bark. The first, a boy with a pudgy nose and big sad eyes, and the second—

She must be dehydrated. Delusional. Imagining faces embedded in a perfectly normal tree. Jillian huddled deeper into the cocoon of warmth the space blanket provided and tried to fall back to sleep. The forest's woodsy scent reminded her of how horribly lost she was, so sleep wouldn't come. She stared at the tree again. A third face appeared in the texture of the old oak. This one had a scarred forehead and a crooked mouth.

Such fanciful thoughts. She snorted. Alone in the woods and she was killing time imagining faces in a tree trunk. Sleep was what she needed. One, two, three, she counted plants on a potting bench in the greenhouse at *Foxgloves* instead of counting sheep—one hundred thirty-two, thirty-three, thirty-four...

Finally, Jillian dozed again.

When she woke a third time, a chill had seeped into her bones. She sat up and pulled the space blanket more snug. The tree looked different in the misty light of morning and another image appeared. This tiny face had an elongated nose and wisps of blond hair dangled across its brow. Jillian covered her mouth to stifle a giggle. She'd recently read a book about faeries and changelings and stolen children. She imagined that the hobgoblins lived in this tree. That stolen boys—

The snap of a branch made her jump. Her stomach knotted.

Standing before her was a gnarled little man. No more than three feet tall, he nearly blended into the surrounding woods. The peculiar clothes he wore matched the colors of the forest. And his dusty brown skin had wrinkles upon wrinkles. Elf-like ears stuck out from beneath a pointed cap. But what startled her most were the unusual blue-green eyes that bore into her.

The man reminded her of a sketch she'd seen while babysitting. Little Allison MacLachlan loved the story of *Rumpelstiltskin.*

Jillian clutched the space blanket in tight fists and gawked at the man. He stared back. Unnerving seconds passed in silence. Abruptly, the strange fellow lunged forward and yanked on the blanket, almost snatching it away.

"What do you think you're doing? Leave my blanket alone." She rose into a crouch, holding tight to the silver cloth while he continued to tug. When the man let go, Jillian fell backward onto her rump. "Dammit."

His eyes narrowed. "Be you a witch?"

"What?" She shook her head. "Of course not."

He circled around. "Then who are you to have spun such a plaid? You are not one of the *Sithichean.* Are you?"

Her thoughts whirled. "A what?"

"A *sithiche*, one of the faeries of these hills." A wave of an arm encompassed the surrounding terrain.

Jillian ran fingers along the edge of the space blanket. "This isn't a plaid."

The man glowered.

Ridiculous. "Who are you?"

"That is none of your mind. My lad be needing that plaid." He grabbed for the blanket again.

She drew it close to her chest, refusing to let go. Jillian wasn't about to let the crazy little man steal it. "I asked who you are."

He raised his chin defiantly. "You tell me first."

"Oh, all right. I'm tired of this game." Jillian threw up her arms in exasperation, dropping the blanket. "I'm Jillian O'Donnell. I'm lost. Perhaps you can direct me to the nearest road?"

A mischievous glint flashed in the man's eyes. "There are none, but if you give me that plaid, I will tell you where to find a game trail."

"Will that take me into town?"

"None here or about. Nearest village is three days walk over that distant ridge." He pointed off to the left.

While she glanced that way, the man snatched the blanket and dashed into the woods.

Jillian ran after him. He was fast, weaving between the trees. She chased him, darting this way and that, dodging brambles and tree limbs. When a branch slapped the side of her face hard, she gave up, bent over, placed hands on thighs, and gasped for breath.

"Damned little man."

She marched back to where her pack still lay on the ground and grabbed it. Jerking the straps over tense shoulders, she glanced at the tree. Strange. There were no face-like images embedded within gnarly wood, just a face-sized cavity marring the bark.

Engrossed in the conundrum of the tree, a sound coming from behind froze her in place.

September, 1513
The Caves of the Gray Women in the wilds of Scotland

There wasn't a spot on Stephen's black and blue body that didn't hurt. The battle had been a bloodbath. Although his wounds weren't too serious, he ached everywhere.

And his leg—'twould be awhile before it healed. Would he ever be able to walk again without aid? That was the question, wasn't it?

He huffed out a breath of frustration and leaned back against the rock wall of the cave. His memory burned with the haunting sight of his dead monarch. Stephen had never expected events to unfold as they had. King James IV of Scotland, dead on the battlefield beside so many of the kingdom's finest warriors.

After lying unconscious among the dead, Stephen had managed to escape the chaos of the field with the help of Munn, the MacLachlan Clan brownie, and found shelter in the caves of the Gray Women. Or so he was told. Stephen didn't remember how they'd managed the feat, how he'd traveled such a great distance with a damaged leg, but here he was, hidden away from those who'd wish him ill.

He'd learned quite a while ago not to be shocked by events involving the fae.

Stifling a groan, he shifted the injured leg trying to find a comfortable position. He stiffened at the sound of footsteps approaching and clutched a dirk at his side. 'Twas only Munn. Stephen dropped the blade and slumped back against the wall.

"What have you there, wee man?" He reached for what Munn had procured. His fingers skimmed over an unusual shiny cloth. "What the devil? Where did you get this bewitched *plaide*?"

Munn quickly looked away. An uncomfortable dread ran through Stephen. The brownie scraped a foot in the dirt.

Stephen's teeth chattered so he wrapped the strange cloth around his upper body. Whether from witch or fae, he was cold and needed any warmth the strange *plaide* could provide.

"Tell me, Munn? Where did you get this?"

"Forest."

"Who did you steal it from?"

"Borrowed." Blue-green eyes flashed. "There be a lass in the wood. Dressed as a lad."

"What were you thinking? We dinnae want to be discovered." Stephen swallowed uneasily. How long had it been since the battle? Had English soldiers infiltrated north? He had no way of kenning. "Is the wench English? Are English soldiers nearby?"

"Nae Sassenachs." Munn curled his body away and looked over his shoulder at Stephen with pursed lips. "Lass foreign. Like Lady Laurie."

Stephen inhaled sharply. *Like Lady Laurie?* Was it possible? "You best fetch her here."

"'Twould be a mistake."

"Why?"

The brownie shrugged and stared at his feet.

"Do as I say. Bring her here. But be careful. We dinnae want the wrong sort to find us."

With a deep grumble, Munn scurried out of the cave.

Stephen scrubbed the stubble on his chin. Could another time traveler have appeared at the *Sithichean Sluaigh*, the faerie mound near Castle Lachlan? If so, how would she have gotten here? 'Twas quite a distance from Strathlachlan.

Hmmm. Would the lass be as intriguing as Lady Laurie?

CHAPTER TWO

*U*nnerved by the snap of a twig, Jillian spun around only to stop short and gawk. Four pairs of eyes stared at her from little faces resembling those she'd imagined within the tree. The boys, dressed in tatters, seemed to range in age from eight to twelve.

"What the…" she stammered. "Who are you?"

The pudgiest and perhaps oldest of the four, with deformed fingers on his right hand, stepped forward; the others huddled behind as if frightened. "We saw you appear from…naught. Be you one of the *Sithichean?*"

The strange little man had asked the same question. *Crazy.* There were no such beings as faeries.

"I'm Jillian O'Donnell. I'm lost."

The child didn't seem convinced. His bulbous nose scrunched up tight, lips pressed together, and grimaced. "But—"

"You dinnae answer his question! Be you one of the *Sithichean?*" A little girl Jillian hadn't noticed—a fifth child, no more than six years old—poked a head from behind the others. "You dress funny. Like a lad."

"I'm nothing more than a lost traveler." Jillian smiled at the little one, trying to hide her shock, hoping not to spook the girl. "I'm dressed for warmth."

The child made a distorted O-shape with a horribly deformed mouth then ducked out of sight. Jillian bit her lip as not to smile at the quick retreat.

"Who are you and your friends?" She directed the question to the pudgy fellow who seemed to be the leader of these poor misshapen children.

He just stared until he stumbled forward a step. He threw a glare over a shoulder at the other children, who took a tentative step back. "Stop poking me."

The boy with an unusually long nose and wisp of blond hair dangling into rounded hazel eyes raised his chin and pointed at the pudgy lad. "We call him Blaney."

"Yeah, and he's Cam." Blaney pointed toward a boy with scars across his forehead and different colored eyes—one bright blue, one dark brown—then to a lad with a head that seemed too large for his child-sized body. "And he's Mack." Blaney then nudged the boy who first introduced him. "This daft lad is Duff."

"And what is your name?" Crouching to appear smaller, less threatening, Jillian addressed the little girl.

The child lowered her head and scraped a dirty, bare toe in the dirt, muttering into her chest. Though bold with her question before, she now acted shy.

"I'm sorry, I couldn't hear you. I'd like very much to know your name."

A soft moss-green gaze peered at Jillian, melting her heart.

"We call her Keita because she is of the wood," Blaney said.

"Keita is a very nice name." Jillian smiled at the blonde-haired child.

The girl giggled and ducked behind one of the boys.

This is crazy. Jillian didn't have time to waste with these ragamuffin children. But the little girl wearing rags on her feet instead of shoes on such a cold morning wrenched her heart. Still... No. She couldn't get involved. She needed to get unlost, find Kyle, and convince him to forget the rest of the cycling trip and head home.

"Do you live nearby?" she asked.

The children looked at each other, but didn't answer.

Okay. "Can you direct me to the nearest town?" Jillian posed the question to Blaney.

The boy seemed confused. A queasy feeling gnawed at her insides. Perhaps the little man told the truth. Was it possible there were no towns nearby? She hadn't checked a map before embarking on this vacation. She'd left navigation for the trip up to her brother.

"We can take you to someone who can help," Duff said.

"Who?"

"The Gray Women."

The other three boys shook their heads vehemently in the negative. Jillian had the feeling meeting the Gray Women wasn't a good idea.

Keita clapped hands in glee. "Aye, aye, let us go to the caves of the Gray Women."

An image of three gray-haired hags smoking corncob pipes hunched over a still, making moonshine popped into Jillian's head. After all, she was in the wilds of West Virginia.

"Mayhap Caitrina will be there," Keita said dreamily.

Jillian's unease compounded. Had she smelled Caitrina's unique perfume, that cloying oriental scent, just before stumbling into the cave—or whatever it was? Could Caitrina have been on the bike trail? Why? And why would she have shoved Jillian?

She smiled at Keita. "Who is Caitrina?"

"A *Sithichean* princess."

Back to faerie tales. The child wasn't referring to Jillian's business partner Caitrina.

Keita took hold of Jillian's hand. "Come. The Gray Women will help you. They help all lost souls."

Present Day
Grandfather Mountain, North Carolina

Far below the mountain trail, a red SUV crawled along the Blue Ridge Parkway. Stopping, crawling, stopping, crawling. Probably leaf peepers or bear gawkers. *Pfft.* "What do you think of the stupid humans?"

Tristan released a shrill *kak kak kak*, lifted one claw then the other, moved his head from side to side, and shrugged a wing before settling again on Caitrina's leather-gloved hand.

"Exactly. Seeing the world through a window rather than experiencing life." Caitrina shook her head, frowned, and slid her gaze over the fireworks display of autumn foliage, letting it settle on the Village of Anderson Creek nestled in the valley below Grandfather Mountain.

Hopefully the tourists would at least stop in the village and spend some serious money in the garden center and restaurants, and perhaps even stay a night or two at the B&B. The villagers could certainly use the income. The local businesses still suffered from the downturn in the economy.

One of many reasons Caitrina hoped not to belong to their ilk much longer. As a *halfling*—half-human, half-fae—she'd never needed money. That was until the banishment by the Queen of the Fae, and resulting punishment, forced Caitrina into life-long service to Mairi MacLachlan, proprietor of the Whispering Pines Inn along with her husband Iain. They and two of their children were time travelers from sixteenth century Scotland living in a modern world.

Anderson Creek was known for an eccentric cast of local characters so the time travelers fit in just fine. Caitrina—not so much. In the past, the clan system kept her clothed and fed. The modern world, however, had many expenses. Aye, she was an owner, along with Jillian and Laurie, of *Foxgloves*, a popular garden center, but her greatest wish was to return to *Tir-nan-Og* and live among other faeries.

And that is where she'd go as soon as the queen's challenge was met. Orchestrate three nearly impossible love matches and she'd be free. Two were complete.

Caitrina inhaled a heavy breath. She must proceed

carefully. The queen enjoyed their game far too much and was prone to cheating. Originally, Oonagh refused to disclose the identity of the next unlikely couple, but finally the potential lovers were revealed. Caitrina already set the match in motion. That's why she needed to return to early sixteenth century Scotland in all haste. She couldn't trust Munn to oversee the meeting and mating. Besides the wee brownie was unaware of Stephen's potential mate.

Tristan nudged her nose with his beak.

"Right. Time is wasting." Caitrina continued up the trail toward the high meadow. She had pressing matters to attend. Wind buffeted them as they cleared the trees and strode out into the open. The bird fussed, eager to dance in the sky.

"I will miss you." She hesitated then released Tristan to the wind. "Fly safe and true, my friend."

The peregrine falcon rose on thermals and soared out of sight. Caitrina crossed her arms in a self-hug, already feeling the loss. 'Twas best he fly wild and free until spring when he would head for northern climes. She was needed in Scotland past.

As she wandered toward the trail heading down the mountain, alarm hummed over her skin. Someone watched. Unnerved, she thought to vanish, but then she wouldn't learn who or what flaunted such intent interest. Trying to appear nonchalant, she scanned the meadow, the rocks, the forest edge, and froze in awe. *What the…*

She closed a gaping mouth and stared.

The silky black stallion reared up on hind legs then galloped away, disappearing into the forest, though not before Caitrina glimpsed the single horn protruding magnificently from the center of the animal's broad forehead. Couldn't be. Wasn't possible. Unicorns only existed in *Tir-nan-Og*. Faerieland. Land o' heart's desire. There were rumors, of course. Stories made up by the local storyteller, Mr. MacNaughton, more than likely. Faerie tales meant to amuse children.

Caitrina rubbed tired eyes, feeling deflated. Dealing with

the queen's matchmaking challenge made her daft. Made her see things that didn't exist. She needed to complete this match and win the game. If only Jillian and Stephen would cooperate.

A large hand clamping on her shoulder made her jump. As she partially faded into the vanishing, a unique scent of earth and wind and animal musk invaded her nostrils. Ah. Said hand belonged to Douglas, the proprietor of the *Celtic Image* shop in the Village of Anderson Creek, and her sometimes lover. The grip tightened on her shoulder, and she jerked back to solid form. She didn't dare bring him along to the past, which would have happened if he touched her.

'Twas bad enough he'd learned her secret.

"Easy, lass. Didn't mean to spook you."

"As if you could." She'd never admit she was so preoccupied that he could sneak up on her. She spun to face him and stepped out of reach. He looked good. Too good. More handsome than any human male had the right.

Unusually tall at six-foot-seven, he towered over her as no other. Long black hair pulled back in a queue brought attention to a penetrating amber gaze and clenched, clean-shaven jaw. He wasn't happy. *Tough.*

As usual, he wore a predominately red and green plaid kilt low on his hips, with a badger sporran at the waist. He hadn't donned a shirt, which tempted her to stare at his muscular chest. She clasped her hands together, stopping eager fingers from petting the smattering of dark hair.

Annoying man. She hated that his mere presence made her wet and needy. Would be hell if he learned the effect he had on her. She assumed her best glower. "What are you doing here?"

"Looking for you." He stepped forward, crowding her space.

She held her ground. "Of course. What do you want?"

"To stop you."

Caitrina's mouth went dry. He couldn't possibly know what she planned. "What are you talking about this time?"

"I ken where you plan to go. There's nae point. You can't win. She won't let you win."

"What are you talking about?" Caitrina bit the corner of her lip.

"The queen. No matter what you do, the queen will have her way."

Today was full of surprises and none of them good. A shiver ran over her spine. What did he ken of the fae queen? The challenge? Caitrina couldn't let Douglas get involved. He was mortal. He could be fatally hurt.

"What do you think you ken?" She swallowed uneasily.

"The queen will not let you win the challenge."

"I dinnae ken what you are talking about."

"Aye, you do. You must let me help."

His strong features softened, the concern for her welfare more potent than a lust-coated faerie dart embedded in her heart. Of all the worst things that could happen, she'd fallen in love with Douglas MacKinnon. *A mere human.*

Crushed by the illumination, Caitrina vanished from the mountain, traveling through space and time to the early part of sixteenth century Scotland in a panic. How could she protect Douglas *and* win the queen's challenge?

CHAPTER THREE

September, 1513
The wilds of Scotland

Jillian paraded along with the children, navigating a narrow game trail, brambles snagging her fleece leggings, nerves tense. They'd better not be luring her into danger.

After about an hour, they left the forest path. She inhaled briny air and hesitated. If she didn't know better, she'd swear they were near the sea. *West Virginia isn't near the ocean.* A large finger lake meandered off to the side and out of sight. She cupped a hand at her brow to lessen the glare from the sun. Tall cliffs rose from the opposite shore, craggy reflections shimmering on the water's surface. Pairs of black and white birds chattered from narrow rock ledges then darted into the air and dove into the water, resurfacing with small fish in their beaks. She'd find the scene delightful, if not feeling unnerved.

They continued along the water's edge until the terrain abruptly sloped upward. The children darted ahead. A narrow rock-strewn trail climbed through a hillside of heather. Some plants still in bloom. Jillian brushed the toe of a bike shoe across a spike of muted, purple blossoms, triggering a light floral scent. She hadn't imagined heather to be so prevalent in West Virginia. Actually, she'd expected more trees.

She shrugged and followed the kids. What did she know having never been there before?

As the trail became rougher and steeper, the children scrambled over boulders like little monkeys. Jillian slipped on scree and cursed her unsuitable bike shoes. Overheating, she removed her wind jacket, stuffed it into her pack, and then drew the red fleece top she wore over her head, tying it around her waist by the sleeves. After tripping and falling a couple more times, short of breath, hands torn and stinging, she caught up to the kids. They had reached a shelf that ran along the cliff face.

Not comfortable with heights, she didn't dare look down. "Just where exactly are you taking me?"

"A hidden way into the caves." Duff smiled from where he negotiated the ledge at her side.

Jillian huffed out a breath. "Isn't there an easier approach?"

"Aye, there is." He shook his head. "Not safe. We dinnae want to run into bad men."

Cripes. "Are there many in the area?"

He nodded, features grim, but then his face brightened with a smile. "Dinnae fret. We ken how to avoid them."

Just great. She hoped they didn't find trouble.

They continued, taking one precarious step after another. Jillian gulped. The shelf they crept along was getting narrower. She gripped the rock face with now bleeding fingers. "How much farther?"

"Almost there." Duff brushed a wisp of blond hair out of hazel eyes.

And then what? Why had she followed the kids? She sighed. Because there was no one else to help her get unlost. All right then. Jillian straightened her shoulders. Might as well follow through.

One after the other, the children leapt over a crevasse, a perilous drop, then disappeared from sight. Duff waited until

Jillian sidled up close. "Just over this gap is the cave."

"Okay." She watched him jump and disappear same as the other children.

Jillian swallowed hard. Easy peasy. Right? Inhaling deeply, she took a leap of faith and tumbled sideways into the mouth of the cave, sprawling on hands and knees.

"Ouch!" Her voice echoed in the cavernous space.

It took a moment for her eyes to adjust to the dim interior, but then she smiled. Blaney and Duff held torches, and three harmless-looking grandmotherly types stood with the children, concerned expressions wrinkling their brows.

"What have you wee urchins brought to our door?" one woman asked.

The three wore strange clothing—long gray skirts with gray over-blouses and dark gray on light gray plaid shawls covering their heads and wrapped around their chests—as if from a different time period. Actually, now that Jillian thought about it, the children's drab rags seemed from a time long past. Her pulse quickened.

"Just exactly where am I?"

One of the women cackled causing gooseflesh to prickle Jillian's arms. "Ach, well, these caverns are kenned by many as the Caves of the Gray Women. Welcome to our home."

"Seems the children have brought us another stray soul in need of help, sisters," said the one who spoke first.

"Best we tell our lad," said the third. "Come, lass."

"Wait—"

The three women abruptly turned and ducked into a narrow tunnel, the children at their heels. Except for Duff and Keita. They waited solemnly.

Could the women help her?

Jillian shivered. Another tunnel. Although these caves didn't feel as threatening as the old train tunnel on the bike trail had. Tugging her warm fleece top back on, she swallowed rising anxiety before it overwhelmed her and smiled at the children. "Shall we?"

A short trek through the rough-sided tunnel brought them

to a smaller cavern. Jillian inhaled sharply when one of the torches shed light on a large lump in the corner. A blond man, wrapped in her stolen space blanket, sprawled motionless on plaid blankets spread over the stone floor with his back to them."

"Stephen dear, we have company."

The man turned slowly and rose to a seated position. He wore an impassive expression, a long, sharp-looking, knife clutched in a big hand.

"How did you get my space blanket?" Jillian curled her hands into fists, anger making her braver than prudent.

The man's head tilted to the side as he studied her, and the blanket slipped revealing a massive bare chest. A terribly scarred chest. The blade disappeared and a smile curved his mouth. Jillian's mind turned to mush. She took a step back and tried not to drool. Though he was scruffy, his gorgeous blue peepers knocked the air from her lungs.

With effort, Stephen blanked his features. 'Twas quite a feat, being he gazed upon the loveliest creature, eyes wide, a hand clutched to her chest. Damn! She was repulsed by the sight of him. He tugged the cloth up, covering the puffy, pink scars on his chest, hoping to ease her distaste.

At least his face hadn't been damaged in the battle.

Her arm dropped to the side, lips parting ever so slightly. Maybe she wasn't offended by his scars? He smiled again.

"What have we here?" he asked, voice gruff from lack of use.

The lass moistened her lips. Becoming aroused, he stifled a groan. Damned luck. Of all times to find a woman to have such an effect on him. *Him* with serious injury and, perhaps worse, handfasted with another. Though loath to have gotten into such a predicament with a lass he disliked and didn't trust, the fact remained another woman already laid claim to him. Refusing to dawdle on that path of thought, he shook off unwanted memories.

The lass standing before him must be the one of whom

Munn spoke. Her garments were strange. Of a type of cloth unknown to him. But it was her heart-shaped face framed by hair the color of the rich earth in Castle Lachlan's garden that left him spellbound. Dark lashes graced warm brown eyes specked with gold that made his insides shiver. And the tip of an impish nose sprinkled with fern-tickles—as if the lass were descended from the fae—begged to be kissed.

Her lips—

Grrr! He'd never be able to fulfill the desire to kiss those sweet lips. Why did she drop into his life now? When he was already handfasted and only half a man?

"Like what you see?" The angry tone of her voice snapped him out of the rude perusal.

"What is your name?" he demanded.

She raised her chin, and he thought she would refuse to answer.

"Jillian O'Donnell. And *you* have *my* space blanket." Her hands fisted on slender hips.

"I never meant… Here." He dropped the odd silver *plaide* and struggled with his crutch to stand. Heat flushed his face and pain burned his muscles. He wobbled before finding secure footing for his wounded leg. He held out the cloth. "Take it."

The lass gasped. Eyes wide, she clutched the *plaide* to her chest. "You're…"

"What? Have you not seen a naked man afore?" *Fool.* Now she kenned the enormity of his injuries.

Without waiting for an answer, he leaned on the crutch and hobbled across the chamber and, less stable than he would have liked, ducked into the tunnel and away from the delectable lass, his powerful reaction to her more than disturbing.

CHAPTER FOUR

*M*unn spun, creating a whirlwind of leaves and forest debris, onto the spot where he'd left the lass. She was gone. He stomped across the ground and sniffed the air, his nose wrinkling with distaste. The lost *bairns* had been there. He didn't have time for their tricks this day.

He furrowed his brow and pursed his lips. Perhaps the lass was with the *bairns*?

Stephen would be angry with him, but he hadn't meant to lose track of the lass. Munn hung his head, kicked at the dirt. What to do? What to do?

Fading from sight, he followed the scent of the *bairns* through the wood, along the edge of the sea-loch, over the heather-covered hill, along the cliff face to the hidden entrance of the caves. He clung to the craggy rock wall and, gripping narrow crevices with fingers and toes, peered over the edge into the mouth of the cave. Had the *bairns* brought the lass to Stephen?

Cloaked with invisibility, Munn crept into the sprawling outer chamber, not wishing to encounter the Gray Women. He inhaled sharply, catching the mingling essence of peony and freesia and sandalwood. *Caitrina*. She must be near.

Was she here to check on Stephen or to play a game piece

on the queen's chessboard?

Munn frowned, annoyed the faerie hadn't confided the identity of the woman in play. Thinking hard, something he hated to do, he pressed fingers against his temples and concentrated. *A lass dressed as a lad, seemingly like Lady Laurie.* He scratched his chin. Ah! She must be the one.

Sporting a huge grin, Munn rushed through the maze of tunnels in search of Stephen, only to be sucked into one of the internal chambers against his will. How dare the annoying faerie? He spun until his rage petered out and he landed on his rump on the cold stone floor at her feet.

"Are you finished?" Caitrina waited, eyebrows raised, emerald gaze filled with scorn.

He clenched his fists. He hated that look.

"I ken who is to be matched with Stephen." Munn stood, puffed out his chest, and brushed dust from his garments. "'Tis the lass from the wood. Aye?"

Caitrina flicked auburn locks over a shoulder and smiled impishly.

Uh-oh! He was in trouble. Her smile didn't reach her eyes. One moment he stared at Caitrina in all her fae beauty and the next a hag dressed in gray. However, the emerald eyes remained the same. Filled with malice.

"I cannot allow you to get in my way." With a snap of slender fingers, she sent him traveling sideways through a void in time and space.

❀ ❀ ❀

Jillian shut her mouth with a snap. The audacity of the man.

But, whoa! He possessed the firmest, masculine backside she'd ever seen in the flesh. Her hands had itched to squeeze the rounded butt-cheeks before he disappeared into yet another tunnel. She touched several fingers to her burning face, confused emotions battling for dominance—anger, lust, sympathy.

"What happened to him?" she blurted. "Never mind. I'm lost and need to find the nearest phone so I can call my brother, or someone who can help me get home."

The women of the cave glanced from one to the other, shrugged, and then stared at her as if she was crazy.

"We dinnae understand," one woman said.

"What is a phone?" another asked.

A dizzy-sick feeling swamped Jillian. *They don't know what a phone is?* "Listen. I need to go home."

"Dinnae fash. Our lad will take care of you," the third said.

"*Him?*" She pointed to the tunnel through which the hunk of a man had disappeared.

The first woman grasped Jillian by the wrists and turned her hands palms-up. "Tsk. Tsk. Your hands are torn raw."

"The faerie pool will make them better," said the second.

"But I need to find my way home," Jillian persisted.

"Oh, aye, our lad will help you find your way," said the third.

Jillian's head started to hurt. She hadn't noticed earlier, but the women had the exact same appearance as identical triplets. She shut her eyes and rubbed aching temples. When she looked again, everything was blurry, the three women blending into one.

"What the—" She shook her head.

Yup. There was only one woman and the children were gone. The remaining woman lent an age-spotted hand to steady Jillian.

"Where did the others go?" Jillian asked.

"Others? Dinnae ken of what you speak. I am the only one here."

"But—"

"My sisters are busy elsewhere." The woman's emerald eyes sparkled. Eyes that somehow seemed familiar.

Couldn't be. Jillian inhaled a deep, steadying breath. Were they playing games with her?

"Come. A soak in the pool will put things to rights."

The woman led Jillian through the same tunnel the man had taken, past several off-shoots, torches set in metal holders embedded in the walls lit the way. The air became warmer and moist and the sound of running water louder as they walked. Finally, the shaft opened to another chamber.

Wow! A powerful waterfall plunged from a hole in the stone ceiling at least seventy-five feet above their heads. Sunlight glistened on wet walls and where the water cascaded into a subterranean pool that took up most of the chamber.

"Bathe. 'Twill heal your hands."

Jillian drew back. "Are you crazy? The water must be freezing."

"Nae. Hot water bubbles from the earth and the cold water from the waterfall makes the pool perfect for bathing and healing what ails you. 'Tis fae magic."

Jillian's hands stung like hell and the pool was inviting. What would it hurt to soak for a bit? Perhaps daydream about the *hot* blond man.

She squatted near the edge and stuck a couple fingers into the water—perfect temperature. "Okay." She turned to face the woman, but the woman had gone.

Somewhat unsettled, Jillian glanced around. Although light came in from the hole in the ceiling, shadows played over most of the cave. Where the illumination was strongest, toweling and a small jar with an ornate bronze lid sat on a niche in the wall. She opened the lid, brought the jar to her nose and sniffed. Heather blossoms. Must be soap.

She wasn't making any headway in getting unlost, yet perhaps she could spare a few minutes for a relaxing soak. She dropped her pack on the floor and kicked off her bike shoes. Careful of her sore hands, she slid the fleece leggings over her hips and stepped out of them. Then extending her arms toward the ceiling in a needed stretch, slowly arched her back, and cracked her spine while tugging off the fleece pullover. Dressed in bike shorts and a t-shirt, she glanced at the water. She didn't want to get her shorts and top wet so she stripped to her bikini briefs and sports bra and folded her clothing on the pack. Making quick work of braiding her hair, she used an elastic from around her wrist to secure it then stepped into the water. *Nice.*

She carefully walked deeper into the pool, dragging bloodied hands through the water. The stinging eased. Sand squished between her toes. The pool deepened then became shallower as she walked toward the far wall, covered in green moss and small plants. Finding a ledge, she sat. Water rose over her breasts. *Ahh! Heaven.* With the warm water and gentle mist from the waterfall soothing her nerves, she leaned back and relaxed.

She must have dozed. Something jolted her awake. She sensed she wasn't alone. A short distance away, water spilled over the edge of the pool and trickled into a stream that ran under a stalactite curtain wall. No one seemed to be there. She held still, sure someone was in the cave with her.

"Who's there?"

Stephen held his breath, not moving a muscle. How could he make his presence known without spooking the lass?

After the shock of seeing her in the chamber where he slept, he'd rudely exposed his ugliness. Guilt tearing at him, he hurried as best he could on his crutch to the falls. He'd hobbled deep into the pool, taking a seat in the shadows, allowing the warm water to wash over his stiff shoulders. The muscle aches and ever-gnawing pain in his leg lessened.

Time suspended, though he didn't sleep. With a warrior's alertness, he sensed the moment she entered the chamber. Why would he feel such a connection to this woman from the future? Like Lady Laurie, that's who she must be.

"I know you're there. Show yourself." Her voice trembled.

Loath to cause more distress, he slowly leaned forward, out of the shadows, not far from where she sat. "I am here."

She jerked her gaze to him, eyes wide.

"I did not wish to disturb you."

"You saw me undress," she accused, her sweet lips curving into a comely scowl.

He held the urge to smile at bay. He'd enjoyed the show immensely, especially the teasing stretch exposing the curve of her back, as the erection he sported proved. The silky garments she wore over her breasts and mound left little to the imagination. Her shapely hips lovely. Her skin ivory perfection. The need to touch her almost more than he could endure.

He cleared his throat, hoping she wouldn't hear the lust in his voice. "I am sorry. I should have made my presence known, but I did not want you to run off before the fae waters healed your hands."

"I'm not afraid of you."

"You should not be."

"Well, I'm not."

"Good."

The silence became awkward. Stephen groped for something to say. "You said your name is Jillian?"

"Yes."

"Mine is Stephen. Stephen MacEwen."

She smiled. More silence.

Of a sudden, Jillian jerked her feet up onto the shelf where she sat. Wrapping arms tightly around her legs, she stared into the water with a frown.

"What is wrong?" Stephen asked, sliding closer.

"Something brushed over my feet. Are their snakes in the water?"

Her horrified expression made him chuckle. "Nae. Just wee toothless fish."

"Oh. Like the *garra rufa* that nibble away dead skin from your feet when you get a fish pedicure at one of the fancy spas in Asheville."

"I dinnae ken about that, but the fish in this pool will not hurt you."

She dropped her feet deeper into the water and smiled. "Tickles."

"Aye. Does." He sounded like the village idiot.

"I'm lost. The children told me the Gray Women would help me find my way to a phone or to a town where I could call my brother, but they keep disappearing. Do you know where I can go to make a call?"

"The women come and go. Mysteriously."

"Why are you here?"

"To heal."

"What happened?"

"Ach. 'Tis a long story."

"You're Scottish. Right? You sound a lot like my business partner's husband, Patrick MacLachlan. He's originally from Scotland." She shook her head, making her braid bob. "Of course, you wouldn't know him. Sorry. I tend to ramble when I'm nervous."

"I dinnae wish to make you uncomfortable." *She kenned Patrick!*

She smiled, and Stephen had to rub an achy spot near his heart. He didn't ken whether it was because she affected him so or because she kenned Patrick. He missed his cousin terribly.

"So? About a phone?" she persisted.

"Phone? Is that something of your future time?"

Her eyes narrowed, brow furrowed. The look clearly stated she believed him simple in the head. He might strive to be underestimated by an opponent in battle, but he didn't like the lass thinking poorly of him.

"Never mind. Where are the children?" she asked before he could defend himself.

"What children?"

She rolled her eyes the way some of the young lasses at Castle Lachlan often did. "The ones who brought me here. They were in the other chamber with us earlier."

"I did not see any children."

"You must have. After I fell in the old train tunnel…" She frowned. "Falling into a well and waking lost in the woods doesn't make sense. I must have hit my head and wandered away from the bike trail," she mumbled, as if talking to herself. She ran a hand over her head. "No bumps." Her frown deepened, and she raised her gaze to him. "I was lost in the woods a couple hours' walk from here."

"You did not travel from Strathlachlan?"

Jillian perked up. "Is that a nearby town?"

"Nae. 'Tis a distant village."

"The children found me and led me here. Blaney and Mack and Cam? Duff and Keita?"

"Ah. The changelings. The lost *bairns* who live in the trees."

"I don't understand."

"The villagers believe that sometimes faeries steal their healthy children and replace them with misshapen changelings. The changelings are later discarded in the forest. Left to fend for themselves or die."

"That is beyond cruel."

"We live in dangerous times. Those who are impaired perish." And if his leg didn't heal, he'd prefer to perish rather than be a burden on others. And if that thought wasn't enough to deflate his cock—

"Wait a minute. There are all sorts of laws protecting children."

"Not in Scotland. Not in the year of our Lord 1513."

The lass's eyes rolled back, and she slid downward. He grabbed hold of an arm and pulled her onto his lap before her head slipped under the water. Now what was he to do?

"Lady Jillian, wake up." He shook her. Her head lolled, but then her eyes fluttered open, and she smiled. He was lost.

"What happened?" she asked.

"You swooned."

"I don't faint."

"Of course not."

The feel of her scantily clad bum against the bare skin of his thighs brought him back to life, made his interest obvious. She blushed, but stayed on his lap, smiling. *Grrr!*

"Um. I guess I should get out of the pool. I'm probably pruning." He didn't remove his arms from around her, and she didn't attempt to pull away. She lifted her hands from the water and stared at the palms. Her mouth fell open. Closed. She raised a confused gaze to him and frowned. "The skin is clear as if never damaged. I don't understand."

"Fae magic."

Her frown deepened. "I don't believe in faeries or magic."

"Then how did your hands heal?"

She thought for a moment. Ran a finger over one of the scars on his chest, making him shiver with delight. "If magic, then why do you have raw scars and a heavy limp when you walk?"

"My injuries brought me near to death. 'Tis taking time to heal."

"What about the children. Why hasn't the water helped them?"

"Fae magic is a mystery. My guess is the children were born deformed. Mayhap if they had been doused in the healing waters at birth, they would have been cured."

"*Hmmm*. Perhaps."

Was it the warmth of the water or the way the *hmmm* left her lips making him feel overheated? Leaning closer, he breathed in her womanly scent and wondered why he was prolonging the torture.

"Do you actually believe we are in Scotland during the year 1513? Is that part of the fae magic?" Soft-brown brows curved into a graceful arch.

"Perhaps magic." He nodded. "Your speech is much like someone I once kenned."

"Really?"

"Lady Laurie MacLachlan. Might you ken of her?"

Jillian gasped. "You *do* know Laurie and Patrick. How?"

CHAPTER FIVE

The approach to Castle Torne, the northern most castle in the Highlands

*U*rgency goaded Prince Dugaid to push his mount to greater speed. The midnight-black stallion galloped effortlessly through pristine snow. Forest and glen and village blurred when passed.

They halted at the edge of the North-wood. The fae horse hoofed the earth, snorted, and blew steam into the frigid air. Dugaid leaned forward over the beast's thick neck and eyed the stone fortress, shrouded in mist, high on the distant sea cliff. To the untrained human eye, Castle Torne appeared a great stronghold, though no more so than many others in Scotland. Something else was at work there. The land and all within charmed by a most powerful fae enchantment.

Its potency pulsed over Dugaid's flesh despite the many layers of garments and furs he wore as protection against the cold. A thrill ran through him; eager for the confrontation ahead.

Prince Torguil, an ancient *sithiche* prince, held court within those massive stone walls. Although a favorite noble of Dugaid's mother, Oonagh, the High-Queen of the Fae,

Torguil chose to reside on earth in this forgotten northern wilderness instead of *Tir-nan-Og*. 'Twas said he pined for his human wife, long since dead and buried.

Dugaid straightened his shoulders. He would need to prove his worth to gain the hand of Torguil's halfling daughter. 'Twas time to stop waiting and put his plan into action. He wanted Caitrina with every fiber of his being. His mother would never forgive him, which made the match all the more perfect.

He scanned the approach to the castle. Out in the open for the distance, he would be exposed, though he doubted Torguil's warriors presented a threat. Dugaid had sensed the fae scouts for the past few days, monitoring his advance. They'd let him pass so far without incident.

Dugaid walked the fine steed across the open moor at an unhurried pace, keeping his senses alert. With each step, the tingling of magic strengthened, and with it his determination.

At the base of the rise to the cliff top, he paused and twisted around in the saddle. Movement within the trees revealed the scouts still watched him.

Ice and loose stones roughened the climb, but the surefooted stallion proceeded unaffected by either the encumbrance or the tremors of magic. If only the enchantment didn't affect Dugaid. Perhaps shifting into his alternate form…

Nae. He couldn't allow others to lay witness to the transformation nor its results. He held the reigns in a tight fist, feeling more lightheaded as they proceeded. He hung on by sheer will alone by the time they reached the massive gates.

Without command, the outer portcullis slowly rose with a loud grating of metal. Dugaid urged the horse forward. The latticed grille dropped behind them much faster than it had been raised, and they were now caught between the two gates. If Torguil wished him ill, this was where the guards could easily take away his immortality and end his fae life with a single, well-shot iron dart to the heart.

"Who goes there?" The voice came from within one of the arrow slits cut into the side wall.

"You ken verra well who I am. Prince Dugaid, son of Oonagh."

The inner portcullis finally rose, opening the way into the castle courtyard. The dizziness faded the moment he cleared the gate. The temperature rose, and Dugaid unwrapped multiple scarves in order to breathe in the briny sea air.

Five muscular fae warriors pounded down the keep steps. The ancient prince wasn't taking chances with his uninvited guest.

"Welcome to the home of Torguil." The leader waved an arm and bowed in greeting.

Although the blond faerie stood taller than his companions, Dugaid, at six-foot-seven, topped him by a good four inches. If there was trouble, Dugaid had the upper hand. A slow smile curled his lips. "I wish an audience with Prince Torguil."

"*Our* prince is well aware of your presence. If you follow me, I will show you to a chamber where you can make yourself presentable."

Dugaid followed the faerie, the other four warriors falling in behind. For Danu's sake what harm did they think he planned?

After a much-needed bath and grooming, dressed in his black leathers, he restlessly waited for a summons. After pacing the width of the chamber for the umpteenth time, a knock sounded the arrival of the blond faerie who'd greeted him in the courtyard.

"Please follow me. I will escort you to Prince Torguil's antechamber."

Upon entrance to the chamber, Torguil strode forward and greeted him with a warrior's embrace. On separating, the elder prince touched the gilt brooch at Dugaid's shoulder. "You are of the unicorn brotherhood."

"Aye."

"Do you bring a message from the high-queen?"

"I harbor nae love for my mother."

Torguil rubbed his chin. "I see. Then why do you grace my hall?"

"I bring a gift." Dugaid removed a wee leather sack secured at his hip and handed it to Torguil.

The elder prince released the thong and dropped the contents onto the table. Thirteen precious gems the size of a man's thumbnail and the color of deepest purple settled on the tablecloth. The flawless amethysts winked in the flickering light of countless candles.

"A rare and exquisite gift." Torguil fingered the stones set before him. "Truly beautiful. Far above par."

"An offering for the hand of your daughter."

"Ah!" The prince's eyes narrowed. "*Caitrina.*"

"Aye." Dugaid couldn't read the impassive expression. Was Torguil pleased with the offer?

"Why should I grant your request? Allow you control over my greatest asset?"

"I am the only man capable of protecting her from Oonagh's wrath."

"Your prowess on the battlefield is well known. I would be proud to call you son." Torguil hesitated. "Yet you dinnae speak of love?"

"I am fae."

"As am I, yet I was verra much in love with Caitrina's mother." The emerald of his eyes—the same color as his daughter's—deepened.

"There is nae time for human emotion. The third set in Oonagh's challenge to Caitrina is in play. I will ensure your daughter wins." Dugaid pounded a fist against his chest. "I will have her as my bride."

"She will fight you."

"I look forward to the taming."

CHAPTER SIX

*J*illian liked the feel of Stephen's arms around her. She almost didn't care he was most probably insane. *Pathetic.* She was starving for attention. What harm was there in enjoying the feel of his body while she could?

She hadn't had a gut-clenching reaction to a man in like forever. Not since…well, since she'd met Finn. He'd had no interest in her, but Stephen seemed to enjoy their interplay.

"Patrick is my cousin," he said solemnly.

"Really?" She jerked her gaze to his, judging his honesty. He seemed sincere.

"Aye. He married Lady Laurie at Castle Lachlan, renounced his claim as chief to the clan, named his brother Archibald chief, and he and Lady Laurie walked onto the faerie knoll in the Fir-wood and traveled, so I believe, to your time. I miss him."

"Archibald you say?" *Unbelievable.*

"Aye." Their gazes held.

Stephen was serious. He seemed to believe the fantasy. She couldn't. Yet, Patrick did have a brother named Archie who lived in Scotland. He and his wife Isobell had reportedly visited the family in Anderson Creek a couple of years ago for Christmas. Jillian had been away visiting with her brother for the holidays. Could it be possible? Did time travel exist?

The terrain she'd traveled with the kids in route to the caves was rather remote. More remote than she'd thought the area around the bike trail should have been. And no one seemed to know about phones. That was just plain weird.

Her heart rate increased. She took a deep, calming breath. She wouldn't freak yet.

Jillian shifted her weight. Stephen groaned. She curbed the desire to smile. He was very sweet.

Was it possible the tale was true? Her hands seemed to have miraculously healed. Even the calluses from using garden tools were gone. *Hmmm*. Many strange things went on in Anderson Creek and, more specifically, with the MacLachlan family. Like when Finn MacIntyre disappeared the first night of the Grandfather Mountain Highland Games and returned three days later with Elspeth MacLachlan, both dressed as if they'd been in ancient Scotland, and Finn with blood on his shirt as if he'd been fighting with his claymore for real.

Perhaps Jillian needed to keep an open mind. She curled into Stephen's embrace, leaning her head against his shoulder. "I shouldn't be sitting on your lap, especially considering your state of undress."

"You should not." He caressed her cheek, settling his palm on the curve of her chin, leaned forward and brushed his full lips lightly over hers.

A heady sensation swirled through Jillian. The taste, the gentle touch—all of him made her feel as if she'd gone to heaven. The kiss was pure magic.

She twined her arms around his neck. Strong masculine arms pulled her in tight. On impulse, she licked the seam of his lips. The corners quirked upward before parting. Everything faded away except the fusion of their mouths and the twirling dance of tongues.

Delicious. Heat shot through her system straight to her core. She wanted, needed—

Giggles near the chamber's entrance demanded attention

and they broke apart, both breathing hard. Several small hands reached from within the shadows along the wall and filched Jillian's belongings.

"Stop!" Her scream reverberated within the chamber.

She leapt away from Stephen and hurried through the water to the other side of the pool. The children were gone. "They took my stuff."

In its place sat a drab colored bundle of cloth. Jillian climbed out of the water, grabbed a thin towel from the niche to cover herself, and rifled through the pile—gray wool maxi-dress, thick woolen stockings, an oversized gray tartan blanket, and underneath the pile, a pair of ancient boots that appeared almost new. *What the hell?*

"What's this all about?" she demanded.

Stephen had followed her across the pool and now floated near the edge, arms crossed in front of him on the stone floor. "Dinnae ken." He shrugged "The garments left behind are more appropriate to this time than your future clothing. Though you deserve to be draped in satins and silks and jewels more fitting to your station as a fine lady."

A warm thrill shot through Jillian. She might like this guy.

"Hand me a drying cloth, lass."

"Sure." She passed him a towel. "I'm in a bind. I need to go home."

It was distressing watching Stephen clamber out of the pool. Pain etched his handsome features. He leaned on the crutch. Jillian raised her gaze to his face to avoid gaping at the beauty of his physique. The healing scars and some older ones made him look dangerously rugged.

"You are now my responsibility," he said, features earnest. "I will help you to the best of my limited ability. We need to travel to Castle Lachlan where you can try to return home from the faerie knoll. Though, I warn you. I have tried to follow Patrick several times. The magic hasn't worked for me."

"How far is it?"

"A long way."

"How can you travel in your condition?"

His eyes darkened, and he frowned.

"I'm sorry I didn't mean to hurt your pride."

"Dinnae fash. I nae longer have any pride." With the towel slung low on his hips, he strode from the chamber.

As he passed beneath the hole in the ceiling, sunlight glistened over broad, wet shoulders. The muscles of his back flexed with each step. Yup, he was gorgeous. Even with the numerous scars.

Jillian grabbed the bundle of clothes and scurried after him, having no clue how to navigate the caves on her own. With his slow, clumsy gait, she quickly caught up. "I didn't mean to offend."

"If I bathe in the healing pool a couple of times a day, I suspect I will improve enough to travel in about a fortnight."

Jillian wracked her brain. Patrick also used such uncommon words. Was a fortnight one week or two? She suspected it was two. Yeah. A sennight equaled one week.

"That's a long time." She didn't want to be stranded here for that long.

"True. I wish I could provide escort sooner, but there are too many dangers. As is, I would be hard pressed to protect you against an armed threat. And my wee man has not returned since I sent him out to search for you and bring you here to safety."

"Do you mean the gnarly little man who stole my space blanket?"

"Aye. I apologize for that. Munn is a *brùnaidh*, the Maclachlan Clan brownie. He tends to be mischievous. Often causes trouble."

"Munn?" She gulped. Little Allison MacLachlan babbled about a funny man named Munn with a wrinkled brown face, like *Rumpelstiltskin*, who visited the family with her Uncle Archie and Aunt Isobell.

Ohmigod! Stephen spoke the truth.

Stephen sensed an inner strength in Jillian. Still, he couldn't

41

allow her to travel alone. He was the only one who understood where she came from and could protect her. Or at least he would be able to if—when—his bad leg healed and he gained his strength back. No one must learn she was a time traveler. She'd be exploited or, more horribly, condemned to death or imprisoned in a deep dungeon as a practitioner of the dark arts.

He refused to allow any of that to happen.

Together they'd journey to Castle Lachlan and the Firwood. She would use the faerie knoll to travel home. Then he would return to Dunadd, another MacLachlan stronghold just north of Lochgilphead, and his unwanted responsibilities.

The plan was a good one, but it didn't sit well. He hated the thought of never seeing her again. Hated the thought of spending the rest of his life tied to Calyn.

If only he'd met Jillian first.

He shook his head. Regrets were a waste of precious time. Stephen awkwardly teetered on his crutch, grabbed a *leine* from atop a wooden chest and tugged it on. Then wrapped a *plaide* around his hips, tossing the end over a shoulder, securing it in place with a bronze brooch lent to him by one of the Gray Women, having lost his during the battle. Though their habits were unsettling, he owed the women a great debt for caring for him.

When he faced Jillian, she had donned the garments left by the lost *bairns*. The sack-like garments didn't suit her, although she would look lovely dressed in anything. When they reached Castle Lachlan, he'd find her something more suitable to wear. He didn't understand why the children had taken her belongings. He prayed to God the future things didn't fall into the wrong hands. He made the Sign of the Cross.

"You must be hungry. There is usually a pot of venison and roots stewing in one of the other chambers. Bread and cheese. Apples. Sweet-tasting heather ale."

"Sounds like a feast. I'm famished." Jillian smiled, and once again he was lost.

The best he could do was take care of *his* lass until she journeyed to the future place. He rubbed a spot on his chest over his heart. He hadn't kenned her long, but had waited for her a lifetime. *Too late.* His desolate future awaited him in Dunadd.

Dammit! Where was Munn?

❀ ❀ ❀

Sands of Time

Munn felt the chafe of sand abrading his flesh before fully awake. Caitrina had done it to him again. Sent him into the endless *Sands of Time.* Hot sand everywhere. As far as he could gaze, and farther.

Last time had not gone well for him.

He kenned better than attempt to return to the earth realm on his own. The effort would bleed away his limited magic and certainly fail.

Sweat coating his skin from the blistering heat, he squinted and, blinded by the sun's harsh yellow light, labored to stand. Did the oasis he fashioned on his last banishment remain? Trudging through the deep drifts, he wandered off in no particular direction. Seconds passed. Minutes. Hours. Days. He didn't ken how long he walked. Time had no meaning in this brutal land.

With no strength remaining, he tumbled to the ground. How was he to protect Stephen? Munn's duty to Clan MacLachlan demanded such. The chief had ordered him to watch over the blond warrior.

He'd failed the chief again.

Unable to move, he lurched into unconsciousness. A nicker near his ear jarred Munn from oblivion. Slow to react, a large muzzle nudged him. Grumbling, eyelids stuck-fast over burning eyes, he rolled away from the intruder.

A shrill whinny blasted his temporal lobe. Munn bolted upright, eyes wide. By Danu! He rubbed unbelieving eyes. The vision remained—*unicorn.*

The magnificent black beast stood at least fifteen hands, unusually large for even a male of its kind. It nickered again, and Munn jumped to his feet, quickly brushing sand from his form.

Ears pricked forward, the noble animal nodded his horned head, then lowered onto front knees.

Munn took the gesture as an invitation to mount. Fisting the silky mane, he hauled his weight up onto the beast's broad back. The unicorn rose, pranced in a circle, and then stretched into a full gallop. Munn leaned low over the animal's long neck, clutching the flowing mane as they raced across miles of sand. Headed to where? Munn couldn't guess. But prayed to the goddess not to fall.

By the time the unicorn slowed to an even trot, Munn was beyond parched and famished. In the wavering distance, he glimpsed the oasis. Was it real or mirage?

With a four beat gait, the unicorn walked into the tropical paradise, past verdant foliage and birds of colorful plumage, stopped, and dropped to its knees on a bed of plush greenery. The fragrance of orchids perfumed the air. Munn slid to the ground, but his legs wobbled and his feet didn't find purchase. He landed on his rump. "Humph!"

Before he could thank the mystical beast, it vanished as if never existing.

Munn licked chapped lips. Leery to approach the pool at the center of the oasis, he hesitated. On his last visit, the fae queen had emerged from the pool and forced him to swear his troth to her. That had cost him dearly. What would she do to him this time when she learned he aided Caitrina with the challenge?

Finally, he succumbed to his physical needs and sat on a flat rock at the edge of the pool. Stiff with fear, he glanced into the water. Tranquil. No image emerged from within its depths. Relaxing his shoulders, he brought handfuls of pure water to his lips and drank deep. Water quenched his thirst and a pear-flavored fruit from a nearby twirling vine satisfied his hunger.

Lightning streaked the darkening sky. The peace of the oasis shattered by rolling thunder. The ground beneath his feet trembled. Munn trembled, too. Had Oonagh found him?

Instead of the queen, a black-haired warrior of royal stature appeared. Garbed in black leather, all manner of weaponry draping his six-foot-seven frame, he could be none other than the Prince of the Black River—Prince Dugaid. Son to the King and Queen of the Fae. Oonagh and Finvarra. More feared than his regal parents.

Teeth chattering, Munn was frozen in place by a fiery amber stare. What did the Dark Prince want with him?

"Dinnae be afeared, wee man." The prince's deep voice sent a shiver over Munn's spine. "You will come to nae harm by my hand."

Munn swallowed uneasily. Then fell into an awkward bow.

The prince laughed. A hearty laugh that crinkled the edges of his eyes.

"Why have you come?" Munn asked.

"To free you. But you must vow to aid Princess Caitrina."

"She does not want my help. She banished me to this barren realm."

"I shall return you to earth and grant you immunity to Caitrina's transference spell for the duration of this match. In return, you will vow to me to do whatever is required to secure a win for Caitrina."

Munn huffed. "Vow to the chief. Vow to the queen. Vow to a prince. I dinnae ken which end is up."

"Are we in agreement?"

"What of your mither?"

"She will not interfere."

Munn clapped hands with glee. "Then we win!"

"Dinnae be too cocky, brownie. Humans retain free will."

Munn bit his lip and hung his head.

Dugaid smiled. "Escort Stephen and the woman from the future to Castle Lachlan unmolested."

"Easier said than done," Munn grumbled under his breath.

"Dinnae fail me. The consequences will be dire."

Munn's stomach dropped at the prince's warning.

Dugaid vanished.

"Wait!" In confusion, Munn glanced around the oasis. Why hadn't the Dark Prince returned him to the earth realm as promised?

Then a wave of nausea sickened Munn further and he propelled through time and space, landing with a thump on his butt in the sprawling outer chamber in the caves of the Gray Women. Weak with exhaustion and fear, he crawled into a dark corner and succumbed to an uneasy sleep, dreams tortured by Stephen and his woman's perilous journey.

CHAPTER SEVEN

*J*illian followed Stephen through the dim maze of tunnels. Torchlight flickered on the walls, flames caught in a fickle draft. As they entered the internal chamber used as a kitchen, the savory aroma of stew replaced the sooty smell of the passageway.

Her stomach grumbled.

Stephen grinned. "Sit. We will get you fed."

"You sit. I'll get the food."

"You dinnae need to serve me. I might be injured, but am capable of filling a blasted bowl with stew."

"Shut up and take a load off your bum leg." She pressed a palm against his chest and gave a gentle shove. He dropped onto one of four bulky chairs at a rough-hewn table. "It will heal faster." *And we can leave these eerie caves sooner.*

"Feisty lass."

Jillian suppressed a smile and searched the nooks and crannies. Aromatic herbs—some she recognized—hung from racks. Wooden bowls, platters, and spoons sat on one of several shelves. A wrought iron ladle and meat fork dangled from a hook next to the source of the tantalizing aroma—a heavy black caldron hanging over a banked fire. Smoke channeled up and out of the chamber through a fissure in the ceiling.

Grabbing a rag from a worktable to protect her hands, she ladled two steaming bowls and placed them on the table.

Stephen grasped her fingers. "I dinnae mean to be surly. 'Tis just—"

"It's okay. I'm used to the grumbles of men."

"You are?" He frowned.

She raised an eyebrow. "I have an older brother."

He nodded. The pout disappeared and curiosity lit his gaze. "Are you wed?"

She snorted. She couldn't help it. Her? Married? "No."

"Betrothed?"

"No." She shook her head adamantly. *Please don't ask if I have a lover.* It would be too embarrassing to say *no* again.

He pointed to a large niche in the jagged stone wall. "The jugs of ale are there."

She turned her back to him and chuckled softly at his adept change of topic. Smart man. The jugs were submerged to their shoulders in a well of ice-cold running water, and secured by rope. She lifted one out, found two cups, and returned to the table.

A Hollywood-worthy smile greeted her. "I procured some bread."

Might he be interested in her? Jillian's pulse double-beat before returning to normal.

Stephen dug into the food. Her stomach knotted and her appetite disappeared at the thought of making love with Stephen. She broke off a piece of bread and soaked up some stew. She swallowed one bite, then another, needing to keep up her energy.

They ate in silence. Although the intense quiet would feel awkward with anyone else, it seemed right with Stephen. Yeah. She'd like very much to make love with him before returning home. It would be a special memory to keep her warm through many a lonely night.

Jillian poured another round of ale. The sweet herb drink helped smooth the rough edges of her psyche. Perhaps she was even getting a tad tipsy.

Stephen took a long swallow and pushed the cup away. "Dinnae want to drink so much as to lose my head."

"You'd look funny without a head."

He grinned, displaying a badly chipped front tooth.

"How did you get so banged up?"

"Ach, well, I guess we have time for the telling of the tale. Not long ago, relations between Scotland and England reached an insurmountable pinnacle. War eminent." He sighed heavily. "My fealty is to my cousins, the chiefs of Clan MacLachlan, and theirs to our king. Patrick's twin, Archibald—our current chief—wife heavy with child, was loath to leave her bedside. He sent me in his stead to lead our lads when King James IV sent runners to summon us to war."

Jillian swallowed uneasily not wanting to hear the rest, but needing to know. "And…"

"We won several skirmishes and became arrogant. At Branxton Hill, we did not stand a chance against the English. The battle raged fierce. Our king died. God rest his soul." Stephen's voice broke, and he made the Sign of the Cross. "Our lads fought hard. One by one they fell. I battled against the onslaught, but received too many wounds to remain standing. My vision blurred. Death hovered. My last memory is murmuring a prayer for forgiveness then waking in these caves far from the battlefield. The Gray Women brought me back to life."

"If we are in the year 1513, how could you have traveled such a great distance with life-threatening injuries and survived?"

Stephen shook his head and shrugged. "Fae magic."

Jillian frowned. "This is really hard for me to fathom."

"It took Lady Laurie a long time to believe, too." Stephen rose from the table. "Come. The hour is growing late."

Stephen shifted uneasily. What had he been thinking earlier? Why had he badgered Jillian about her marital state? *I have nae right.*

"Where shall I sleep?" Her question shook him free of the chastising thought. Though more than likely a mistake, he wanted her to sleep with him. Jillian crossed her arms over her chest and shivered "It's getting cold."

"Aye. We can lay together on my pallet to keep warm." Her body cuddled close to his, again, 'twould be torture worth enduring.

She nodded with a yawn and plopped onto the pallet.

Stephen unraveled his *plaide* and joined her, covering them with the wool and then her silver cloth. She lay on her side, facing away, shivering with the chill.

He slid her back against him. His nose in her hair, he inhaled a sweet hint of fruit mingled with the scent of woman. "Mmmm. You smell good enough to eat."

Jillian chuckled, and the vibration against his chest spiked his desire for the lass. Saints be praised, it felt good to hold her.

"I'd imagine I smell like a sweaty locker room after a rugby match considering the amount of exercise I've gotten over the last several days."

"I dinnae ken of what you speak, but you dinnae smell like sweat." He inhaled deeply. "Ripe green apples and woman."

"That's my shampoo—soap."

"Verra nice."

Jillian wiggled her bum against him and his arousal throbbed. He wouldn't take her. Nae. 'Twould be wrong. He was handfasted to another. But he'd keep Jillian warm through the night.

She rolled over and faced him. Her lips trembled. A liquid, questioning gaze searched his. She must have gotten the answer she wanted. She kissed him. A sensual breath across his lips. His balls tightened and his determination faltered. What harm was there in a few kisses? He needed this. Wanted this. He wrapped his arms around her and returned the kiss with a greedy intensity that released much of the raw emotion hidden within his heart.

He claimed her lips, tasting the sweet heather ale from their meal. She opened for him like a flower and their tongues twirled in a mating dance. Logic slipped away and deft fingers untied the laces of her gown, folding aside the cloth to reveal her precious bounty. He took one breast in hand. A handful of lusciousness. He massaged the taut nipple.

A soft moan escaped from deep in her throat. He'd burst if he couldn't have more. She arched, pressing her womanly mound against his hard cock. Intense sensations rocked him. He thought he'd explode in a blaze of pleasure.

Rolling her onto her back, he hovered inches above. If only he could see better in the dim light seeping into the chamber from the tunnel torches. With a growl, he sank between her legs and lowered his head to a breast suckling the pebbled nipple, while teasing the other with his fingers. She made the most erotic sounds as she undulated beneath him.

His free hand skimmed the length of her calf, the skin silky smooth. He eased up the wool covering her feminine core, and brushed the flesh of her thighs with eager fingers.

"Stephen, please!" she begged.

"Easy, sweetling. I will provide what you seek." Honor blurring, he was more than ready to stake his claim.

Cold air swirled over his bare backside, stopping him mid-motion. Jillian halted, too. Munn whirled into the chamber, landing on the floor beside the pallet with a smack.

Stephen rolled off Jillian covering them with a *plaide* at the same time. He didn't ken whether to thank Munn or curse the wee man his timing.

"Urgh!" Jillian growled, breathing heavy. "Where did he come from?"

"Shhh," Stephen whispered into her ear.

She, once again, lay on her side with her back to his front. He rubbed a hand in a circle over her shoulder blades, hoping to ease her ire.

"Where have you been?" he demanded of Munn.

"Searching the wood for the lass."

"The lost *bairns* brought her here."

Munn's snarl would make Stephen laugh if he wasn't sporting a rock hard erection with no relief forthcoming. 'Twas for the best. He shouldn't have carnal relations with Jillian. She didn't deserve to be so dishonored.

An image haunted him of waking in Calyn's bed, both of them naked, and not kenning how he'd gotten there. Her father and brother glowering from the bedchamber doorway, swords raised in menace. Tears and claims he'd stolen her maidenhead. Hours spent in Allain of Dunadd's study, trying to talk everyone down, only to give in to her father's demands. Then the rushed handfasting.

He'd never shown interest in Calyn, nor she in him. How had he ended up in her bed two nights before he was to leave for war? And worse—handfasted to the wench the next day.

She'd claimed he'd bullied his way into her bedchamber and pressed her to submit. He'd never in his life taken an unwilling maiden. His honor would never allow such. What had really happened that night?

There were no bruises on her pale skin. Not that he would ever harm a woman. No sign of forced entry to the chamber. No proof to support her claim other than the fact he woke naked with her in the same bed.

Would he ever learn the truth?

She'd been more than happy to make the handfasting pledge. Did Calyn carry his *bairn*? The thought deflated his cock like naught else could. They'd not been together since. If no *bairn* was conceived on that one night, the handfasting would end in a year and a day.

It would be too late to pledge his love to Jillian, she'd already have returned to the future, but at least he would be free of Calyn. And, perhaps, he could try yet again to pass through the faerie knoll to Jillian's future.

"Stephen?" Her hand softly brushing his cheek startled him out of the grim reverie.

"Aye?"

"Munn has gone. We can…"

Stephen grabbed his crutch and hauled himself up. "I need to soak my leg."

He wasn't worthy of Jillian's touch. 'Twas wrong to dally with her. He would see her safely to the *Sithichean Sluaigh* and naught more. Then return to Dunadd and make inquiries about the events of that ill-fated night.

CHAPTER EIGHT

*S*tephen leaned back against a smooth section of stone wishing to soak away the chaos in his mind. The warm water and gentle mist did little to ease his troubled heart. Jillian lured him like moth to flame. When she kissed him—

Deep grumbling heralded Munn's entrance into the waterfall chamber. "Ach, the stench of the lost *bairns* lingers. So they guided the lass here? Dinnae trust them."

"Aye, they ran off with her belongings. Things that will cause trouble if discovered by the wrong someone, if you ken my meaning."

"Nary a soul will find the things. The *bairns* hide their horde well. In a hollow tree surrounded by a dense thicket. Concealed by fae magic."

"Munn, you ken the *bairns* are not truly changelings. They possess nae magic."

"Each are gifted. Protected by the fae."

Stephen sighed. "There are other problems. I dinnae wish to stay overlong in these caves. Maclay once used them as a hideout. Who kens if the reprobate might return? In my debilitated state, I would be hard-pressed to protect the lass."

"Maclay hates our clan."

"Aye, he does. If he learns we are here and vulnerable, he

might try to get even with Patrick and Clan MacLachlan by hurting Jillian."

"Or you."

Stephen wasn't worried about himself. He didn't have much to live for beyond seeing Jillian safely to the *Sithichean Sluaigh*. His future with Calyn unfurled before him like a living hell.

He stretched his bad leg. It improved with each soak in the pool. "If only we had horses. We could ride to Castle Lachlan and Jillian could return to her own time before something perilous happens to her."

Munn stared at the ground and scraped his foot back and forth.

"Can you get horses, Munn?"

The brownie's gaze jerked up. "Mayhap. Will cost dearly."

"I dinnae care what must be sacrificed. I will see Jillian safely home."

The wee man spun in a circle then vanished amid a litany of fading grumbles.

Stephen shook his head. "Damned brownie."

Caitrina reclined amid amber grass, relishing the noontime sun. 'Twas late in the season yet a smattering of heather remained in bloom, perfuming the air. She loved the Highlands in late September.

This was not a day for frowns, but her lips curved into a fierce one. Damn that meddling brownie. His plea for an audience skittered over her skin like a mass of recently hatched spiders. How had he gotten free from the *Sands of Time?*

She vanished from mortal sight and traveled with haste from the hillside on an anger-induced wind, landing on the plush green grass of the *Sithichean Sluaigh* in the Fir-wood not far from Castle Lachlan, the home of Archibald, known to family and friends as Archie, Chief of Clan MacLachlan. Caitrina retained the cloak of invisibility, waiting.

Munn spun onto the faerie knoll, grumbling as usual. "Where is that infuriating *sithiche?* Appear now!"

Caitrina shimmered into corporal form, hands arched on hips, fire sparking at her fingertips. "Why are you here?"

"Need horses."

"Not where you are going." She waved her arms, working the transference spell. Naught happened. Munn remained on the knoll, feet planted apart. "Grrr! Why are you still here? How is this possible?"

He rocked back and forth on the balls of his feet and smiled smug-like. "Ha! That's where being arrogant gets you. Nowhere."

Her eyes widened. Blood thundered in her ears. "How dare you!"

"You look lovely today, Caitrina." Munn grinned. "I need three fae horses."

"You presume to make demands." She waved her arms again, concentrating her power into the spell. Naught happened. "Why do you remain?"

"I have powerful protection so dinnae think to do anything else to me. If you want to win the challenge, provide the horses."

Who dares shield him? Oonagh? Sparks shot from Caitrina's fingertips, setting a patch of grass afire. Within seconds the flames petered out and, as if they watched a time-lapse film, lush green grass replaced the scorched earth. A fresh, earthy scent replaced the acrid smell fouling the air. She gnashed her teeth. "Who protects you?"

The brownie fisted his hands at his sides, leaning forward. "Give me fae horses."

"Why should I?"

"Stephen wants to bring the lass from the future here to the knoll, so she can return to her time."

"And how will that help me win the challenge?" Caitrina demanded.

"They will fall in love while traveling here. Stephen is already randy." Munn grinned and uncurled his hands.

"Is he?"

"Aye. And the lass is receptive." The wee man nodded like an idiot.

"More reason for them to stay at the caves. The chambers and pools are conducive to my objective." She flicked a dismissive hand.

"Trust me. The prince made me vow to help you."

"Prince?" Caitrina stiffened. Certainly not her father. "Who?"

"Aye. Dugaid."

"You made a pledge to the Dark Prince? Are you mad?" A shiver of acute interest meandered down her spine. Was the prince as handsome as rumors boast? 'Twas hard to believe the infamous Dugaid, one of the acclaimed unicorn brotherhood, would lower his exalted self to converse with a wee brownie, never mind request said brownie's help. The stakes must be high.

They were for her, of course. But why the prince?

"Nae choice," Munn said. "He is verra persuasive."

"And he's the queen's son."

"There is that."

"You dinnae believe the prince is on my side, do you?"

"Well, aye. Prince Dugaid wants you to win. He said so. Promised there would be nae interference from the queen."

"You wee fool." She shook her head. "You believed him?"

"Aye." Munn pursed his lips.

"Since Oonagh vowed not to interfere, she must have drafted her son to thwart me." *But why?* Caitrina paced in a circle then threw up her arms. "Dinnae try to help, Munn. You will just make a muddle of things."

"Want to help," he said. "Give me the horses."

"Nae!" Weary of the conversation, Caitrina flashed into the vanishing. Why had Prince Dugaid taken an interest in the outcome of the queen's challenge?

Both intrigued and apprehensive, Caitrina rode the wind in a whirl to a private mossy glen, needing to contemplate the significance of such an important development. Crossing swords with the Dark Prince could be exhilarating. Heat flashed her chest, anticipation coiling in her gut.

Or, could bring about her demise.

❀ ❀ ❀

Jillian shivered under the covers. Frustration along with the cold making her miserable. Why had Stephen hurried off after the little man appeared and then disappeared? Perhaps she shouldn't have been so forward as to kiss him. Maybe should have played harder to get. *Cripes*. Her come-on had been poorly timed and reckless. Though he'd been more than receptive of the kiss, and she almost found release in what came after.

Some men disliked aggressive woman. Before Finn married, he'd reinforced that truth each time he ignored her advances only to take up with pretty debutants from New York City—simpering fools—with D-cups. That wasn't totally fair. His wife, Elspeth, was beautiful, and no one's fool.

Jillian cringed. She'd been so jealous of Finn and Elspeth's relationship. Until she met Stephen.

Stephen didn't appear the type to shy away from a woman's advances. From the gleam in his eye, the reverence of his touch, and the semi-erection that seemed permanent, she didn't doubt his desire. So why did he hobble off?

Had she repulsed him too?

A scuffing sound nettled Jillian's already strung out nerves. She wrenched the covers higher as if they'd protect her. "Who's there?"

After an uncertain moment, Duff slipped from the shadows. "We dinnae want to sleep in the trees tonight. 'Tis too cold."

"We?"

Keita poked her head out from behind the boy, sad eyes imploring. "Can we sleep with you? Please."

Jillian's heart melted, but these were the same kids who

stole her stuff. "What did you do with my clothes and pack?"

"Naught," they said in unison vehemently shaking their heads.

"We did not filch anything," Duff said.

"Who did?"

"The others," Keita chimed in.

"Can you get my things back for me?"

More of the head shaking. Jillian let out a heavy sigh. What was she to do? Well, it didn't seem as if Stephen would return to keep her warm. She lifted the blankets and the children burrowed under the covers beside her.

"We like you," Keita said.

"You do?" Jillian smiled.

"Aye. You dinnae stare like other folk."

Jillian felt a twinge near her heart again. This poor child must be scorned for her disfigurement. All of the children had some sort of deformity. Except Duff. Other than having a long nose, he looked like a normal kid.

Keita and Duff wiggled restlessly.

"Perhaps a story will help us fall asleep." Jillian sat up and Keita crawled onto her lap. "Once upon a time there was a baker who wanted to seem more important in the eyes of the king so he claimed his beautiful fair-haired daughter could spin gold from straw—"

"Could she?" Keita asked.

"Well, let's see how the story goes." Jillian brushed fingers over the little girl's blonde hair. "The king's man escorted the maiden to a chamber high in the castle tower containing straw and a spinning wheel. She was left with the threat that if she could not do as her father bragged, she would be condemned to life in the deepest, darkest dungeon."

"That is a terrible punishment since it was the father who told the lie," Duff said.

"How do you ken 'tis a falsehood?" Keita demanded.

"'Cause no one can spin gold from straw except, mayhap, one of the Fae."

"Is that true?" Keita bunched a handful of Jillian's dress in her small fist.

"Let's hear the rest of the story, shall we?" Jillian tapped the tip of a pert nose, and the little girl smiled, gaze alight with interest. With a wistful breath, Jillian proceeded with the tale. "Tears spilled from the maiden's eyes for she was unable to spin straw into gold. But a short wrinkled man residing in a neglected part of the castle heard the sobbing and snuck into the chamber unnoticed by the other castle inhabitants. How will you reward me if I spin this straw into gold before the night is through, he asked. The maiden offered the bronze brooch securing her shawl, though she would miss it dearly for it had belonged to her deceased mother."

"Was the wee wrinkled man Munn?" Keita asked.

"He cannot spin gold. He's just a wee brownie," Duff said with an indignant huff.

"Shall I proceed?" Jillian asked.

"Please," the children answered in unison.

"In the morning when the king came to the chamber, the man was gone and a pile of gold coins sat on the floor next to the spinning wheel."

Keita gasped then made raspberries at Duff, who stuck his tongue out in return.

"The king was a tad on the greedy side so he ordered his steward to take the maiden to a larger chamber where there was twice as much straw and a spinning wheel," Jillian continued. "When left alone, the maiden cried because she couldn't spin straw into gold. The little man appeared, again, and she offered him the bone bracelet from her wrist if he would spend the night spinning."

"Sounds like a lot of work," Duff groused.

Jillian chuckled. "The king was so pleased to find the gold in the morning he escorted the woman to a third, much larger, chamber filled with straw and a spinning wheel. He told her if she spun the straw into gold during the night, he would make her queen and she would never need spin again. She waited and waited but the little man didn't make an appearance."

"He has to help her," Keita shrieked.

"Finally, as she wept with despair, he appeared in the chamber and asked what she would give this night for his service. She had nothing else to offer. I will take your firstborn son as payment, he said, and he spent the night spinning."

A shadow blocked the dim light coming from the tunnel entrance. Jillian glanced up. Stephen had returned.

Stephen halted in the entranceway, listening to Jillian's sweet voice spinning magic for the *bairns*. He rubbed his chest. Damn. How, in such a short time, had she found a vulnerability within his heart?

"What is this tale you tell the children?"

"It's a Grimms' faerie tale I often read to Patrick and Laurie's daughter at bedtime when I babysit."

"Please, continue." He leaned against the rough stone wall with crossed arms.

"Aye." Keita begged. "What happens next?"

"The king kept his promise and married the maiden, making her queen. She enjoyed her life in the castle, especially walks in the garden. When their son was born, joy filled her heart. She had forgotten the promise to the gold-spinner. But the man came to collect the child without delay, demanding payment. The queen couldn't bear to give up her child so offered the man riches beyond the imagination. The wretched man scoffed, having no desire nor need for wealth. He wanted the boy for his own."

Duff snorted, and Stephen laughed.

"After much debate, the man finally agreed to forsake his claim to the child if, and only if, the queen guessed his real name before the full moon three nights hence. For two days the queen's attempts failed. At dusk on the last day, she secretly followed the man into the forest to a grassy hill—"

"'Twas probably a faerie knoll," Duff said.

"Where he danced in a circle." Jillian ignored the boy's remark. "Then he chanted a name three times before vanishing from sight. Moments before the full moon, he came to the queen at the castle, ready to collect the child. The queen shouted the name she'd overheard in the forest—*Rumpelstiltskin.*"

"Then what happened?" Keita asked in a breathy voice.

"The man was so angry his face flamed red, he spun in a circle and disappeared, never to be heard from again."

"Are you sure the tale is not about Munn?" Duff asked. "'Tis just like something he would do."

Stephen ruffled the lad's hair. "Enough. 'Tis time everyone is abed."

He joined them on the large pallet. After a short time, he was the only one awake. Jillian cradled Keita in her arms, and he had an arm around the sleeping Duff.

He felt content for the first time in he couldn't remember how long. If only he hadn't agreed to the handfasting, he'd be begging Jillian to be *his* forever love.

I need to find a way to end things with Calyn. He prayed she wasn't with child.

CHAPTER NINE

*M*unn stood on the mound in the Fir-wood, hands fisted on hips, staring at the spot Caitrina had vacated. *Infuriating sithiche!* He stomped a foot. Caitrina was too proud to accept his help. He should forget this whole affair and find a nice spot for a nap.

Munn slumped. His vow to the Dark Prince sat heavy on his shoulders. What was he to do?

He paced and thought and paced some more. How was he to aid Caitrina when she didn't want his help? He should forget the faerie princess and concentrate his efforts on assisting Stephen and the lass from the future. By so doing, Caitirina would win the challenge, and he'd fulfill his vow to the prince.

But where could he secure the mounts Stephen requested? Munn scratched his head. Where? Ah! Archibald would provide horses. The chief would want to help Stephen.

Munn spun in a circle. As he faded, he heard the sniggers of the lost *bairns*. He should stop and investigate what sort of mischief they stirred this day. Instead, he traveled through the nether to the stables at Castle Lachlan landing with a *grumph* on the muck-covered floor of Archibald's favorite warhorse's stall. He rolled to a sitting position and sniffed the shoulder of his *leine*. The reek of dung burned his nostrils. *Crap!*

Archibald laughed, but it was a hollow sound. "Ach, wee man. 'Tis good to see you."

His features sobered and he extended a hand, helping Munn to his feet. Munn stared into the chief's gray eyes. Eyes that glistened with grief.

Munn fretted. He hated for the chief to be distressed.

"We heard the word from Branxton." Archibald shook his head, slammed a fist against a thigh. "Such a waste. The loss of so many fine warriors. Most of our lads are dead. God keep them." He made the Sign of the Cross. "I will feel their death in my heart for the rest of my living days."

Archibald sucked in an audible breath. What could Munn say to lessen the chief's sorrow?

"Duncan is devastated by the loss of Jamie," the chief continued, a hitch in his voice. "And Stephen…"

Munn bounced on his feet unable to contain his delight in the news he would share. He would make the chief smile again. "Stephen lives!"

Archibald swayed. Leaned on the stall's half-wall. "How? Where?"

"Wounded. Caves of the Gray Women."

Tempered relief replaced some of the pain clouding the chief's eyes. "How bad are his injuries?" He cleared his throat. "How did he get there?"

"Caitrina."

Archibald's eyes widened. "The faerie?"

"Aye." The chief must remember Caitrina. She once guided him to the caves to rescue Lady Laurie from the clutches of Maclay. And she was with them in the future when they visited one Christmas.

"And Stephen's injuries?"

"Cuts from swords. Bruises. Crushed leg. Cannot walk without a crutch."

"Dammit!" Archibald ran a hand through his chestnut hair.

Munn sighed. "Getting better. The fae pool helps with the

healing."

"Has Maclay been seen?"

"Nae." Munn shook his head, and the chief seemed to relax.

"Let me go to the keep and tell Isobell the good news, kiss our newborn son, round up some lads, and then we can be off to retrieve Stephen."

"Needs horses."

"More than one?"

"Aye." Munn shuffled his feet. "He found a lass from the future."

Archibald's brows rose into his hairline and he gripped the stall half-wall again. "The future, you say?"

"Aye."

"Then we must travel to the caves in all due haste."

Tir-nan-Og

Dugaid paced his mother's antechamber. He'd always hated the overindulgence cunningly displayed to intimidate visitors. Silver columns and crystal walls, brilliant sapphire gemstones in cut-glass bowls, luxuriant royal blue velvets and silks draped about, all to enhance the silvery splendor of the Fae High-Queen.

A sharp inhale and exhale fortified his patience, and he loosened tight fists. Might as well get this over with. He strode to the open wall draped by lucent curtains and drew aside the diaphanous fabric interwoven with threads of finely spun silver to view the pool beyond where his mother entertained her current lover.

Dugaid ground his teeth. *Ach! And legend tells tales of Finvarra's unfaithfulness. Tit for tat. Aye, Mother?*

Oonagh's gaze reached him. Surprise flared and a pleased smile curved her lips. She whispered something to Gabriel then released the lesser fae from a wanton embrace.

With a tight rein on his control, Dugaid ignored the glare

sent his way as Gabriel climbed from the pool and padded past and out of Oonagh's chambers.

She emerged from the glistening water in all her naked glory. He should look away from her lissome form glimmering with a fine dusting of silver powder. Away from her pert breasts and the smug smile playing on sensuous lips. Away from the gleam of sexual desire in her gaze.

He refused to show such weakness, maintaining a mask of indifference.

"My son." She glided across the white marble tile to stand before him.

How easily her interest shifted. She caressed the curve of his cheek. Slender fingers skimmed the muscles in his arms, across his chest, stomach, to land on his groin, where she gripped the family jewels. Dazzling blue eyes burned with lust then anger when his cock didn't harden beneath her palm.

He felt naught but hatred.

"Clothe yourself, Mother."

She twisted away with a shrug of a slender shoulder as if his lack of desire didn't matter.

He kenned better. She was an incestuous bitch.

Lounging on the white brocade chaise in the center of the chamber, she positioned her ankle-length blonde hair to best advantage, leaving breasts and feminine mound open to view. She taunted, hoping to get a rise from him. She'd be waiting 'til the world and all its realms no longer existed.

He remained behind an impassive facade.

Oonagh scrutinized him through narrowed eyes then grasped a crystal pawn from the ebony and ivory chessboard. "What brings you to the palace, Dugaid? You have not bothered to visit your mother in many a decade, preferring to cavort with those of the earth realm. Perhaps you are more of their ilk than fae."

"Unless you care to admit to lying with a human, Mother, which we both ken you will not do, my status as a pure-bred faerie cannot be disclaimed."

"So why are you here?"

"Aye, Mother. Let us cut to the chase." He hesitated, locking stares with the bitch. "You will not interfere with Caitrina and the challenge any further."

"That is none of your affair, Dugaid."

"Aye, 'tis. I have recently left Torne Castle and Prince Torgil, where I signed a betrothal agreement in *fae* blood for Caitrina's hand."

"You fool!" Oonagh rose and quickly clothed herself in argent silk, meeting him head on. "How dare you go behind my and your father's back to negotiate a betrothal?"

"Finvarra could not care less. And as for you, I will only provide this one warning. Dinnae interfere with Caitrina. She will be my wife. The mother to my faelings."

Oonagh snarled, transforming her features into something unexpectedly ugly. "You dare mix your royal blood with that halfling's?"

"This discussion is at an end. Remember my warning."

Dugaid slipped into the vanishing, but as he faded his mother let fly a parting volley, "She'll never forgive your deceiving her."

Every muscle taut, he appeared in the palace stables where he retrieved his fine stallion and three other mounts then whisked them away to the earth realm. He rolled his shoulders, relieving some of the tension. In time, he would make Caitrina understand why it had been necessary to deceive her these many years. She'd forgive him.

Seeking the hum of fae protection magic—his mother's magic—he zeroed in on the hidey-hole of the woodland *bairns*. A child's voice tittered on the breeze. The imps must be nearby. "I ken you are here. Come out. I will not harm you."

Three deformed lads slipped from the trees, near to quaking where they stood.

"I have a heroic task for thee."

Three sets of eyes widened, and the boys shuffled closer. He handed each a set of reins. "Take these fine beasts to the caves of the Gray Women and present them to Stephen

MacEwen. Dinnae sell them. Dinnae dawdle. Travel with haste and hand them over to Stephen. Nae other." Dugaid looked each child in the eye in turn. "Do you understand?"

The three lads nodded, and he handed each boy a silver coin snatched from his mother's chamber.

"Dinnae fail me."

The lads grinned. The pudgy fellow stepped forward. "We will do as you request, hoping you will look kindly upon us in the future."

Cheeky kid. Dugaid chuckled. "Fare thee well."

A week had passed and a severe case of cabin fever, or cave fever as it be, drove Jillian bat-shit crazy. Stephen refused to allow her to leave the caves, claiming it was too dangerous to go outside without an armed guard since a madman, more than likely brandishing a sword or some other relic weapon, scourged the countryside. The same man who had supposedly kept her business partner, Laurie, prisoner in these caves several years prior.

A shiver snaked up Jillian's spine. Could it be true? Laurie had never mentioned it. Why would she? She hadn't told Jillian about the time travel thing either.

Jillian paced the sprawling outer cavern, frowning. And why did Stephen avoid being alone with her? He seemed to make sure if they were together the two kids, Keita and Duff, were with them, too. They were becoming quite the little family unit. The children had burrowed into Jillian's heart, but she wanted some alone time with Stephen.

Thank God, each day he was getting better. Stronger.

Stephen entered the chamber with barely a limp, carrying a claymore, a green gemstone that looked very much like an emerald winking from the cross section. She'd seen enough of the Scottish swords used by the men in the Anderson Creek reenactment group to know exactly the name of the long pointy weapon.

"Your recovery has been truly miraculous," she said. "I'm

becoming a believer in your fae healing magic."

His quick grin was electric, and it sent a shiver of awareness through her body, culminating in the clenching of her sex. She stepped close to Stephen, placed a palm on his bare chest. The children were off to who knew where, and she was determined to take advantage of their absence. Jillian rolled onto the balls of her feet and planted a kiss on Stephen's lips.

He stiffened, but then got with the program. The sword dropped with a clatter to the floor and his arms came around her in a crushing embrace. He repositioned his head and sought her tongue. The heady sensation curled her toes. She clutched his firm ass. God, he tasted good from the medicinal herbs the women made him eat. When the kiss ended they pressed their foreheads together and just breathed.

"Ach, lass, you make me want things I must not have."

"What do you mean?" She leaned back and held his gaze. "I know we haven't known each other long, but sometimes it only takes a moment to feel an undeniable attraction that might blossom into more. I feel that with you."

He ran a hand through his overlong blond hair. "You are so sweet..."

"But..."

He opened his mouth, though before he provided an explanation a crashing noise came from the entrance. Stephen dove for the sword, and she swirled to face the opening.

Blaney rolled into the cave, landing at her feet.

"What are you doing here?" Jillian fisted hands on hips. "Where are my things?"

Stephen placed a gentling hand on her arm. "'Tis better for your future things to remain hidden out of the clutches of those who might accuse you of practicing the dark arts."

"*Witchcraft?*" At his nod, she swallowed uneasily, remembering hearing stories at a Celtic festival about false accusations of sorcery leveled against women and men alike in Scotland. Many were burned at the stake. "I thought politics were behind accusations of witchcraft."

"In some cases," Stephen agreed. "Fear of those different in most."

"Okay. We leave the things hidden."

Blaney's gaze ping-ponged between Jillian and Stephen.

Stephen patted the boy on the shoulder. "What brings you to the caves today?"

"Prince Dugaid sent us."

Jillian gave Stephen a questioning look. He shrugged and returned attention to Blaney.

"Dinnae ken the man."

"The Prince of the Dark River. The son of the King and Queen of the Fae."

"Oh, my," Jillian squeaked.

"He gave us horses to bring to you," Blaney said. "He said we mustn't give them to anyone else. Just you."

"Where are these horses?" Stephen asked.

"Mack and Cam are tending them at the edge of the wood."

"You are in luck, lass." Stephen grinned, squeezing her hand. "With horses, we can leave for Castle Lachlan as soon as we pack provisions for the journey."

This was good news. Finally. Jillian sighed with relief.

"Can we come too?" Keita begged. She and Duff must have silently slipped into the cavern while they were busy talking with Blaney.

Jillian shot Stephen another questioning glance. She'd hate to leave the children behind, but he'd have to deal with them once she returned to the future. And maybe that was why he kept putting on the brakes. Why should he be with someone who was going to leave him?"

"Aye." Stephen patted Keita's blonde head. "You may come with us."

❀ ❀ ❀

'Twas best the children traveled with them. Stephen didn't ken how he'd keep his hands off Jillian during the journey otherwise. He wanted her in a way he'd never wanted another woman. If it wasn't for Calyn, he'd beg Jillian to stay in this time with him or he'd force the faerie knoll to take them both to her future place.

The three lads faded into the wood while he and Jillian loaded the horses, the *bairns'* ability to disappear without sound unnerving. The other two children were bursting with excitement, eager for an adventure.

Stephen placed his hands on Jillian's waist and lifted her onto the roan horse. Duff found a tree stump and mounted his horse.

"Keita, do you want to ride with me or Jillian?"

The wee lass stuck her thumb in her mouth.

"How about you start out with Jillian and when she grows tired you can ride with me?"

Keita nodded, and he lifted and placed her in front of Jillian.

He was about to mount his horse when an unsettling sensation came over him, as if he'd forgotten something important. "I will return shortly. Must retrieve something from the caves."

Carefully traversing the cliff ledge, hopeful his leg wouldn't give out, he wondered what he could have forgotten that made the back of his neck itch. He strode through the outer cavern, through the tunnels, to the kitchen. One of the Gray Women, the one with timeless emerald eyes, sat at the table.

"Good morrow, good sister," he greeted.

She inclined her head, and he glanced around, searching for whatever drew him back to the caves.

"These are what you seek." She pointed to two leather sheaths on the table from which she removed two short, ornate knives etched with flowers. Each handle decorated with small emeralds matching the one in his claymore.

"I dinnae understand." He picked one up, measuring its heft and balance. "'Tis too light for my hand, too beautiful, but I thank you just the same."

"Foolish lad. They are for your lady-love."

He stiffened. "Calyn does not deserve such a generous gift. Nor can I afford such."

"These are not for Calyn but Jillian. And they are a gift from me and my sisters."

The air whished from Stephen's lungs, and he staggered back a step. What did this woman ken? Was she a seer?

"Dinnae look so startled. You ken you have fallen in love with the lass."

"But I am handfasted to Calyn."

"Though your future is not yet set in stone, 'tis unlikely you will share it with that unfaithful wench."

"But—"

"The tips are dusted with fae magic. See Jillian learns to use them."

Moisture blurred his eyes, making him blink. When his vision cleared, the woman had gone, leaving behind the exquisite knives.

CHAPTER TEN

*T*aking one of the B&B's horses for meandering trail rides in the forest behind the *Whispering Pines Inn* in Anderson Creek was nothing like riding cross-country in the wilds of Scotland 1513. Jillian shifted her weight in the saddle, trying not to wake Keita, who snuggled on her lap. Because of the children, Stephen's healing leg, and her inexperience, they halted every couple of hours to rest, eat a snack, and take care of personal needs. With the days getting shorter, Stephen had said they would stop early afternoon since they had much to do before nightfall. When they finally halted for the day, Jillian had sore muscles she'd never known existed.

Stephen limped over. Even he suffered from the arduous activity. He collected the sleeping Keita. "You must be tired, too. I will come back and help you dismount once I have settled her on the bedroll."

"No need. I can get myself down." Or so she thought until her jelly legs gave out and she crumbled to the ground in an aching mess. She hauled herself up while Duff slid from his horse, also wobbling when he hit the dirt.

"I am hungry," the boy whined.

Jillian's stomach growled in commiseration, but several tasks needed accomplishing first. "After we set camp."

The lad groaned, but he and Keita helped with the chores. After packs were unloaded and horses cared for, Stephen made a small fire, and Duff heated oatcakes. Jillian hadn't thought she'd ever wish for pre-packaged backpacking meals, but she did now.

After the sparse meal was finished and the extra food and cooking gear stowed, Stephen dropped onto the blanket beside her. "I have a gift for you from the Gray Women."

"For me? Really?" Her eyes widened. "I can't imagine why they'd give me a present."

His impassive expression made her feel jittery. Her fingers trembled. He placed a tied roll of deerskin between them then released the knot and spread the leather flat to display two sheaths containing ornate handled knives.

She locked gazes with Stephen. "What are these for?"

"Protection."

"I don't know how to use them. Even if I did, I don't think I could."

Stephen unsheathed one of the knives and held it out to her. "Take it."

"Don't want to." She shook her head, lips pressed tight into a frown.

"Take it," he repeated, his tone firm. She hesitated, but finally gripped the handle. "Be careful of the sharp tip. 'Tis coated with faerie dust."

She rolled her eyes. She couldn't help it. Even though she'd started to believe in magic, faerie dust seemed over the top. "Now what?" she asked. "I feel squeamish just holding a weapon."

He ignored the complaint and stood. Grasping her left hand, he hauled her up beside him. "I stuffed moss into a cloth and hung it on that tree trunk to use as a practice target. Since you accepted the blade with your right hand that must be your dominant side. I will train you to throw from the right."

"I can't do this."

"You can. We need you to ken how to handle the knives.

If something happens to me, if I am injured or killed, you will need to protect yourself and the children."

"I'm not sure." Now was a fine time to wish she'd gone to martial arts classes with her brother years ago.

Stephen grasped her arm with a firm grip. "I have faith in you. You can learn to throw."

"If you say so."

"I do." Stephen's encouraging smile did funny things to her insides. He believed in her. She could see the confidence in his gorgeous blue eyes. He made her want to believe, too. It was a new experience having a man show faith in her. She hoped she wouldn't disappoint.

He grasped the second knife. "They have good balance."

Keita and Duff sat on a nearby log to watch. Jillian tilted the knife in her hand from side to side as Stephen had done, unsure what she was supposed to feel. The blade was beautiful, etched with flowers, and from the handle glinted several small emeralds. The knives should be displayed as works of art, not used as weapons.

"Since the handle is heavier than the blade, you will need to throw from the blade. Grasp it like this." Stephen demonstrated.

She attempted to hold the knife as directed.

"Not exactly. Here, let me help." He dropped the knife he held onto the blanket then stepped in close from behind, placing a hand on her left hip. He leaned in tight, hard chest pressed against her back. He smelled good—of fresh air and woodland. She felt the definition of each of his muscles and had to suppress a sigh. He grasped her right wrist, and her pulse spiked. "Loosen your grip, lass. Aye, like that."

Easy for him to say. His breath whished over her ear, causing delicious shivers to spread. Her breasts felt heavy, nipples beaded. She wanted to forget the knife and spin around and kiss him. But the children were watching. And she wasn't sure Stephen wanted her advances. He'd kept a metaphorical distance between them for the past few days. Until now.

"Plant your right foot like so…" He released her hand and gripped her thigh. Ripples of sensation tingled up her leg, making her sex clench. Making her needy. Making her want to reach back and take Stephen into her hand. He seemed unaffected. "Point your toes toward the target. Good. You will throw the knife, following through with your back foot to provide more power."

She released the knife. The effort fell short of its mark. Stephen stepped away, taking his warmth with him, yet leaving her hot and bothered.

"Let me demonstrate." He grabbed the knife from the blanket, stressed each step as he went through the motions, and threw. The knife sailed through the air in a blur. The blade imbedded in the target with a twang.

The children clapped.

"Easy for you," Jillian groused.

"You can master knife throwing, too." He retrieved the blades and handed her one. "Now, move through the steps with me."

"Okay." Though she'd rather have him up close and personal again.

"The trick is to get the knife to tumble, blade over handle, so it doesn't bounce off the target but enters soft flesh."

"I don't think I can throw a knife at a real person."

"What if one of the *bairns* is threatened?"

Jillian glanced at the children and frowned. Brow furrowed tight. He knew her weakness. She would do anything required to protect the kids or protect Stephen. "Okay, I'll try."

"That is a good lass."

He moved her closer to the target. She threw again. She kept at it until her arm ached with the repetitive motion, but not once did she hit the mark. One more throw. If she missed the target, she was giving up. She repeated the steps and threw. The weapon fell way short of the target again.

"Grrr. Told you I couldn't do this."

Stephen chuckled. "Have faith. We will practice each

afternoon after we make camp and finish our eve'n meal."

"If you think we must."

"I do." He kissed the tip of her nose.

Stephen didn't ken why he'd planted the impulsive kiss on Jillian. Her bemused smile tore at his resolve to keep her at a distance. Being close to her and inhaling her feminine scent while instructing her near made him forget the need to temper his desire. 'Twas proving difficult to stay detached from the lass.

Jillian dropped onto the log next to the *bairns*. Moisture pricked the back of Stephen's eyes. These three were becoming important to him. He wished he could keep them.

"Darkness is upon us." His voice sounded gruff so he cleared his throat. "Duff and I will alternate keeping watch."

The lad perked up at the announcement, eager to help.

"I can take a turn," Jillian offered, but exhaustion surrounded her eyes.

"Nae need."

"You require sleep more than I do since you are still healing from your wounds."

"Mayhap another night. For now, Duff and I will see the task done. Come, lad, let us walk the perimeter of camp to ensure all is secure and plan our defense."

They checked on the horses then found a raised spot from which they could observe anyone approaching the small campsite.

"Can I take the first watch?" Duff pleaded.

"Aye. I will stay with you. Wake me when you grow tired." Stephen hunkered down on a scattering of pine needles, huddling into his *plaide* for warmth. Duff did the same, but kept a sharp eye. Stephen gave the lad his trust and slept. Duff shook him awake near dawn.

Stephen cracked his neck with a twist. "You should have awakened me sooner. You will be too tired to ride."

The lad shrugged then yawned.

"Go. Join Jillian and Keita. Get some sleep." Stephen sent

the lad off. When the sun rose over the horizon, he tended the horses and rekindled the fire.

The previous night, Jillian had found a leaf-strewn spot close to the fire to cushion the large bedroll. She and the children were cuddled under several *plaides* and her strange future cloth. He scratched the itch at the back of his neck and pursed his lips. Though the silver cloth provided extra warmth 'twould be best to destroy the thing before a zealous stranger saw it and mistook it as the work of Satan.

Stephen sighed. He'd need to speak to Jillian when she woke and convince her of such. She wouldn't be happy to give up another possession.

How dare Prince Dugaid interfere? With fae horses, Jillian and Stephen would travel the far distance to Castle Lachlan and the *Sithichean Sluaigh* in half the normal time.

Caitrina wanted them to spend more time together not less. They needed a chance to fall in love.

Caitrina shed the glamour of a Gray Woman, smooth skin replacing that of the wrinkled hag. Thick auburn hair replaced stringy gray. Drab garments disappeared, and she ran a sensitive touch over the much preferred, gauzy, green silk dress that molded to her tall, slender frame. She retrieved a gold brooch intricately crafted with thistle designs and amethyst gemstones from a hidden pocket and secured it at the shoulder of the green and purple tartan sash, interwoven with shimmering golden threads, draping the gown.

She fisted her hands, allowing free rein to her anger, almost missing the subtle change of vibration tainting the air. Evil skulked nearby. Not the darkest evil of hell yet evil just the same. Fading into invisibility, she traversed chambers and passages to the land-side mouth of the caves opening high on the hill. She caught the scent and followed the foul smell.

Dammit! Maclay stalked the three lost *bairns*—Blaney, Mack, and Cam. What would he want with the lads?

Malcolm Maclay hesitated behind a broad oak. The three

misshapen lads scurried through the wood, making nary a sound. Yet Malcolm was known as a gifted tracker and able to move as silently. He easily followed their serpentine wanderings.

Caitrina hovered behind him. Should she intervene? She'd need be careful and not interfere with freewill.

"Damn eerie place," he muttered and rubbed the back of his neck, darting a glance over a shoulder. "Have the lost *bairns* stolen a bauble from the Gray Women? Mayhap, I can snatch the trinket to use in trade."

The man was in desperate need of resources. Of that she was sure.

Malcolm stalked to the next large tree. She stayed with him. Protection magic hummed over her skin. *Oonagh.* The *bairns* must have hidden something of import for the Queen of the Fae to conceal it within spell magic. *Jillian's things?*

Why would the queen protect Jillian's things?

The rustle of brush brought her attention back to the *bairns.* First one lad, then the second, lunged into a tight thicket of bushes and small trees. The third—the pudgy *bairn* with the deformed right hand—used his left to drag a fir bough over their tracks. Then he, too, disappeared from sight.

"There it is!" Malcolm snickered. "The changelings hidey-hole."

He glanced at the branches above. 'Twould be the perfect place from which to wait for the *bairns* to head off again. Although the tree leaves had long ago fallen, chances were slim the lads would notice Malcolm high up in the branches. He climbed the tree and secured a spot at the crook of a fat limb, enfolded his upper body within the excess drape of his *plaide* for warmth against the chill breeze, and watched.

She would wait, too. Caitrina settled on another branch.

CHAPTER ELEVEN

*S*everal days into the trip, Jillian woke and shared with the others a breakfast of dry oatcakes, apples, and cheese. *Ugh. Again.* Stephen passed around a skin of heather ale. Afterward, as Jillian packed the saddlebags, Keita tugged on her skirt. She peered down at the little girl. "What is it, sweet pea?"

The child stared bug-eyed as if astonished by the endearment, and then smiled. "I want to ride with Duff."

Jillian glanced at Stephen. He gave an abrupt nod then returned to adjusting the horse's tack. He'd been acting differently toward her since they'd left the caves. He'd not shared the warmth of the bedroll at night, preferring to sleep enwrapped by his plaid while keeping watch with Duff. She'd offered to take a turn at guard duty, but repeatedly Stephen shooed her away, telling her to take her rest with Keita.

Perhaps he found traveling with her and the children a burden. She sighed and returned her attention to Keita. "Sure. You can ride with Duff for a while."

The delighted girl spun in a circle, skirt swirling around her ankles, and skipped to Stephen.

He lifted the child onto the boy's horse as if she weighed less than a feather. Stephen seemed to be growing stronger daily. Thank goodness he no longer needed the crutch and only showed a trace of a limp when walking. The speed of his healing truly amazed Jillian. Made her a believer in faerie magic.

As he passed, he leaned in close. "Keep an eye on her. When she tires, one of us can take her on our horse."

"Of course." Did he think Jillian wouldn't watch after the children? *Cripes*. She was beginning to feel cranky.

He helped her mount, though not as familiarly as on previous occasions, then mounted his stallion, and they reined the horses out of the small clearing onto an overgrown game trail. With her skirt bunched up for riding astride, brush and twigs tugged at and caught on her exposed woolen stockings. Seemed like every dozen feet, or so, she needed to halt and detangle the wool cloth from a bramble.

After an hour or so, they entered a broader trail. The earthy smell of fallen leaves reminded Jillian of home, of the Blue Ridge Mountains and the trails surrounding the garden center. Would she ever find her way back to *Foxgloves*? She could only hope.

For the moment, her future was in Stephen's hands.

Several hours passed before they broke free of the forest. The noonday sun warmed her shoulders. They climbed a hillside with a scattering of cheerful yellow blooms.

"Lovely, is it not?" Stephen said.

Jillian jerked a surprised gaze in his direction. They were the first words he'd uttered since leaving camp this morning. Maybe he felt cranky, too.

"Yes, I'm surprised to see gorse in bloom this late in the year."

"Always some in flower. My ma used to say, when the gorse is in bloom, 'tis kissin' season." He laughed and his blue eyes twinkled. "You should see the golden hillsides near Castle Lachlan in springtime."

She stared at his lips, wanting to kiss that sexy mouth. But then she glanced away. Hopefully, she'd be home in North Carolina way before spring.

"I will miss you, lass," he said as if reading her thoughts.

She twisted toward him. "You will?"

"Aye," he said, gravely. The horses had slowed and Jillian tried to read the emotion in his eyes, getting lost in their depths. She would miss him, too. More than she wanted to admit. Perhaps, if only he—

The children rode up and shattered the moment. "We are hungry."

Jillian shook her head. She shouldn't consider staying.

"Then we better feed you, aye?" Stephen said, as if he hadn't just sent her world off axis and into a wobble. Could Stephen possibly want her to stay?

After dismounting, Jillian spread one of the plaids on the hillside in the sunshine, craving warmth. Stephen dropped beside her. Keita chased Duff over the hill, burning off excess energy.

"Meant what I said earlier," Stephen said. "I will miss you."

Jillian lifted her face to the sun, feeling awkward. "I don't know what to say."

"There is nae need to say anything." He squeezed her upper arm. "Just wanted you to ken it has been my greatest joy meeting you. I wish you well in your future place."

What was he saying? Or, what was he not saying? She bit her bottom lip. Did he want her to stay here in the past with him, but feared asking? She couldn't stay. Could she?

"What if I can't return to my own time?"

"Nae worries. You will."

"What makes you so certain?"

He shrugged. Maybe he wasn't convinced at all.

What would happen to her if she were stuck here in the past? Would Stephen marry her? He hadn't declared his love. He said he'd miss her. Like a friend?

There was so much she liked about him. He was sexy as all get out, yet there was so much more to the man. He treated her and the children with gentle consideration. He'd taken them under his wing even though they were not his responsibility. She loved his honesty.

Did she love him? She was beginning to believe so. Or was that just her being needy?

If she was stuck here and he didn't want to marry her, what would she do? She'd perish on her own without a way of earning a living. How could she possibly take care of herself?

Keita ran toward them, jounced on the blanket, and handed over a small bunch of golden flowers, drawing her attention away from Stephen and her jumbled thoughts. Jillian inhaled the blooms' coconut-like scent careful of the prickly stems. "Thank you, sweet pea."

"Why do you call me that?"

"Because I think you're a sweet little girl."

Keita beamed, leaned forward and kissed Jillian's cheek, and then dashed off after Duff again. The child was such a dear one. Jillian glanced at Stephen. Major creases lined his forehead.

What was he doing? Stephen scrubbed a hand over his face. Why hadn't he kept his thoughts to himself? Kept his mouth shut? Kept a distance? He shouldn't encourage any sort of special accord betwixt him and Jillian, as much as he wanted to do just that. 'Twould be unfair to lead her to believe he could offer her more than...

More than what? He had naught to give.

A tumble in the heather? She deserved more than that.

He leapt from the blanket, strode to the horses, and made busy loading their saddlebags. He needed to remember he was obligated to another. And though he wasn't happy with that circumstance, he couldn't dishonor his vow and lay with Jillian as he wanted. It would be wrong.

She sidled up beside him and grasped his hand, making everything within him still. "As much as I don't understand how or why I came to be here. I'm glad I had the opportunity to meet you and the children. Thank you for helping me."

She'd lumped him in with the children. Did she not have

deeper feelings for him?

"I can do naught else." And wasn't that true?

"I wish I could stay and spend time getting to know you better. But…I don't belong here."

He swallowed hard. It was only right she'd want to leave. "Let us be on our way so we can get you back where you do belong."

She nodded. They mounted and rode on in silence. The children started to bicker and before long, Keita once again rode with Jillian.

When they came upon a small glen with a *burn* running through it, they stopped for the night. After setting camp and eating, he put Jillian through her paces, making her practice throwing the knife. She'd made progress, hitting the target one out of every three throws. Not as good as she might need to be, but a marked improvement, and better than he had hoped after such a short time.

"Hope this is a waste of time," she said. "I don't want to need to use the knives."

"I ken. Slit the bottoms of the pockets in your skirt. Then lift the skirt and strap a knife to each thigh."

She raised her brows. "Why?"

"You need to have them within easy grasp."

She did as instructed then eyed him suspiciously.

She read him well. "'Tis time to teach you how to protect yourself if you are physically attacked."

"I won't need to face that. Will I?"

"Not if I am able to protect you. However, there are many dangers in this time. Remember, if things turn ugly, if I cannot come to your aid and you need to fight hand to hand, expect to get cut. Ignore the pain. Keep fighting. Your objective is to make the bastard bleed. Slow him down."

Her beautiful face scrunched up with a deep frown. He hated that he'd caused her distress.

Stephen hugged her. He knew immediately 'twas a mistake. Made him want so much more—a future with Jillian.

He stepped away. Cleared a suddenly parched throat. "I

ken you dinnae want to stab anyone, but your life may depend on it. May I attack you?"

Bored beyond measure, Caitrina massaged aching shoulders. She repositioned her weight on the limb and released a heavy, though silent sigh. What were the *bairns* doing for so long in their hidey-hole? Gloating over their treasure like a dragon with its horde? How long did Maclay plan to wait?

Another hour passed. The sun crept over the horizon, shades of vermillion painting the sky. Soon 'twould be dark. She could barely remain still. Her knee jounced. Fingers tapped.

Maclay scratched the back of his neck, glanced around as if he sensed her presence. She placed her thumbs in her ears and waved her fingers at him. Stuck out her tongue and blew soundless raspberries in his direction. Ha! He couldn't hear or see her; she remained invisible.

They were both distracted when the lads popped out of the thicket and darted away through the trees. With a frustrated growl, Maclay dropped to a lower branch then jumped to the ground, springing into a full-out run as he dashed after the children.

Caitrina laughed. The *bairns* were good at evading grownups. He didn't stand a chance at catching them.

She lowered to the leaf covered ground and stole to the thicket. Oonagh's strong magic skittered over her skin. There was no need to fear Maclay would find what was hidden.

Jillian's stuff from the future would remain safe.

Caitrina vanished into the evening breeze and traveled to Strathlachlan and the *Sithichean Sluaigh* to await Stephen and Jillian's arrival.

CHAPTER TWELVE

*T*hey traveled for several days and set camp late each afternoon. Exhaustion taking its toll, Jillian fell into a deep sleep along with the children after a meal of freshly caught trout. Loud voices roused her to semi-consciousness. She tried to shake off the cobwebs of slumber, sensing a strong need to wake up. Something pinged her cheek. Then again. She brushed a hand over her face and over the blanket. Pebbles? There were tiny round stones on the bedding.

Was she dreaming? Disoriented, she jerked her eyes open. Early morning light filtered through the mist. Panic set in when she realized the children were gone from the bedroll and the fervent voices belonged to angry men.

She rolled to the side and froze in place. Eyes wide, she focused on the four men near the cold fire ring. A man with a badly scarred face brandished a claymore, pointing the darn sword at Stephen while two other men held him by the arms. Stephen's desperate thrashing did little to throw off the men. He stilled, glare leveled at the man with the blade.

"Ach, now, MacEwen, how does it feel to be a member of the high and mighty Clan MacLachlan? My prisoner?" The scarred man's bark carried on the moist air to where Jillian pretended to sleep.

"What are you after, Maclay?" Stephen's voice held a chilling calm.

Maclay? Shit! This was the ruthless man they sought to avoid.

"I plan to take your lass to replace the one Patrick stole from me."

Jillian's gasp blended with the noise the men made and went unheard. Thank God.

"Lady Laurie never belonged to you. You kidnapped her," Stephen retorted.

"I was supposed to wed Lady Laurie. Patrick was to wed Lady Isobell. You cursed MacLachlans got them both."

"You ken verra well Patrick never agreed to that arrangement. Be off with you. Leave us in peace."

The scarred man's howling laugh made the hairs on Jillian's arms rise. She needed to do something to help Stephen. But what? She was powerless against three armed men. Fortunately, they seemed to believe she remained sleeping. Or perhaps didn't consider her a threat.

"Your time is at an end, MacEwen. The lady from faerieland is mine."

"Faerieland? You make nae sense."

"Oh, aye, I do. My men followed Isobell to the *Sithichean Sluaigh* and watched her disappear. I saw Archibald vanish from the same spot with my own eyes. I ken the knoll is a passageway to faerieland."

"Then use it and go there," Stephen spat.

"I cannot." Maclay precariously waved the sword as he spoke. "The magic will not work for me. I need the lass to show me the way."

"What makes you think she can take you?"

"She is like Lady Laurie. I ken Patrick traveled to the other side with his wife."

"You are a fool. They live in France."

"You lie. All MacLachlans lie. They went to faerieland and so shall I with the help of that lass." The four men stared in her direction.

Jillian snapped her eyes shut, feigning sleep, sneaking a peek from beneath her lashes.

"Mighty comely lass. Methinks to have my way with her first. Perhaps I will let you watch."

"Ye promised to share," blurted one of the men holding Stephen."

"Aye. I will." The scarred man leered, upper lip curled.

A shiver of fear shot through Jillian and she swallowed uneasily. How would they get out of this mess? Adrenaline surged in her veins. She needed to do something. But what?

Stephen struggled against the arms holding him. They held firm. "Why would she help you after you abused her?"

"To keep you alive." The man's spittle spattered Stephen's shirt.

Stephen didn't flinch. He locked gazes with Jillian, sending her strength. She knew he'd protect her with his last breath. Jillian must do the same for him.

The man with the sword lunged forward, blade pointed at Stephen. Jillian reacted without thought as Stephen had taught her. She grasped one of the knives from its sheath on her thigh and threw, grabbed the second and threw. The first blade embedded in the scarred man's forearm. He howled and pulled out the blade, tossing it on the ground. Blood flowed down his wrist, covering the sword hilt gripped in his hand. The second knife hit one of Stephen's captors in the belly. He doubled over then fell to the ground. His body convulsed then stilled.

Stephen took advantage of the disruption and threw off the remaining man holding him, rolled over the ground, and secured his claymore.

The scarred man and the uninjured man melted into the trees and disappeared.

"*Life or death!*" Stephen bellowed and ran into the woods after them. The oath sounded very much like a war cry.

Jillian scrambled to her knees. The man on the ground clutched his stomach, eyes wide with shock. Blood oozed from his mouth and he made funny gurgling sounds.

Ohmigod! She'd done that. Probably killed the man.

She crawled to the edge of the clearing and vomited. Once the nausea passed, she brushed hair away from a sweaty face with trembling fingers and scanned the camp. Where the hell were the children?

Stephen returned, tossed aside his sword, and lifted her to her feet. He wrapped her in a bear hug of an embrace. She could feel the rapid beat of his heart keeping time with hers.

"I am so verra sorry. Sorry you needed to do that." His palm cradled the back of her head.

"What about the man on the ground? Is there something we can do for him?"

"Aye." Stephen released her and slashed the man's throat. "May his soul rot in hell."

A rush of nausea hit Jillian and she retched again.

"My poor lass." Stephen wet a small cloth from a flask and wiped her face and her neck, his touch gentle. He offered the flask. "Here. Take a small sip and rinse the foul taste from your mouth."

She did as told and attempted a weak smile.

He held her close. "There, there. We only did what needed to be done."

Jillian sobbed into his chest. He hugged her shaking body. Rubbed her back. Kissed the top of her head. She took comfort in his strength.

On a hiccup, she murmured her fear into his chest.

"What? I did not hear you."

"The children are missing," she repeated.

"I ken."

She leaned back and searched his gaze.

"They snuck away into the wood as soon as the men showed themselves. Maclay did not care about the *bairns*. He let them go."

"I don't think they left right away. I think they threw pebbles at me first to rouse me from sleep."

Stephen smiled. "They are resourceful."

She sniffled. Glad the children woke her. Glad they hadn't

stuck around. Glad they hadn't witnessed what she'd done.

"Why did the men run off?" she asked.

"They ken I am the better fighter."

"Even with your bad leg?"

"They dinnae ken I was injured." He released her from his secure embrace. "We better break camp and go into hiding for a wee while."

Jillian felt lost without the comfort of his arms. Taking the flask of water, she gargled and thoroughly washed the awful taste from her mouth. Ugh. Toothpaste or a mint would be great right about now. She started to pack, but the dead man still lay there on the ground, watching her through sightless eyes. She burst into tears.

"Turn away, lass. I will drag the body into the brush so you will not need to look at it."

"Shouldn't we bury him?"

"Nae. Let the scavengers have him. He deserves nae better."

She swallowed hard and continued to pack. Stephen returned with a pronounced limp.

"Are you okay?"

"A minor setback. Stiff is all." He stepped close. "I will be fine. Here, let me help."

Jillian handed him the bedroll to tie onto one of the horses. "Why did they attack us?"

"Maclay wants you. And wants me dead."

"But why?"

"Revenge against Patrick. Maclay also seems to believe you are from faerieland. Mayhap, he thinks you are a faerie." He smiled, trying to make light of the situation.

"I heard him. He wanted to rape me."

"Dinnae think of it."

She knew Stephen was trying to ease her mind, but it wasn't working. "What are we going to do? How will we find the children?"

"Each night, Duff and I agree on a nearby place of safety. He took Keita to some caves not far from here. We will head there and regroup. Perhaps remain a day or two. Hopefully, Maclay will think we moved on and search for us farther abroad. Though I doubt we have seen the last of him. We will need to be more vigilant." He embraced her again. "You saved my life."

"I was so frightened." She hugged him back. "I thought they were going to kill you."

"They would have." Stephan ran a palm over the curve of her face, and she melted into the caress. "Your throws were well done. I am proud of you."

Acid burned Jillian's stomach, anxiety replacing the false moment of calm. She didn't want to think about what she'd been forced to do. Being in the past was no longer fun. She wanted to go home. Now.

They broke apart. Stephen had cleaned her blades and he held them out. Her hands shook, and she closed her eyes.

"Take them," he said, softly.

Jillian bit her lip. She didn't want to touch the knives, but finally took the pair and returned them to the sheaths strapped to her thighs. They finished loading the horses and mounted. Before they left the clearing, Jillian reined her roan mare next to Stephen's stallion. "Do we truly need to go into hiding? Couldn't we make a run for it? Hurry to the place where you think I can travel home from? I don't want to stay here any longer."

"Trust me." He patted her thigh. "I vow to keep you safe."

And he would, by the Saints. Stephen wouldn't let Maclay get hold of Jillian. The bastard would destroy the goodness within her. Hurt her for his pleasure. She meant more to Stephen than did his handfasted wife. His honor felt tarnished by the admission, but the truth was the truth. He wouldn't lie to himself.

He tensed his jaw. When they reached the caves, he planned to commit a sin of the flesh. Being near to death a couple of times, add the risk of nearly losing the one he loved, well, ach, the fear was enough to make a man rethink his convictions.

He stole glances at Jillian as they rode. They got twisted around a few times, searching for the caves Duff had described. Not a bad thing. The crossed tracks would confuse anyone following them.

A light snow began to fall. That, too, would help hide their tracks.

Although the caves were well hidden, the mouth easily handled the horses' height. He and Jillian dismounted and led the animals through the opening. A large hollow carved into a side wall proved perfect for securing the beasts out of the bad weather.

After making a torch and lighting it, he and Jillian explored the few inner chambers, holding hands. Felt right to guide her in such a personal manner. Especially considering the decision he'd made.

"The children aren't here. Do you think Maclay caught them?" Jillian scraped pearly white teeth over her bottom lip.

His body hardened in reaction. He wanted to plant a kiss on those sweet lips. "What?"

"The children?"

"The *bairns* ken the woods better than most. They are used to running free. Mayhap they have grown tired of traveling with us."

Her eyes misted.

He squeezed her fingers. "I am sure they will come to us again."

Upon returning to the horses, they unloaded the saddlebags, brushing against each other in the process. His body awakened, stiffened with each touch. He couldn't wait to hold her in his arms. Make slow, passionate love to her. Sleep with her at his side. He hoped the children stayed away, at least through the afternoon.

He slung the bag with the food over a shoulder. "Bring the bedroll, we will find a dry spot to rest and eat. You must be famished. I am."

He was hungry. Just not for food.

Stephen led Jillian deeper into the caves with only one thought in mind. He needed the feel of her body against his. Proof they both still lived.

They selected a chamber where a previous cave visitor had constructed a stone fire ring and left behind a pile of dry wood. While Jillian rolled out the bedding, he lit a wee blaze, the smoke escaping through a narrow fissure in the ceiling. He removed his *plaide*, and after they sat, spread the wool cloth over their laps.

He offered a cold oatcake, but she shook her head. "Not hungry."

What happened at camp this morning must still have her upset. "Perhaps some ale?"

She gifted him a tentative smile and accepted the skin. A long pull made her choke.

"Easy, lass." He slapped her back. "Not so fast."

"I'm fine. The ale went down my Sunday throat, is all."

She took a slower sip then handed him the skin. His brow tightened in confusion. "Dinnae understand."

"That was sort of a saying my father used to repeat when I drank too fast and inhaled the liquid instead of swallowing. As if it went down another throat and made me choke, a throat only used on the Sabbath. He could say it on any day but Sunday." She smiled for real this time.

His chest tightened. He couldn't wait any longer. Stephen leaned forward and, with the lightest of touches, pressed a kiss to her mouth. Soft brown eyes flared, gold specks sparkling, then closed as his lips continued to caress. He sucked on her bottom lip and caught a sensual moan. Wrapping her in a gentle embrace, he slid her onto his lap.

"Jillian, I wish to do more than kiss you, if you will permit." Her eyes fluttered open. The tenderest of moments. He kenned the answer without her speaking.

"I'd like that very much. Though first, a question. How do you suppose I was able to strike those men when I found it difficult to hit the target on a tree? Was it fae magic? You said the knife tips were coated in faerie dust." Jillian drew wee circles on his chest with the tip of a finger.

Her touch was distracting. Stephen would prefer to think about pleasure. He hesitated in answering wishing her thoughts hadn't travelled back to the attack. He didn't want her upset. And if he admitted what he believed to be true— he didn't want her to think he disparaged her marksmanship.

"You won't insult me."

"Ach, well, magic may have played a wee role."

Jillian smiled. "You are a diplomat, Stephen MacEwen. I like you very much."

She kissed him. Not a soft, gentle kiss, but an all-consuming, shocking kiss. Her tongue slid between his lips, and she tasted of the sweet ale they'd shared. Gaze locked on his, she grasped his shoulders and pushed him back against the bedding, straddling his hips, continuing with the kissing, tongues entwined and dueling.

He stiffened, ready to roll her over and become the aggressor. Her tongue grazed his teeth, and he nearly bucked. What was she doing to him? His erection throbbed. His heart beat as if he'd run a long distance without rest. He'd never had such an adamant lover. Felt good. Very good. He growled deep in his throat and responded in kind.

She broke the kiss and tugged his *leine* up over his chest. "You have way too much on."

He raised his arms and allowed the cloth to be dragged over his head and tossed aside. "As do you."

She giggled, and he reached for the hem of her plain wool gown. Shortly thereafter, divested of clothing, they tumbled on the bedding in a snarl of arms and legs, stroking and kissing. Each caress heightening desire. Stephen didn't think he could hold out much longer, but he wanted this one time with Jillian to last in his memory for a lifetime.

Using fingers to stoke the flame, he brought her to a fevered pitch. She arched, gripped the *plaide* beneath them in tight fists, and screamed his name with her release. Her joy echoed within the cave.

Her eyes glossy with satiation, his chest expanded with the knowledge he'd brought her such pleasure. His own need could no longer be denied. He slid between her legs, leaned his forehead against hers and struggled for control, struggled in search of gentleness.

His lass wanted none of that. In a quick move, she rolled them over and mounted him. For the love of… Her tight sheath slid over his cock, then withdrew, causing aching need. Exquisite pain. Blinding pleasure. Drawing him in, stroke after stroke, she moved with a rhythm that possessed, took him higher than he'd ever been before. Urgency drove him to the edge. Sweat broke out over his forehead. Almost. Almost there. He fisted the cloth beneath them. With Jillian's name on his lips, he exploded with a rush that burned through his chest, bled his cock, made him come and come and come.

They stayed entwined in a loving embrace for the longest of time, Jillian's breath teasing over his moist skin. Stephen hated to shatter the moment, but guilt nagged at him. He needed to explain the situation with Calyn. It wasn't fair to keep the handfasting secret.

He rolled away and sat up, feeling horribly unworthy. Jillian deserved so much more than he could offer. And what made him think she wanted anything more from him? "Jillian, I need to tell you—"

"We are back!" Keita ran into the chamber, arms full of clothing, and lunged onto the bedroll, landing between Jillian and Stephen. Duff also carried a pile of clothes.

"What's all this?" Jillian sat up while pulling the *plaide* up to the neck. She swiped snarled hair from her eyes and gave Stephen an amused sideways glance. He tugged a *plaide* over his privates. His chest constricted. She looked thoroughly bedded and utterly beautiful.

"'Tis getting colder, and you need warmer garments for the remainder of our journey," Keita said, sounding very grown up for a wee lass.

Duff rolled his eyes.

"Well, that *is* what the man said."

Jillian ignored them and rummaged through the pile. There were woolen undergarments, wool-lined boots and gloves, and a high-necked velvet gown. The deep green gown was of the finest quality and perfect for Jillian, as was the matching hooded, wool cloak lined with red fox. Expensive garments indeed.

She caught his eye and raised a questioning brow.

He rubbed his chin. "Duff, who gave you these things?"

CHAPTER THIRTEEN

*D*ugaid stared at the compromised hidey-hole, a snarl curling his lip. How dare his mother remove her protection from the lost *bairns*? Oonagh was a beautiful woman, sought after by many a man, both fae and mortal, but she lacked even an iota of motherly tendencies. Had the Fae Queen put the *bairns* in harm's way?

His pointed ears perked at a commotion deeper in the wood. A lad cried out as if in pain. Cloaked in the glamour of invisibility, Dugaid followed the scuffling sounds.

Two of the woodland *bairns* huddled together on the ground, faces battered and bruised. Dugaid fisted his hands. No one had the right to hurt children.

An explosive outburst of nature heralded his anger to the world. Lightning sliced the darkening sky. Thunder reverberated over mountains, hills, and glens. Hail pounded the earth. The pungent smell of ozone sharpened the air, making his nostrils flare.

Maclay's gaze shot to the ominous sky, and the man frowned. Returning attention to the third *bairn*, the one he held by the shoulders, he shook the battered lad. "Tell me!"

When the *bairn* didn't answer, Maclay knuckle-slapped him hard across the face.

The lad cried out. Blood spewed from a broken nose.

Red also wept through a rag wrapped around Maclay's wrist, but didn't hinder the man from inflicting pain on those weaker. "Tell me what you ken of the lass traveling with MacEwen, unless you wish for more of a thrashing."

"Nae. Dinnae hurt me anymore," the lad pleaded. "She is from the future. 'Tis all I ken."

Maclay thrust the lad away, grabbed the backpack from the ground, and strode away from the whimpering *bairns*. Dugaid's rage boiled. The storm intensified. One especially jagged streak of vertical lightning pierced the ground at Maclay's feet.

The villain leapt back, tossing weight from leg to leg, attempting to find balance as the ground rolled and splintered around him. Spider cracks spread from long narrow slits. Trees and rocks tumbled into deep crevasses. The backpack Jillian had brought through the time gate slipped from Maclay's nerveless fingers. It tumbled into a fissure, got caught by the strap on a branch, and dangled just within reach.

He dove to retrieve it, but the earth pitched with a violent shudder. The pack dropped into the hole while the vibration joggled Maclay precariously close to the edge. He crabbed backward scarcely in time. One more quake closed the opening.

In a flash, Dugaid placed a vanishing blanket over the *bairns*, making them invisible.

Maclay stood, paced in a small circle, and punched a fist in the air. "Where are those cursed changelings?"

Unable to release his frustration on the *bairns*, the nasty devil strode away from the scene of destruction, muttering obscenities. Dugaid hated allowing the man to leave, but there were certain covenants to which he must adhere. As much as he so desired, he mustn't kill a human.

Dugaid waited until the man had traveled a great distance before uncloaking himself and the lads. "Can you all walk?"

"Aye." The lad with the mismatched eyes helped the

older, pudgy fellow, who'd taken the worst beating, rise to his feet.

"Hie tail to the Caves of the Gray Women and use the pool to heal your injuries."

"Many thanks for coming to our aid," said the lad with a head too large for his child-sized body.

"You are verra welcome. Now run along and forget you saw me." Dugaid watched them leave, chanting a spell of protection to keep them safe.

Then he, too, vanished, traveling through the nether in search of Caitrina. She would never win the challenge if she didn't keep her mind on the task at hand. He was more than ready to give her a lengthy scolding.

Outside the smaller caves where Stephen, Jillian, and the children had taken refuge, fingers of fog wove through the trees. Jillian swirled the wool cloak over her shoulders and secured it at the throat with a large emerald brooch found in one of the deep pockets. Someone had seen to her every fashion need.

"You look like a queen," Stephen said.

She felt beautiful for the first time in her life, but thought it had more to do with the time spent with Stephen than anything else. Dressed in the layers of fancy clothing given to the children by a mysterious dark-haired man, Jillian brushed a palm over the growth of beard covering Stephen's face. "Thank you. You're sweet."

His smile made her insides go liquid. She stood on tiptoe, placed a kiss on his velvety lips, and sighed. What a marvelous two days they'd spent in the caves.

The children raced around them, restless for more adventure.

"Must we leave?" After making love with Stephen, Jillian wasn't so sure she wanted to return to the future. "Perhaps..."

"We must and since the weather has turned cold, we will

need to take shelter instead of sleeping in the greenwood." Stephen stepped away. "We are about a day's ride from Dunoon Castle, a royal stronghold under Campbell control as the hereditary keepers. One of their ilk, still friendly to the MacLachlans even after the debacle over Elspeth's handfasting to Finn MacIntyre, is in residence there and surely will allow us safe haven for a night. Actually, Sir Robert is Elspeth's grandfather."

Jillian's thoughts flashed to Elspeth and Finn. She'd been so jealous of Patrick's younger sister when the woman arrived in Anderson Creek with Finn and they announced their upcoming wedding. At the time, Jillian fancied herself in love with Finn. Now, she knew it had only been infatuation. She wouldn't be developing such strong feelings for Stephen had she truly loved Finn.

Melancholy swept over her. She'd never see Stephen again after she returned to the future. Did she really want to go after falling in love with him? She couldn't seem to drum up the nerve to tell him of her feelings, fearing he didn't share the same deep affection. If she managed to tell him she loved him, might she convince him to travel through the time gate with her? He claimed to have tried passing through but failed. Perhaps that nasty man Maclay had inadvertently come up with the trick of it. Might *she* be the key? Maybe if Stephen were with her when she attempted to return home, they'd both travel through to the future.

He seemed to like her. Maybe even love her. She needed to get over her sense of inadequacy and trust in her instincts.

Yet there was a chance all these mental gymnastics were a waste of time. Who knew if either of them would be able to travel through the gate?

"Jillian?"

"Oh, I'm sorry. I zoned for a moment. What were you saying?"

He creased his brow and pursed his lips.

"Oops. Future talk."

"You will need to be careful what you say in front of

others while we are at Dunoon. We dinnae want to draw unwanted interest."

"How will we explain my sudden appearance in Scotland?"

"I will introduce you as Lady Jillian O'Donnell of Ireland. You were visiting with Patrick and Lady Laurie in France and they suggested a visit to Castle Lachlan before returning home to Ireland. Your guards took ill on the crossing and when we met by chance, I suggested my escort."

"My hero. You really know how to spin a story."

Stephen blushed. He looked so darn cute, she wanted to kiss him again, but then she'd drag him back to bed and there was no time for that.

"Dinnae look at me that way." The desire reflected in his eyes turned her to mush. He grasped her elbow. "Shall we be on our way, my lady?"

She giggled then tried to recover dignity by inclining her head in a queenly fashion.

As they walked to the horses, she brushed fingertips over the velvet gown. "I feel as if I'm going to a swanky New York hotel's masquerade ball. All I need is a bejeweled mask."

He raised a brow.

"I know. No more future talk."

They helped both children onto Duff's horse, then Stephen assisted her onto the roan, careful of her fine gown. He mounted his stallion and sidled alongside.

"We will stay to the main trail to make better time."

She raised the hood of the cloak over her head and followed him, the children trailing behind. They rode for about an hour when the sound of galloping horses carried to them on the moist air.

Stephen signaled a halt. "Into the wood. Hurry!"

Jillian's stomach clenched as they guided the three horses off the trail and walked them deep into the trees. She prayed the approaching riders didn't notice hoof prints in the dirt, or broken branches from their passing.

Stephen held a finger to his lips for quiet. She turned to check on the children, but they had melded with the forest, becoming invisible. They had an amazing knack for going into hiding. The thought of what brutality had taught them such wariness tore at her heart.

The thunder of hooves pounding the ground grew louder. The riders were getting closer. Jillian held her breath. The moment of fear stretched into infinity, panic ratcheting up her heartbeat.

The riders stopped at the spot where they'd entered the woods. *Cripes.* Her worst fear come true. Her horse skittered to the side, tossed its head, tugging against the reins Jillian clutched in a tight fist. She rubbed the mare's neck with trembling fingers, trying to calm the animal, hush it to silence.

Branches snapped. Someone must have entered the woods in search of them. Her wide-eyed gaze jerked to Stephen.

"Come." His sharp whisper set her into motion and she followed him deeper into the trees, farther away from the main trail.

They'd only gone a hundred yards or so when a rider appeared directly in front of them like an impenetrable wall. The very large, ginger-haired man wore a huge grin.

Jillian squeaked.

Stephen grabbed the reins from her hand before she bolted to the left. "'Tis a friend."

"And mighty glad to have found you," the man said.

Friend. Jillian felt flushed with relief.

"Do you ride with the others, Duncan?"

"Aye. We have been searching for you for days. Brought you horses. From the look of things, you are not in need of the beasts." The man's curious gaze swept over her. His cheeks reddened before he looked away to Stephen. "Your mounts are mighty fine."

Stephen whistled three high notes. Within a few moments, Duff and Keita rode into sight.

The man Stephen addressed as Duncan raised several

fingers to his mouth and let go a warble of a birdcall. A series of similar notes came from the direction of the main trail they had left. Not quite a cell phone or walkie-talkie, but it seemed to work for them. They made way through the trees to where a group of men draped in woodland-hued plaids waited. Relieved smiles greeted them as they emerged, easing the tension knotting Jillian's stomach. There were about fifteen men plus the annoying little man they called Munn. The one who'd stolen her space blanket what seemed like an eternity ago.

Déjà vu made Jillian shiver. The man striding toward them looked exactly like Patrick, her partner Laurie's husband; Jillian did a double take. Although this man's eyes were more gray than blue. Still, must be Patrick's twin, Archibald, current chief of Clan MacLachlan.

Stephen slid from his horse, and the two men grasped forearms. The man dragged Stephen into a masculine hug. Then the bear of a man who'd found them leapt from his horse and embraced Stephen. A lot of backslapping came next, along with manly grunts.

Stephen broke away and helped her dismount. He stood at her side, arm wrapped around her back, hand resting on a velvet-covered hip. She could feel his heat through the layers of fabric. It almost seemed as if he communicated possession. Her face flushed with the intensity of the other men's knowing stares.

Archibald's eyes narrowed, and he frowned. "Is that the way of it?"

Stephen stiffened then gave an abrupt nod.

"A fine mess." Archibald paced away from the others.

Stephen winked at her before following the other man. *Mess.* Why? Did he think poorly of her? Quiet words passed between them. Archibald looked in her direction a couple of times while the two men continued to speak in hushed tones. It appeared Stephen was doing a lot of explaining. At one point, he dragged a palm over his face. Then Archibald slapped a fist against his thigh, and Jillian thought she heard the name Maclay growled.

Several more minutes passed before they returned to the group.

Archibald approached her and bowed. "Excuse my lack of manners, my lady. I understand you are, Lady Jillian O'Donnell from Ireland, a friend of my twin brother and his lady-wife."

She nodded, unsure how else to respond. For the first time, Jillian really felt lost in a world not her own. As if sensing her unease, Stephen stepped to her side, lending moral support.

"Stephen tells me you have had quite a trial of it. You are welcome to spend as long as you wish at Castle Lachlan. My sweet lady-wife, Isobell, will be delighted to make your acquaintance and hear news of our niece and nephews. Unfortunately, I must bid you farewell as my men and I pursue the fugitive Maclay."

He abruptly turned, signaled to his men with a raised hand, and they all mounted with exception of four. Munn, the ginger bear, and two others remained.

"They will provide added security for the remainder of the journey to Castle Lachlan," Stephen answered her questioning glance before lifting her onto the roan horse.

With an uneasy frown, Stephen mounted his horse, as did the other men. Archibald had voiced displeasure with the turn of events. The chief didn't want trouble with Calyn's kin.

Stephen didn't either, but he couldn't give up Jillian. Not after she risked all to save his life. Not after finding love in her arms. Such love too precious to throw away. Life too precarious. He would figure out a way to convince Calyn to release him from the commitment.

Munn whirled in a circle and disappeared without comment. Unusual for the wee man not to voice an opinion. Just as well. Stephen didn't want to hear a litany of his failings.

The two MacLachlan guards rode to the front. Stephen

signaled for Jillian and the children to follow, and he fell back to ride at Duncan's side. The big man brooded but held his own counsel, which gave Stephen ample time to brood himself, to remember the misery of the battlefield and recall Jamie's death.

Finally, he felt the need to break the silence. "I have much sorrow for your loss."

Duncan's watery gaze snapped to him. Grief lined the man's features. "Ach, well, you look fit and hearty."

Stephen stiffened, but understood the man's rage. Duncan had lost his twin while Stephen lived. Sometimes the same anger plagued him—the injustice.

"He fought valiantly for Scotland and king. The end came quickly. He dinnae suffer long." Little consolation for Duncan's loss.

The big man gave a curt nod, and they continued along in silence. After a time, his speculative gaze fell on Jillian and lingered. Stephen couldn't blame the man his interest, but still—

Duncan jerked a glance his way. "How did you come to be here with her?"

Stephen shrugged. "Dinnae ken the all of it. I was badly injured."

The man's brows scrunched tight, forehead wrinkled, lips curled downward. His reluctance to believe was understandable. Stephen could hardly believe all that occurred since the battle.

"I was saying my final prayers when darkness stole over me. I woke in the Caves of the Gray Women with cuts and bruises and a worthless crushed leg. Dinnae ken how Munn got me there to safety, but am thankful for his resourcefulness." He ran fingers through his overlong hair. "Spent several days soaking in the fae pool, healing and regaining strength. Then the lass arrived and..."

Surprise transformed the big man's face, and he visibly shivered. Poor Duncan had spent several days a few years back in the caves being tortured by Maclay's band of renegades.

"You ken she is like Lady Laurie, aye?" Duncan's gaze jumped to Jillian and back to Stephen.

"Aye." That knowledge was the gist of the problem. Handfasted to a woman he disliked and in love with a woman from the future. A woman he shouldn't want, but needed for his heart and soul to mend.

Duncan snorted. "She will take you on a wild romp as Lady Laurie did with Patrick. Do you plan to go to the future too?"

Stephen cut off the intended retort. Jillian and the children had slowed and were within hearing.

"The children and I need a respite," Jillian said, as he and Duncan approached.

"A wild romp," Duncan repeated in a whisper as they halted, the man's wolfish chuckle raising Jillian's brows.

Stephen shrugged, masking his features, then whistled for the forward guards to return to them. They dismounted and Jillian and Keita headed for some privacy in a nearby grove of trees.

A chill breeze blew across the moor, a beckoning of colder weather to come.

They didn't remain in the unprotected spot for long. Huddled in their outer garments, they set a faster pace. Several hours later, a cold wind buffeted them as they galloped along the Firth of Clyde, closing in on their destination, the stronghold seated on a hillside position with its three circular towers in a triangular formation—Dunoon Castle.

CHAPTER FOURTEEN

*N*ear gloaming, with long shadows trailing, the small party of weary travelers passed through the castle gate without challenge. Muscles clenched, Stephen remained wary. A sentry posted in one of the towers must have reported their approach for Sir Robert Campbell and his personal guard awaited them on the stair to the keep. The sound of hooves against stone grated the edge of Stephen's already fraught nerves as his party crossed the courtyard to meet with the keeper of the castle.

"*Fàilte gu* Dunoon." Sir Robert descended the stone steps to greet them.

Stephen dismounted and shook the man's forearm. "I was not sure of our welcome after the disagreement between Alexander and Archibald over the betrothal to Elspeth, but we are in need of lodging this night."

"Ach, nae worries, lad. We are pleased to accommodate you and your people. 'Twas my granddaughter's choice to make. Neither man should have tried forcing her into an unwanted marriage. MacLachlans are always welcome here. And you should ken, Alexander is a changed man. As a matter of fact, he was expected to arrive today, but the snowy weather to the north has detained him and his entourage."

Of that, Stephen was glad. He'd not been fond of Alexander even before the dispute. Although bad weather didn't fit with his plan to escort Jillian to the faerie knoll.

Sir Robert's gaze slid over Duncan, the guards, the *bairns*, landing on Jillian. "And who have you brought with you?"

Stephen hoped Jillian didn't say or do anything too future-like. "May I present Lady Jillian O'Donnell. She has recently travelled from France and is en route to Castle Lachlan for a wee visit with Lady Isobell MacLachlan before proceeding home to Ireland."

"*Fàilte*, my lady." The man grasped Jillian's extended hand and kissed the air above her fingers.

"Thank you." Jillian lowered her gaze demurely, praise the saints.

"May I assist you from your mount?" She nodded, and the gallant Sir Robert placed large work-hardened hands on her hips, lifted her from the roan, and placed her gently on the ground.

A pang of unexpected jealousy sliced through Stephen. He cursed under his breath. He was young and virile and should not be envious of a weathered, gray-haired man.

Sir Robert grinned as if reading his mind. "Let us get Lady Jillian and the *bairns* out of the cold, shall we?" He clasped Jillian's elbow and guided her up the steps, leaving Stephen to give orders to the MacLachlan guards and herd the *bairns* into the keep.

Duncan laughed. "You will need to keep a keen eye on that squirrely old man or lose your lady-love."

Stephen snorted. By the time he entered the great hall, Duncan and *bairns* in tow, Jillian was out of sight. Sir Robert signaled to him from across the hall.

"Let Duncan tend the *bairns*. Come. Sit by the fire, Stephen, and tell me of the devastating events at Branxton." As they took seats before the hearth, Sir Robert waved over a young *ghillie*. "Bring whisky."

Stephen scanned the great hall. There no sign of Jillian, but the appearance of a familiar man tipping ale, seated at one of the tables below the dais nearly made his heart still. He stiffened. Ciaran, one of Calyn's brothers, shot him an angry glare.

"I requested a maid take the lass to a guest chamber to rest before the eve'n meal," Sir Robert said.

Stephen jerked his gaze back to the older man.

Sir Robert raised an eyebrow and continued. "You will bed down with Duncan and the *bairns*?"

"I thank you, though I believe Lady Jillian will want the wee lass with her." Stephen said naught more, unwilling to feed the man's speculation.

Both Sir Robert's brows rose. "I imagine there is a story there, but for now, tell me of the battle."

The serving lad arrived with the whisky and poured. Stephen accepted the drink and sank into the chair's velvet cushion, the warmth of the fire relaxing tired muscles.

Sir Robert lifted his cup. "*Slàinte mhòr.*"

"*Do dheagh slàinte.*" Stephen raised his. He swirled the amber liquid, inhaled its unique aroma, and took a sip. *Uisge-beatha*—water of life—splashed over his tongue, its flavor rich. Damn, it tasted good. With the salutation to good health completed and the brace of good whisky in his gut, he described the events leading up to the fateful day at Branxton. "Mayhap if James hadn't wasted time at Ford, enjoying the favors of Lady Heron. Ach, well, who kens what might have taken place instead of what did happen."

Stephen furtively glanced at Ciaran. The lad garnered attention, glaring in Stephen's direction. Even a village idiot could sense the coming confrontation. Resigning to the inevitable, Stephen returned full attention to Sir Robert and the telling of the tale.

"The battle turned brutal, nary a *Sassenach* spared a Scot, nor we, them. James fought valiantly, but should not have been at the front. We lost Duncan's brother Jamie, too." Stephen swallowed hard, the loss overwhelming.

Another glance at Ciaran's clenched jaw and dagger glare proved the man had a bone to pick. Stephen would need keep the lad and his damning tales away from Jillian.

The castle steward approached, leaned forward, and whispered in Sir Robert's ear. The man stood. "Please excuse me. I must confer with my man."

Sir Robert and the steward left the hall and Stephen looked to Ciaran, but the lad no longer sat with the other men. There was no sign of him anywhere in the hall.

Stephen rose and headed toward the circular stair to the upper level. He would search out Jillian and confide the sordid details of his life to her before she learned of them from someone else. On the first landing, Ciaran stepped from a tapestry-draped alcove.

"You dare travel with a mistress? Flaunt her, here at Dunoon, for all to see? When your wife, my sweet sister, pines for you in Dunadd, believing you dead?"

"I near lost my life during the battle." Stephen didn't believe for a moment Calyn yearned for him. He still didn't understand why she'd pushed for a handfasting.

"Ha! Where are your battle scars, warrior? Perhaps you are naught but a coward. Did you flee the battlefield before our king was slain?"

"Careful, lad. Dinnae disparage my character with accusations of things of which you dinnae ken." Stephen swallowed rising anger, not wanting to appear guilty. "Lady Jillian O'Donnell is not my mistress but a gentle woman. A noble woman from Ireland. She is a friend of Patrick MacLachlan and his lady-wife. Lady Jillian's escort took ill on the crossing. 'Tis my duty, as sworn to the MacLachlan, to see her safely to Castle Lachlan." Stephen kenned how to stretch the truth.

Ciaran's hands fisted. Stephen rolled onto the balls of his feet, flexed his knees, ready for an attack.

"I thought you were leaving, Ciaran." Sir Robert joined them. "Make haste. Your captain plans to sail with the tide, hoping to beat the storm."

The lad's jaw clenched. He pushed past Stephen and descended the stairs, the angry pounding of boots rapidly fading.

"Where is Ciaran headed?" Stephen asked.

"Glasgow."

Great. Stephen should have time to escort Jillian to the *Sithichean Sluaigh* without the need to burden her with his problems, and then ride like the devil to Dunadd to resolve the matter of his unwanted wife.

"The cook will serve the eve'n meal shortly. Retrieve your lass and dine with me at the head table. Perhaps she could share word of Elspeth and her rascal of a husband." Sir Robert continued down the stair, and Stephen ascended to the upper level, where a maid directed him to the bedchamber assigned to Jillian.

Jillian brushed fingers over the furs covering the bed, taking pleasure in the luxurious feel. She wouldn't believe she was in a medieval castle if it wasn't for the fact there wasn't a single modern convenience. No central heat. No electricity. No running water. The maid had lit a fire in the hearth along with lighting two braces of candles. One sat on the hearth's mantel, the other on a large chest next to the enormous four-poster bed, luxuriously curtained in red velvet. As to the water, the maid had left an urn for washing and directed Jillian to a garderobe.

The privy smelled awful.

If *they* couldn't travel through the time gate and she remained in the past with Stephen, could she handle the lack of everyday modern things previously taken for granted? The thought that scared her most—the lack of advanced medicines and medical care.

She scanned the room, doubting Stephen possessed this kind of wealth. After all, Dunoon was a royal stronghold. Though he did have a large emerald in his sword, so he mustn't be too poor.

Jillian frowned. She didn't really know all that much about him. He was a good man, of that she was sure. He could have left her wandering aimlessly.

She cringed. She wouldn't think of what could have happened if she'd not met the children and Stephen.

Seated in one of two velvet-cushioned chairs placed before the hearth, she took off her boots, and warmed her stocking feet by the fire. Leaning her head back, she slipped into a doze. A rapping on the door jerked her awake.

"Jillian, are you there?" She jumped up at the sound of Stephen's voice and ran to the door. Throwing it wide, she leapt into opened arms.

Stephen lifted her off her feet, carried her into the room, and kicked shut the heavy oak door. His lips crashed against hers in a sinfully delicious kiss that sent a thrill down her body to curl her toes.

"I missed you," he said.

Her thought exactly. She'd hated even the very short separation. How would she be able to leave him for the rest of their lives?

"Sir Robert has invited us to dine with him."

"What if I trip up? Make a mistake?"

"Dinnae fear, but keep in mind, the castle walls have ears, so check your tongue."

Jillian's spine stiffened even though his meaning was clear and she shouldn't take offence. He softened the blow by kissing her again, and she forgot the misplaced indignation.

Stephen descended the awkward circular stair in front of her. Still, she feared tripping and falling in the long gown. She raised the hem with her right hand while leaning into the wall to her left with a palm against the gray stone, keeping as far from the drop on the right as possible. She understood the rationale from a security perspective. Patrick and his father Iain had once explained that since most men were righties and you wanted enemies to be at a disadvantage if they breeched the castle walls and ascended the stairs, with the wall to the right, the attackers would be forced to wield a sword with their less dominant hand. But it made the steps precarious for woman expected to wear long gowns. Perhaps she could find a lad to lend her some clothes. Wouldn't that shock the castle inhabitants?

She released a sharp breath when her booted foot took the last step, and they entered the noisy great hall. Young lads carried trenchers heaped with bread to the many tables.

Stephen guided her to the head table where he seated her two chairs away from Sir Robert, and then sat between them to the older man's right in the seat of honor. Once they sat, the room became silent, the servers stilled, and everyone stared. Jillian worried her bottom lip, wishing they hadn't drawn so much attention.

Sir Robert clapped his hands and activity resumed. She supposed *they* were the topic of discussion among many of the castle folk. She was glad when the meal arrived shortly thereafter consisting of a heavily seasoned roast—which Jillian overheard was deer meat—and vegetables. She'd tried venison before and liked it very much. This roast tasted of rosemary and garlic and perhaps some spices or herbs of which she was unaware. Delicious.

After making a report on the health of Elspeth and her family, the conversation turned to a discussion of the weather and an anticipated storm expected from the north. That didn't bode well for the continuation of their travels. Jillian shifted her weight on the hard chair. She hoped they wouldn't be stranded here.

After the meal finished, Sir Robert rose. "Stephen, I would like a word in private. Lady Jillian, please excuse us, a maid will provide escort above stairs. I am afraid the men are not used to having a highborn woman at the castle. They can be rather rowdy. I am sure you will be more comfortable in your chamber."

"No need to bother a maid, I can find my way." She curtsied as Stephen had instructed and left the hall.

Jillian made her way along a passageway in search of the chamber she was given, looking forward to spending the evening with Stephen in a real, authentic castle. How cool was that? But she'd gotten twisted around and wasn't sure which way to turn. Taking a right around a corner, she stopped short. A blond man blocked the way. She moved to the left. He moved with her. She stepped to the right, as did he. "Excuse me."

"Nae."

"I beg your pardon?"

"Why should I let the whore who sleeps with my sister's husband pass?"

"What?" She leaned forward. She must have heard wrong.

"Ignore him." Keita popped out from behind a tapestry and clasped Jillian's hand, tugging her in the opposite direction. "He is a drunk. Hurry. We need to stay away from him."

They hustled along another passageway. Jillian glanced back. They were alone in the corridor. The man hadn't followed. Perhaps he was too drunk. Maybe that's the kind of behavior to which Sir Robert alluded.

Keita opened a door and, sure enough, it was to the room Jillian had been in earlier.

"What was that all about?" she asked.

"Naught but a drunk. Dinnae worry about him." The little girl slid home a metal lock on the door. "Stephen said I can sleep with you."

As much as she loved Keita, Jillian had wanted to sleep alone with Stephen. Guess he had other plans. Her chest ached with disappointment.

CHAPTER FIFTEEN

Castle Lachlan

Caitrina awoke to a slow awareness of sensation—the warmth of the linen sheets from her body heat, the smooth velvet of the coverlet against bare skin, and the plush feel of fur delighting sensitive fingers.

Oh, aye. She remembered. She'd traveled to Castle Lachlan, arriving late during the night and had fallen asleep in Elspeth's old bedchamber, now used for those visitors of highest rank. To Caitrina's mind, that included her, as the daughter of an ancient *Sithichean* prince.

Dull light filtered through slots in the shuttered window, marking dawn. She stretched languorously. A familiar smell tickled her nose. She must have dreamt of Douglas and conjured his unique, masculine scent. An ache at the core of her womanhood proved as much. She missed her human lover. She could almost taste his satiny lips.

Urgh. Caitrina rolled to the side seeking cooler sheeting.

What is that? Her fae hearing detected a subtle sound, a swish of heavy fabric, soft as a breeze. She froze, pupils dilating, fae vision adjusting to the dimness with speed. She wasn't alone in the richly appointed chamber. A large figure draped in a hooded cloak stepped back into the shadows, impenetrable to even her gaze.

Why hadn't she been aware of his entrance? How long had he stood there, watching her, undetected? Was she losing her fae gifts? Couldn't be. She grew stronger with each day closer to achieving her goal.

She slid to a sitting position, dragging a fur pelt up to her chin, as she'd slept nude beneath the covers. "You have me at a disadvantage, sir, for I cannot see your face."

The annoying man remained mute.

"Who are you?" she asked, more curious than frightened.

"I am known as the Prince of the Dark River." *The Dark Prince*. Oonagh's son. His voice, of a spicy dialect that heightened sexual desire, slipped over her defenses and coiled deep into her soul.

Her heart sputtered then raced—intrigued. Had his mother sent him? Or might he be interested in a tryst with her?

"Why are you here?"

Dugaid stood frozen in place. Enthralled. First light cast a gentle glow, enhancing Caitrina's beauty. How had he forgotten the effect she had on him? He'd been obsessed from the first time he'd seen her shortly after her flowering.

One foot edged forward of its own volition to take a step out of the darkness, but he curbed the desire to go to her. He didn't want to be recognized.

Dugaid drew the voluminous hood of his cloak farther over his face, hiding his features.

He'd misled himself. Planned to punish her for recklessness. Instead, he received the punishment. Desperate need gnawed at his insides, hardened his loins. He inhaled sharply. The allure of her fae scent—peony and freesia and sandalwood—almost had him tossing away caution and revealing his secret.

Too soon. He must have her within his control first.

She rose from the bed, teasing him with luscious breasts

and…

The desire to bury his cock deep within her core made him dizzy.

"Do you plan to stare at me all morning or will you answer my question?" Caitrina inquired, tone sharp.

That acid voice snapped him out of the stupefaction possessing him. He hardened himself against her allure. "Clothe yourself."

"Dinnae growl at me. You are the intruder here."

"Your father would be appalled by your whorish display."

"I doubt that. And what do you ken of my father?" She stepped toward him. With a wave of her fingertips, a gauzy green gown floated over her curves, sparing him further distraction.

"'Tis of nae consequence at the moment." He moved deeper into the gloom. "Why are you allowing my mother to win?"

Caitrina's eyes narrowed. "She is not winning."

"Oh, but she might. Her last move placed your victory in peril."

"What do you mean?"

"Oonagh removed her protection from the lost *bairns* of the wood. Maclay had his filthy hands on Jillian's things. And—"

She clutched his arm, and with a thought, he slipped a silk mask over his face, ignoring the thrill from her touch. "I handled the matter, but not before Maclay learned Jillian is from the future. Will not take him long to deduce the secret of the *Sithichean Sluaigh*."

Caitrina laughed. "Only centuries. And he will not live that long."

"You can only hope."

She shrugged a graceful shoulder. "I am not worried."

"You should be. Take care, Caitrina. As you ken, my mother is a gifted adversary. Would be in your best interest to pay better attention to the chess pieces in play on the board."

"How dare you chastise me?" Her hands fisted. Emerald

eyes smoldered.

Overpowering lust hit him like a gut punch.

"Why do you wear a mask?" Caitrina asked. "Are you horribly deformed?"

"Heed my warning, Caitrina!"

Dugaid faded into the vanishing before giving into a primal desire and acting out his favorite fantasy with Caitrina bound to the bed by faerie-spelled, silken scarves. One day soon, he'd make her beg for his touch.

CHAPTER SIXTEEN

Castle Dunoon

*J*illian woke to chattering teeth. *Hers.* The room was frickin' freezing. Even with all the covers and the child burrowed against her side, Jillian shivered. She missed Stephen's warmth.

The barest amount of weak light filtered through the shutters. Must be near dawn. She hated to get up, but someone needed to tend the fire or they'd freeze to death.

She padded across the cold stone floor, hopping from bare foot to bare foot. Cold drilled up her spine. A few embers still glowed. She added tinder and kindling. After the tinder flashed and the kindling lit, she added a piece of chopped hardwood from a stack near the hearth. She tugged on wool stockings and boots, twirled a length of tartan over her shoulders, then made a dreaded trip to the privy.

When she returned, Keita stood on the window seat, shutters flung wide, staring out. The little girl turned and, after rubbing sleep from her eyes, smiled brightly. "'Tis snowing."

Jillian rushed over to look. Sure enough. Heavy snow fell. From the amount of accumulation on the ground, it appeared as if it had been coming down for a better part of the night. *Cripes.* There was little chance they'd travel on to Castle Lachlan and the faerie knoll during a snowstorm. More time lost.

A soft tapping on the door interrupted her perturbed thoughts. She opened the oak panel to find the maid who'd escorted her yesterday, carrying a tray. "I have brought something for you and the *bairn* to break yer fasts. A party of travelers arrived shortly before dawn with a large contingent of fighting men. Sir Robert requests ye spend the morning in yer chamber until everyone is settled."

Jillian nodded, and the maid left the tray.

After donning her gown and eating, she paced, bored to tears and getting more agitated by the moment. Just where was Stephen?

An hour or so later, the door pushed open, and Duff lurched into the room carrying a flat wooden box, the lid checkered like a chessboard.

"Sir Robert gave me draughts. He said 'twould keep us out of trouble." Duff placed the box on the table between the two chairs and opened the lid. The gold and black pieces stored inside looked somewhat like checkers. "Do you ken how to play?"

"Sort of. I know the basics."

"The board and pieces came all the way from the Continent," the boy enthused. "Sir Robert said Alexander Campbell brought it back when he traveled to France on em-embassage for the king. The one that died in the battle. The battle Stephen fought in."

Keita perked up. "I want to play."

"You are too wee."

"Am not!"

"Are too."

"How about we play girls against Duff?" Jillian jumped in before the argument could escalate. Keita smiled and nodded.

"All right," Duff agreed rather belligerently and dropped into a chair.

"Which color do you want?" Jillian hid a smile and sat across from him.

"Black, like the black leather the man wore who gave us your garments."

Jillian started to place the gold pieces on the red squares in front of her. Duff didn't seem to know what to do with his pieces so she laid them out on his side.

"Now what?" Duff asked.

"Well, the objective of the game is for you to try to capture all of my game pieces, or for me to capture all of yours, or for one of us to force the other into a position where we are unable to move."

"What about me?" Keita asked, bottom lip pushed forward in a crooked pout. If only she could take the child to the future where a doctor could fix her deformed mouth.

"Come here, sweet pea, and sit on my lap." The little girl climbed up, and Jillian gave her a gentle squeeze. "Duff, you go first since you chose to play black."

He moved a piece to a white square.

"Only the red squares are used. Move your game pieces diagonally."

"Why?"

"I don't really know. It's just the way the game is played."

They played until the children grew bored—not very long—and Jillian's nerves wore thin. Duff discovered walls could be built with the game pieces and then knocked down. The children were entertaining themselves thusly when a heavy hand knocked on the chamber door.

Jillian raced to open it. Stephen stood on the threshold looking more handsome than any man had a right. He'd bathed and wore clean clothes, a fresh plaid draping his shoulder. Even with his hair still straggly and in need of a cut and beard overlong, he made her stomach do somersaults. The rugged appearance looked gorgeous on him. Sparkling blue eyes—

Damn him for being so desirable.

"Where the hell have you been?" Jillian snapped before

she could stop the angry question.

His eyes flared, then he chuckled. "Is that any way to treat the man who came to fetch you for the midday meal? Sir Robert has requested we dine with him and a few others in his private hall."

"Of course. I'm sorry." She was just disappointed he hadn't come sooner. "When will we be able to continue on to the time gate?"

He shushed her and taking her arm, ushered her back into the room. He shut the door and leaned close to her ear. "I warned you the castle walls have ears. Be careful of what you speak."

His whispered breath teased her flesh and she shivered. "Okay. When can we continue our journey?"

"On the morrow or day after. Not sure."

Ugh. Possibly stuck here for a couple of days—she'd go stir crazy.

He turned his attention to the children. "Duff, take Keita to the kitchen for your meal by the back stair, and be wary of men roaming the passageways."

Duff inclined his head and grasped Keita by the hand.

Stephen weaved his arm through hers. "Shall we go, my lady?"

The smile in his blue eyes made her insides do a shimmy. She allowed him to lead her, barely remembering to mark the route they took. They crossed the great hall and stepped through a doorway into a smaller, more ornately appointed inner hall, cushioned chairs at one end encircling an inviting fire in the large hearth and a dining table at the other end, the room obviously meant for entertaining important guests. Duncan was already seated at the table, but no one else. Stephen sat her next to the big ginger teddy bear.

"I must leave you in Duncan's care while I tend to a wee bit of business."

Jillian watched him leave. Where was he going? With whom was he meeting? What was the purpose of his business? Did it involve her?

With an irritated sigh, she turned attention to Duncan. He leaned back in the chair, arms crossed, a closed expression on his face. Not the most approachable body language, but since they were alone perhaps a good time to question him. She wanted to learn more about the children, and he might be just the person to ask.

"So, Duncan, what do you know about where Duff and Keita and the others they call changelings come from? What are their stories?"

A judging gaze zeroed in on her. "Why do you wish to ken?"

"I'm curious. And wondered if there might be a way to help them."

"Most people shun them for their deformities."

"Well, I don't."

Duncan scowled, and she thought he wouldn't say more.

"Each child holds a story of their own," he said. "Poor Keita was born with a deformed mouth. Her superstitious parents, howbeit, believed a devious faerie came during the night and took their perfect wee *bairn* and replaced her with our deformed Keita. They left her in the wood. I dinnae ken how she survived until now. I guess the older *bairns* somehow care for the younger."

"She has stolen my heart."

"Aye, she is a sweet wee lass." His expression softened, and he spoke with affection. "Now superstitious folk see Cam as an abomination, with his mismatched eyes of blue and brown, as if evil faeries or the devil hisself cursed the lad. 'Tis believed by common folk that if his family kept him, they would be cursed, too."

"How unfair." It shocked Jillian that people could cast out their children when she wanted a child so badly to love. Wow. She'd not admitted that before. Not to anyone. Not even to herself. She shifted in her chair, unnerved by the unexpected realization.

"Unjust, but reality just the same," Duncan said.

"What about Duff?" Jillian pressed. "He has no detectable

deformity. Just a long nose."

"Duff's is the saddest of the tales. As you said, he has nae affliction except lacking the same appearance as his father and brothers. Duff's da, fearing his wife had lain with another, cast off the child before others could see her sin in her son's face."

"Genetics doesn't work that way." Jillian scoffed, feeling as if she'd choke on the indignation. "Not every child will look like their father or siblings."

Duncan glanced around the room, then lowered his voice. "Dinnae ken of what you speak, but the lad's appearance was enough to get him banished to the wood. Many believe the Queen of the Fae helps the *bairns* survive. Another reason to fear them."

"Why doesn't anyone take them in? Why doesn't your chief protect them?"

"Ach. 'Tis difficult to explain." Duncan scrubbed a hand over his face. "The *bairns* are feral creatures, you ken? They dinnae take well to domestication. They prefer to run wild."

"But—"

"Duff and Keita are playing with you. One day you will wake, and they will be gone, taking with them what they can carry."

No. Jillian couldn't believe that of the children.

"What about the others? Blaney and Mack? What are their stories?"

The sound of voices approaching the door kept Duncan from responding.

Two men and a woman entered with Sir Robert and Stephen. The most conservatively garbed of the men seated the flamboyant woman, whose red velvet gown clashed with fiery-red hair. He then took the seat of honor for himself. Sir Robert and a peacock of a man also sat.

Stephen stood at her side. He glanced at her with warning before resting his gaze on the man at the head of the table. "Lord Campbell, may I present Lady Jillian of the Irish Clan O'Donnell. She recently made the crossing after visiting

France and my MacLachlan kin. When her men and traveling companion took ill, I offered my services as escort."

"How gallant," the woman twittered.

"Please, feel free to call me Alexander." Lord Campbell gave Jillian a devil-may-care grin. The woman at his side frowned before a brittle smile curved her lips. He ignored her displeasure. "Then you have met our Lady Elspeth and her husband, Finn?"

"Aye. I have." Jillian attempted to sound like the others. What sort of game did they play? *Intrigue.*

"Are they well?"

"Aye. Very."

The brightly dressed man chortled. Lord Campbell shot him an annoyed glance. "Where are my manners? Please let me present my companions. "Lady Jonet Stewart and her brother, Ninian, Sheriff of Bute, and Keeper of Rothesay Castle."

"My pleasure." Jillian inclined her head. Something unsettled her about both men, but especially the sheriff. His black hair, swept back in a tight queue, made his features appear hawk-like. A chill slid along her spine when his dark gaze swept over her then narrowed in calculation.

Sir Robert cleared his throat. Alexander raised a hand and a server appeared from the shadows of the room. Stephen squeezed her shoulder and sat in the empty chair at her side. Wine was served in jeweled goblets and bread passed round.

"Are you journeying to Castle Lachlan then?" Alexander dipped a piece of bread in his wine. "The heavy snow has made travel difficult."

"Aye." Stephen nodded. "I imagine it has. We wait for the storm to pass."

"Could be a couple of days."

Jillian tensed, and Stephen patted her thigh under the table. She appreciated the comforting gesture though she hated the thought of being stuck here, playing this charade for much longer.

The remainder of dinner was a quiet affair with light

conversation. Although Jillian didn't completely relax, she enjoyed the meal. Afterward the small group gathered before the fire, and her skin prickled with unease at the speculative glances directed her way by Lord Campbell and the sheriff.

There was something unnerving about the way both men watched her, making no effort to display discretion.

"You must be a good friend of our Lady Laurie," Lord Campbell said. "Your speech is much like hers, yet she is French and you Irish. A conundrum to be sure. You must have spent much time together..." His eyebrows rose, and he let the words trail off.

Stephen tensed. She wanted to clasp his hand, but feared touching him would send the wrong message.

"Yes." She attempted to appear serene, unaffected by the direction of the conversation. "I've lived several years with...Lady Laurie and her husband in France."

"Quite." Lord Campbell smiled, but his eyes remained hard. "You ken there was a time I thought the lady a witch."

"Lord Campbell, I—"

He raised a hand. "Please call me by my given name—*Alexander*."

"Well—"

"I met Patrick's wife once—a bewitching creature surely," the sheriff interrupted. "As are you, Lady Jillian."

"Dinnae tease the woman," Lady Jonet admonished. "You both ken verra well there is nae such thing as a witch."

"Of course there is not, my dear," Alexander said. "Yet some believe it true."

No such thing as a witch. Jillian shivered and shifted her gaze from man to man to woman. Why did they study her so intently?

CHAPTER SEVENTEEN

*"G*et up!" A large hand grasped Stephen's shoulder and shook.

Thank the good Lord for a warrior's agility. He rose in a flash, gripping the hilt of his dirk, ready to face a threat. Munn's weathered brown face greeted him. An unpleasant sight of which to wake certainly. Blinking and shaking his head, Stephen chuckled. "You are lucky I did not skewer you. You ken better than to wake me thusly."

"Humpf." The gnarly wee man fisted oversized hands at his waist. "If you had not drank yourself into your cups with Campbell and Stewart the last several eve'ns, waking you would have been easier."

"Ach, I needed to keep them busy. Did not want them to pay too much attention to Jillian and her unusual ways."

"That's as it may be, 'tis time to leave."

Stephen jerked his gaze to the unshuttered window and beyond to the clear blue sky. *Amen.* The storm had ended. They could be on their way.

The air coming from outside felt warmer, lightening his mood. He dressed in woolen *trews* and *leine*, and strapped on an array of weapons. "Where have you been, Munn? I thought you had gone ahead to Castle Lachlan."

"Nae. Hunkered down in the stables. Saw things."

"What did you see?" Stephen hesitated in the fastening of the large claymore to his back.

"Calyn's brother did not leave on the galley traveling to Glasgow."

Stephen pinned Munn with a penetrating stare. "Explain."

"Headed out on horseback toward the inland track."

"Why did you not stop him? Come to me directly to relay the lad's activities? Follow him?"

Munn shrugged. "Someone needed to guard the fae horses. I be tell'n you now."

"Damned devil's spawn!" Stephen pulled the sheath's leather strap tight and stomped to Jillian's bedchamber.

Ciaran would ride for Loch Fyne. But would he turn left toward Castle Lachlan or right and head for Dunadd?

If Ciaran rode hard for Dunadd, Calyn would hear of Stephen's traveling companions before he had a chance to reach her and explain the status of his affairs. Ciaran would certainly corrupt the tale. Then again, the storm would have slowed the lad. Perhaps Stephen still had enough time to escort Jillian to Castle Lachlan and the *Sithichean Sluaigh*, and then ride like a *banshee* chased him to Dunadd and explain things to Calyn. Once she learned he loved another woman, she'd certainly release him from their commitment. Wouldn't she?

Jillian was packing when he arrived at her chamber. She glanced up from the task and smiled.

The sight made him grin. "I see you have been informed of our departure."

"Duncan stopped by."

"Here, let me help with those." He grabbed a saddlebag from the floor and together they descended the stairs.

They gave thanks and said their goodbyes to Sir Robert, collected the two MacLachlan guards, Duncan, and the *bairns* on the way through the great hall, and rode out the castle gate through the slushy snow before the morning escaped them.

Once out of sight of the castle folk, Munn appeared,

riding the rump of Duncan's horse.

As the sun continued its arc across the cerulean sky, the day grew warmer and the snow covering the ground continued to melt, making the trail muddy and difficult to traverse, but they plodded onward. By late afternoon, the small group was weary and ready to take their rest for the night. Stephen guided them through a hilly area where a small cave lay hidden within an outcrop of rocks. With a nod from him, the other men ensured no wild inhabitants had taken up residence.

"All clear," Duncan yelled.

Stephen handed Duff a bedroll. "Go and help Duncan set camp."

Keita trailed after the lad.

Stephen placed his hands on Jillian's waist and lifted her from the saddle. She slid down his front, thrilling him, trapped as she was between his body and the horse. He kissed the tip of her nose. To his surprise, she plundered his mouth, making his blood run hot, his cock harden. *Grrr.* She would be the death of him.

He savored her unique taste. Her scent. *A very enjoyable death at that.*

"My legs are wobbly," she murmured.

Her lustrous gaze, full of desire, sent his heart into a rapid thumping. He swallowed hard and stepped away. Hand in hand they strolled into the cave.

Duff glanced up. "Lady Jillian's shiny *plaide* is gone."

"You must be wrong." Jillian dropped Stephen's hand and squatted beside the lad. "It was rolled inside these." She lifted each of three blankets. The silver cloth was not there.

"Shite." Stephen rummaged through the remaining *plaides* and furs. He knew he should have destroyed the damn thing.

"It was with these others when we arrived at the castle," Jillian said, tone tentative.

"Ach, well, 'tis nae longer." He ran a hand through his snarled hair, yanking at the ends. "Someone must have taken it. The question is who? And what do they intend to do with it?" He trailed his gaze across the others to Munn. "Do you ken who might have taken the cloth?"

"Several people come to mind."

He could just imagine. "Go back. See what you can learn."

The wee man spun in a circle and vanished.

Jillian held a palm over her heart. "He freaks me out every time he does that."

Stephen didn't bother reminding her not to use such words. The fear of the future *plaide* falling into the wrong hands gnawed at the inside of his chest. He gazed at her beloved face.

Jillian frowned, noticing the deep furrows in Stephen's forehead. Why did he seem so concerned about losing the space blanket? They had enough wool blankets and furs to stay warm now that the weather had warmed. If she wasn't upset, he shouldn't be.

"How many more days until we reach the time gate?" she asked.

"Two. Mayhap three."

That seemed like an eternity, but they'd come this far, she could wait a few more days, especially if she spent those days with Stephen.

They ate a light meal and bedded down, rising early to continue the trek.

On the third day out, they rode from within the shade of forest trees onto a sundrenched ridge. Jillian let out a gasp. A large loch reflected the clear blue of the early afternoon sky and the deep green of the fir-covered hills from the opposite shore. The pungent smell of tidal water teased her nostrils. Just off the near shore, nestled upon an islet within a small bay, sat a faerie tale castle.

"Castle Lachlan?" Jillian asked.

"Aye, lass, we have arrived." Stephen's voice held a smile.

Jillian didn't savor the thought of dealing with more snotty castle lords and ladies. She really wanted to go home. Now. "Can't we go directly to the time gate?"

Over the last few days, Stephen had once again kept her at a distance. He obviously didn't feel for her as she did for him. It was inevitable she would miss him. But like ripping off a sticky bandage, she wanted the pain over. Staying longer, enjoying his company, wishing *if only*, would make her miss him all the worse in the long run.

"From what we ken, the faerie knoll only works on full moons," Duncan said, joining them. "Three nights hence."

Stephen tugged on his reins, and Jillian followed him down the hill to a large stable. Duncan, the children, and guards trailed behind. After the horses were taken away by young boys who threw her curious glances, they descended the remainder of the hill to a pebbly beach, where water lapped against several small boats made of wicker and skins.

"What are these boats called?" she asked.

"*Currachs.* We use them to come and go from the castle. You can only ride a horse across during an unusually low tide."

They loaded their gear into three of the boats. Keita scraped a foot from side to side in the grit, staring at the ground. Duncan tilted his head toward the child, and Stephen squatted next to her. "Do you want to come to the castle with us?"

She bit her crooked lip and glanced at Duff, worry in her mossy green eyes. He gave an abrupt nod, then she smiled and nodded with vigor.

"Let us be on our way then." Duncan picked her up and placed her into one of the boats, then Duff climbed in. Duncan pushed the boat into the water, jumped aboard, and rowed toward the castle. The guards took the second.

"Shall we?" Stephen grasped Jillian's hand.

She inhaled a deep breath and stepped into the third boat. After dragging the craft into the water, he joined her, taking oars to hand. What new misadventure did they row toward?

"Nae worries, lass. Nae one at Castle Lachlan means you harm."

She hoped that was true as they approached the massive

structure and a chill skittered over her spine.

"Welcome!" A woman with dark amethyst eyes, shrouded in a matching cape with thick white fur peeking from the hood, hurried toward them. "Welcome to Castle Lachlan. So good to see you, Stephen. I had hoped to find Archibald with you."

Stephen bowed over her hand. "He chases Maclay."

"Should have expected as much. He is determined to bring Maclay to justice." She shook her head, a deep frown darkening her features, then she glanced at Jillian and her demeanor lightened. "And who is this you brought with you?"

Jillian dropped into a curtsy, feeling awkward and out of place. Stephen took hold of her hand and tucked it under an arm. "Lady Isobell, 'tis my pleasure to present Jillian O'Donnell, a friend of Patrick and Laurie."

"Oh dear." The woman's gaze narrowed. "You came through the faerie knoll?"

Jillian gasped. Threw an annoyed glance at Stephen. He barely suppressed a grin, the corner of his lips quivering.

"Not exactly." She glared at him.

He sobered. "'Tis a long story. Mayhap the telling could wait until we are inside."

The woman grasped Jillian's free arm, drawing her away from Stephen and toward the castle gate as they walked together like schooldays friends. "We have much in common."

Jillian doubted that.

CHAPTER EIGHTEEN

*C*astle Lachlan wasn't as large, nor perhaps as lavishly adorned as Dunoon Castle, but as Jillian stepped over the threshold into the great hall, something within her warmed to the place. Made her feel comfortable. Tension in her shoulders eased. This was a home. Men and women and children dressed in colorful tartans of red and green with yellow crossed the stone floor covered here and there by woven rush mats, greeting one and other cheerfully as they went about their business. Several acknowledged her with a tentative smile, showing only mild curiosity, then continued on their way. Much different from the audible whispers exchanged behind raised hands at Dunoon.

"Come and sit by the fire. You must be exhausted from your travels. I am eager to hear of them." Lady Isobell directed her to a grouping of chairs before a hearth taller than Stephen by more than a foot, and wide enough that several men could stand within. A welcoming fire burned with a crackle and pop.

The raven-haired beauty dropped to a green velvet-cushioned chair and propped her legs on a small embroidered footstool with a heavy sigh of relief. The skirting of her purple gown hiked up, providing Jillian a glimpse of a pair of very modern-looking Fair Isle knit leg warmers made with synthetic fibers. Certainly not of the time period.

"I have recently given birth to a fine son." Lady Isobell's smile glowed with happiness. "My ankles and hands still swell on occasion."

Jillian shut an open mouth with a snap.

When the other woman noticed where Jillian stared, she smirked. "Do you like my leg warmers? They were a gift from my mother-in-law, Mairi, when we visited my husband's family in a place called Anderson Creek a couple of Christmases ago. Have you heard of it?"

"Uh…yeah. I live there, Lady Isobell."

"No need for formality. Please. Just Isobell. I am sure we will become bosom friends." Isobell beamed. "Do you ken the MacLachlans? Mairi and Iain? Patrick and Laurie? Elspeth and Finn?"

"I know them all. Laurie is my business partner. We own *Foxgloves Garden Center* along with our friend Caitrina."

"Ah. That explains much." The woman's violet eyes brightened. "I have fond memories of the orchid room."

"Yes. It's lovely. Full of color, especially in winter." This was all too bizarre. *Had she fallen into a 1960's episode of Twilight Zone?*

"And so verra warm." Isobell fanned herself as if the memories made her hot.

"The orchid room has state of the art environmental controls encouraging peak performance from the plants."

"The plants? Oh, aye, they are nice. And the cushions are verra comfortable, if you understand my meaning."

"Oh." Jillian raised both eyebrows. Had the woman and her husband used the orchid room for a…sexual encounter? Obviously, based on the suggestive expression Isobell wore.

She patted Jillian's arm. "Now, you must tell me all about my niece and nephews. I miss the wee *bairns* terribly. It has been some time since we visited."

"You make it sound so normal. Time traveling, that is." Jillian swallowed uneasily.

"Far from normal, but I have come to terms with fae activity since marrying Archibald, having our wee adventure, and living at Castle Lachlan."

"It boggles my mind." Jillian looked beyond her hostess to scan the hall, wondering what happened to Stephen and the children. Not seeing them, she returned her attention to Isobell. "You mentioned the faerie knoll. Is that how you traveled back and forth from…" Jillian glanced around again to see if anyone listened to their conversation. No one seemed to pay them any mind. "Anderson Creek?"

"Oh, aye. But only once. According to my father-in-law, a person can only travel through the portal once in each direction. Our faerie knoll sent us to Laurie's garden then the garden gate returned us to the knoll."

"That isn't how I came to be here."

"Nae? Do tell."

"It all started in a cave of sorts with a deep well, which I fell into." *Or into which I was shoved.*

"Interesting."

"Indeed," Stephen said as he joined them by the hearth.

"Jillian was just telling me how she came to be here, traveling with you." Isobell studied Stephen. He seemed to squirm. "I was delighted to hear you survived that foolish battle." Isobell sobered. "So many others died."

There was a heavy silence then Isobell pinned Stephen with narrowed eyes, the hint of an unspoken question in the intent gaze. "You do look hale. Are you leaving Jillian in my care and traveling on to Dunadd to see—"

"I will see Jillian to the faerie knoll on the full moon," Stephen cut the woman off.

She didn't seem to mind. "Well, then, I guess I should have Aine prepare a chamber for our Jillian."

"Nae need. She will stay with me in my chamber." Stephen's blunt statement provoked a raised brow from Isobell and surprise from Jillian. Over the last few days, she'd thought…he'd lost interest. Perhaps she'd been wrong. The thought of being alone with him sent a thrill through her system.

"I see..." Isobell's lips quirked and she fought a smile.

A flush crept up Jillian's chest, flaming her cheeks. What must the other woman think? Oh, what did it matter? Jillian would soon leave and she wanted to spend the last few nights of her stay in the past in Stephen's bed. Without the children.

He presented a hand and helped her from the chair. "I will show you the way. I am sure you would like to bathe before the evening meal."

"I would. You will excuse us Lady—"

"No *lady*. Please."

"Isobell then."

"Stephen will take good care of you, Jillian." Their hostess smiled. "He is braw. Is he not?" She winked.

Jillian nodded. Embarrassment heated her chest yet again. Oh yeah, he was a handsome blond devil. As they walked through the great hall and climbed the narrow circular stair, Jillian pondered over what Isobell might have been about to say when Stephen cut her off. She would ask him when they arrived at his bedchamber.

But when they entered the room, he spun her around, pushed her back against the hard oak door, and kissed her senseless, the kissing all-consuming. The feel of his satiny lips and velvet tongue working her mouth made her sex clench and weep. She clutched the hem of his shirt, desperate to feel his skin. Breaking off the kiss, she yanked the soft fabric up and over his head. His throaty chuckle made her bold. She skimmed impatient fingers over his abdomen. Splayed her hands on the heated flesh of his chest, relishing the flex and ripple of honed muscle as he moved and wrapped her within a tender embrace.

Without a word, he lifted her into strong arms, carried her to the large canopied bed, and seated her at the edge.

"What about the bath?" she asked.

"I instructed the lads to take their time heating the water."

"Well, then." She ran an appraising gaze over his fine form. "I want you naked."

His eyes flared. "Ach, lass. You ken just what to say to a man."

His wool pants dropped to the floor, the belt buckle clunking the stone. His plaid landed on top. His erection jutted forward. The sight pebbled her nipples tighter, and she reached for the ties on her gown.

"Allow me." He made quick work of divesting her of the heavy gown and undergarments then tenderly laid her back on the mattress. He rose over her and, leaning in, took possession of her mouth. A kiss that left her breathless, wanting more, wanting everything, wanting forever.

His lips whispered over her flesh like fine silk, skimming along her neck and chest and latching onto a sensitized nipple. Overwhelming pleasure shot to her core.

She ran her fingers through his tangled hair, holding his head to her breast. She arched. Moaned. A needy sound that took her by surprise. Oh, man. She wanted him deep inside. Her muscles tightened and her sex throbbed.

"I want you *now!*"

His deep chuckle was so damn sexy.

"I dinnae want to rush. I want to savor every last taste of you." He switched the sinful torment to the other breast.

She burrowed her heels into the mattress. Clutched the coverlet, fingernails digging deep. Stifled a scream as an orgasm took hold, built to a crescendo, and bliss wrapped her in its loving embrace.

"Ach, you are beautiful when you come for me." Stephen released her breast and kissed her mouth, hard, going deep with his tongue.

She'd never come like that, not from a man just sucking on her nipples. She felt raw and tender and needy. Still primed. She pulled Stephen's hair. "Now!"

"Aye, lass, as you wish."

He entered her with a quick thrust that threw her into a second orgasm. "Oh. Dear. God. Stephen, what are you doing to me?"

He grinned and continued with a leisurely lovemaking. As

the burn hit her, his speed increased and they both exploded at the same time. His arms tightened around her and she didn't understand the torrent of Gaelic words he murmured in her ear, but loved his touch and the sound of his voice.

How would she ever leave this man?

"*Mo chridhe. Cha d'fhuaireadh facal Gaidhlig mar.*" My heart. My only true love. Stephen couldn't hold Jillian close enough to his heart. In the very short time since they'd met, she'd become a part of him. He needed her with every breath. She'd become his sole reason for living.

He'd find a way for them to be together. For always and ever. No one would stand in his way.

"Stephen! Someone is banging on the door." Jillian slipped out of his embrace.

"I am coming." He raised his voice to be heard through the thick oak.

Jillian arched a graceful eyebrow and gave him a smug grin. Ach, his words held a double entendre. He shook his head with a laugh.

"Must be the lads with our bath water." He rose from the snarled bedding and threw a cover over Jillian's nude form. "I will return shortly."

He tugged the bed curtain closed, hiding the most delectable woman in the world from view. Donning his *leine*, he padded barefoot across the cold floor whilst still chuckling over his faux pas and opened the door. Several young *ghillies* entered, burdened with buckets of hot water. The big metal tub was dragged from the curtained alcove and set before the fire. One of Isobell's many improvements to Castle Lachlan. After spending time in that future place of Jillian's, Isobell insisted each bedchamber have its own tub. A major expense, but although they sometimes debated over the changes, Archibald mostly always gave in to Isobell's requests. Theirs was a true love match. As he prayed he would have with Jillian.

A bucket of hot water was hung within the heat of the

hearth for later use before the lads departed. With the door bolted for privacy, Stephen strode toward the bed eager to bathe with his lady-love.

CHAPTER NINETEEN

*M*unn blinked into substance near the hidey-hole of the woodland *bairns*. He sniffed the air, and sniffed again. Fae and human essence lingered in the area. The strongest was the musky scent of a male faerie. He scratched his chin. Had the Prince of Darkness been there?

His nose twitched. Caitrina's sickening oriental perfume fouled his breath. As did the filthy body odor of Maclay. The slight whiff lingering of the *bairns* proved they hadn't visited the spot this day.

With another deep inhale, he caught another scent, one Munn had only recently become acquainted with—Ciaran.

How had Calyn's brother found the place? At least, he was days away from Dunadd and his sister. She wouldn't hear of Stephen's activities anytime soon. Munn would follow the lad's scent to ensure no tales were spoken, but first...

He scurried into the thicket. Sharp thorns scratched exposed skin, and he grumbled aloud even though no one could hear the complaint. Magic vibrated and hummed. An unceasing ringing assaulted Munn's sensitive ears. Translucent colors shimmered and swirled. He extended a hand. Slowly. Ever so slowly. Hair on his arm bristled. He touched the covering of the stash. Ouch! He yanked his hand away, the tips of his fingers singed.

He stuck them into his mouth. An acrid taste made him gag. He rubbed his hands on his *trews*. Shite! The stinging pain remained. Dark magic protected the *bairn's* treasure trove. *Dugaid?*

With a grumble and a moan, he backed out of the thicket, receiving more scratches for his trouble. *Stephen better appreciate my efforts on his behalf. And as for Caitrina—*

A shrill sneeze cleansed the stench of burned flesh from his nostrils. He needed to concentrate on just one scent. With a sharp inhale, he spun and spun and vanished on the breeze, following Ciaran's trail through the wood.

Stephen drew aside the bed curtains. His heart lurched. Desire spiked. Jillian reclined on the mattress, eyes closed, silky brown hair—now much longer than when she appeared at the Caves of the Gray Women—fanned a pillow. *Exquisite.* Her state of undress combined with the scent of their previous lovemaking made him hard and wanting; tempted him to join her for another tumble in the furs.

She slowly opened her eyes. A tired gaze touched him, made him rethink the carnal impulse. Instead, he assisted her from the bed. "Come, lass, your bath awaits."

"Thank you." She leaned on him and clambered into the tub.

"Shall I summon a woman to attend you, or might you honor me with the task?"

She squeezed his fingers. "I'd like to just soak a bit and think."

"As you wish."

Stephen made busy tending the fire so he wouldn't act upon the longing to drag Jillian to the bed for another round of lovemaking, though that was exactly what he wanted to do. He couldn't get enough of her. When he turned back to the tub, she was leaning against a wet drying cloth, eyes closed, arms hanging limp on the rim. He should have realized how tired she'd be after their trek and given her time to rest before coming to her like a rutting beast. Though she'd seemed to enjoy their loving.

He rubbed an ache in the center of his chest. This woman had come to mean so much to him. He couldn't imagine a life without her smile, her scent, her touch. He wanted to go with her to the future.

Mayhap she feared asking him to join her, uncertain of his intentions as he was unsure of hers. He needed to declare his love. But how? He'd never been so powerfully charmed by a lass. Never before had his stomach been knotted with self-doubt.

What if she rejected him? It would tear his heart asunder. A risk he must take. "Jillian, I—"

"Stephen, I was…" Jillian chuckled. "I'm sorry, what were you about to say?"

"Nae worries. It was not important." *Although it is of the utmost importance to me.* "You?"

"I was wondering. Do you think I could take Keita with me through the time gate to the future? I believe the doctors—healing men and women—of my time could fix her mouth. Make her look normal."

His heart tripped. *She has decided to leave with no invitation for me to join her?*

"I dinnae ken." He rubbed a hand over his face. He hated the thought of being left behind. He'd be a shadow of a man without her bright light. "You should speak to Keita. She may not want to leave Duff. And what would you do with her once she is healed? You might not be able to send her back. The faerie knoll is a fickle place."

He should know. He'd tried to follow after his cousin many times and failed.

"I'd treat her as my daughter, of course. Adopt her if need be. I can give her a better life."

"You ken naught of her past."

"It doesn't matter. Only her future matters." Lovely shoulders set firm, Jillian seemed determined to take the lass.

142

"What of Duff and the other lads?"

"I'm willing to take Duff, also, if he wants to come, but I can't take them all."

"Ach, well, then you best speak to Keita and Duff. The full moon is two days hence."

A smile lit her face. "Thank you, Stephen. I feared you'd nix the idea."

"There is nae need to thank me. It is up to the children to decide if they want to join you." What about him? How could he garner her love? He grabbed a washing cloth from a nearby table, needing something to do while his thoughts whirled. "Lean forward, sweetling. I will scrub your back."

His hand shook. She glanced at him strangely, brow furrowed, then did as requested. With a deep breath, he went about the task at hand. His mind was in such turmoil he hardly noticed the glorious curve of her neck. The softness of her skin. The scent of lavender wafting from the water.

Jillian had such a kind heart, he couldn't help but love her. And that was both a pleasure and a problem. He needed to convince her to take him to the future. To be his forever and always love. There must be a way to make the faerie knoll accept all of them. He couldn't lose Jillian now that they'd found each other.

Mayhap she was the key. Mayhap together they could make the faerie knoll work.

Yet guilt gnawed. Conflicting emotions near to choking him. What of his handfasted wife? He'd never believed he'd lain with Calyn. She couldn't be carrying his *bairn*. If he left with Jillian and the children, disappeared from Scotland as he knew it, Calyn would find another in which to sink her claws. He brushed away the niggling remorse.

Ach, his dithering would drive him mad.

"I ken I am being presumptuous." He hesitated, unsure. Mouth suddenly dry. What if Jillian didn't feel the same for him as he felt for her? *Grrr! Just ask.* "Would you consider taking me along?"

Relief swept over Jillian. Stephen wanted to come, too. She'd hoped. Prayed. Even considered remaining in the past with him, but wasn't sure he'd wanted her to stay. Might he feel the same for her as she felt for him? She'd fallen heels over head in love.

"If your answer is nae, I understand. I ken I dinnae have much to offer you in your time. But I have a strong back and am willing to work hard. I love you. I want to spend the rest of my days and nights with you."

She stood and lunged into his arms, water sloshing over the side of the tub and onto the floor. She kissed his face. His lips. Hugged him tight. "I love you, too."

"Easy, lass, I dinnae want to slip and drop you." He stepped away from the wet floor, swung her in a circle, kissed the tip of her nose, and deposited her on the rush mat.

She accepted the large towel he offered and wrapped it sarong-like, tucking the ends at the top. Joy made her giddy. "Of course I want you to come with me."

"I am glad." Stephen hugged her, holding her close for several breaths, then he stepped into the tub, a large smile curving his lips. "Now 'tis time for my bath."

"You can't mean to use the same water. It's become cold. And it smells of lavender."

He laughed as he sat in the same water she had bathed in. "'Tis common to share bath water. Though usually men bathe first, then women, and lastly *bairns*."

"I'm happy you want to go forward with me. I've been agonizing over the matter for days. I think I would find it difficult to live here permanently. Life in my time is very different. Easier. But if you wanted me to, I'd stay."

His eyebrows rose. "Truly?"

In answer she kissed the tip of his nose, as he had hers a moment before, then skipped away.

"Easier you say? How so?"

"Well, it is and it isn't. It's hard to explain. We have many conveniences that make life easier. Yet many people are overly stressed due to the fast pace of the time."

"Was it my willingness to work hard that made you decide in my favor?"

She danced back to the tub and squeezed the muscle in his bicep amazed at how well he'd healed since they'd met. "Do you think the children will want to go with us?"

He climbed out of the tub and wrapped a towel around his waist. "Shall we dress and go find the *bairns* to learn their answer?"

A timid knock had them both turning toward the door.

"Aye?" Stephen stalked across the room and partly opened the panel, protecting Jillian from prying eyes. Keita scuffled through the gap, hugging a bundle of cloth to her chest.

"What have you there?" Jillian crouched in front of the child.

"Lady Isobell sent the most beautiful garments." A pair of kid slippers slid from within the bundle. "And pretty shoes."

Jillian picked up the slippers and took the clothing to the bed. She held up the embroidered burgundy gown. Breathtaking. She carefully laid it across the mattress.

"Sweet pea, come sit by the fire. We need to talk to you."

Keita climbed up onto one of the chairs, and calmly waited.

Jillian didn't know where to start. How to explain. Finally, she just spoke from the heart.

"I'm going home soon and I'd like very much for you to come with me. You would become my daughter. There are men and women with great healing powers I believe can straighten your mouth. Stephen is going, too, and if you want, we can ask Duff to join us."

Keita just stared. Eyes wide. Several minutes passed then she smiled. A beautiful crooked smile. Her nod was abrupt, but melted Jillian's heart.

Suddenly, the tapestry on the wall behind the little girl moved. The massive peridot-colored dragon undulated as the fabric wavered. She stepped closer to inspect the heavy cloth.

"Duff!" Jillian jumped back and clutched her chest when

the boy popped out from behind the tapestry. "Where did you come from?"

"How did you find the secret passageway?" Stephen asked, voice gruff.

"There are many in the castle." The lad shrugged, feigning innocence. "Even one behind the carved wooden wall in the council chamber."

"How much did you overhear?" Jillian asked.

"All of it." He raised his chin. "I go wherever Keita goes. I am her champion."

Stephen patted the boy's shoulder. "As you should be."

"I would love for you to come, too, Duff. Where I live is much different than here. You would become my son. Live with me and Stephen in a small house." She glanced at *her man* hopeful he was onboard with living together. His nod and grin released a knot of tension within her chest she hadn't realized she'd harbored. She returned her gaze to Duff. "No more living in the woods."

"Will Keita be even prettier if she gets her mouth fixed?"

"She will."

"Then we both are coming with you."

"It is settled," Stephen said. "We leave in two days' time. You cannot take aught from here except the clothes you wear. And 'twill be our secret. Aye?"

Both children nodded, expressions earnest.

"Good. Now scoot along and allow us to get ready for the evening meal." He wrapped his arm around Jillian and elation made her buoyant.

CHAPTER TWENTY

Stephen escorted Jillian into the great hall. He teemed with pride as clansmen's heads swiveled, following their progress across the chamber to the dais and head table. Beautifully garbed in a burgundy gown, Jillian's skin glowed with health. Beams of amber candlelight streaked her brown hair with gilt, making the locks glisten. And she smelled of heavenly lavender.

He couldn't help but chuckle; he also carried the feminine scent.

"Welcome to my board." Isobell smiled in greeting. "I hope you find dinner pleasing."

"I'm sure we will," Jillian responded with genuine warmth as he seated her to the right of Isobell as honored guest. Stephen sat next to his lady. Duncan took the seat to Isobell's left, providing protection seldom required within the walls of Castle Lachlan.

Although, not long ago, Archie's sister, Elspeth, had been kidnapped from her bedchamber by way of a hidden passage. Duncan, as MacLachlan captain, took nae chances with his chief's lady-wife in Archie's absence.

Their hostess leaned close to Jillian and whispered, "I requested Cookie make something *similar* to what you might find in your time. Will venison stew baked in pastry and stewed apples appeal?"

"You needn't have made a special effort."

"Nae trouble." Isobell waved a hand. "It is our desire to make your stay at Castle Lachlan pleasurable and memorable."

Jillian glanced at Stephen, her lips curved in a satisfied smile. He grinned, wondering if she, too, recalled their earlier loving upon the furs.

Several young *ghillies* served dinner. He took little notice of the meal, content to be with Jillian. As they served the last course, the tower horn bellowed a warning. A party crossed the bay headed for Castle Lachlan.

"I do hope it is Archie." Isobell rose. "Please, finish your meals."

Stephen frowned. "You ken the horn would have blown a different sequence of notes to announce the chief's arrival."

"He may be traveling with others. In secret."

"It is late." Duncan stood. "If it please you, Lady Isobell, I will go and greet the newcomers."

"Aye, that would be best," she conceded with a sigh, and dropped back to her chair.

They waited in tense silence. A short time passed and a group of men stomped into the hall with Duncan. The Sheriff of Bute and several of his guardsmen. What the hell was Ninian Stewart doing at Castle Lachlan?

Jillian stiffened at his side as the man approached the dais. Stephen grasped her hand under the table, hoping to ease her concern. He didn't care for the presence of the sheriff either. Seemed odd considering they'd left the man at Dunoon Castle mere days ago and there had been nae mention of planned travel to Castle Lachlan.

"Good eve'n, m'lady." Ninian bowed over Lady Isobell's hand then an inscrutable gaze took in each individual at the high table in turn. "Lady Jillian." He nodded in her direction. "MacEwen."

"What has you traveling north again?" Stephen asked,

working to keep his voice dispassionate.

The sheriff ignored the question. "Lady Isobell, please excuse my arrival at this late hour. It is with great urgency I must speak with Archibald. Is he here?"

"My husband is away, patrolling our borders since no one seems capable of bringing the fugitive Maclay to justice." The lady's voice dripped scorn.

Ninian stiffened at the taunt, but kept a cordial smile in place. "Then may I confer with you in private, m'lady?"

"You cannot," Stephen blurted.

"As you are championing the lady, I will take nae offence. Howbeit, keep your head, MacEwen. Lady Isobell is perfectly safe with me."

Isobell raised a brow before standing. "My woman, Aine, will accompany me. You can say what you will in front of her. And Duncan will stand guard at the door."

"As you request, m'lady." The sheriff assisted her from the dais. Then he pinned Stephen with a hard stare. "You and Lady Jillian are spending the night?"

"We are."

"Then I look forward to breaking my fast with both of you on the morrow." He gave Isobell a coy smile. "That is if you will offer me and my men hospitality for the night, m'lady."

Isobell regarded the man, eyes narrowed, lips thinned. "We are naught if not purveyors of Highland hospitality."

"So right." Ninian waved an arm toward the north door. "Shall we?"

Isobell lifted the hem of her gown and marched across the hall, the sheriff keeping pace, a flustered Aine and a frowning Duncan in their wake. Near the door, one of Ninian's lads handed him a leather-wrapped parcel as the foursome departed the hall. Two of the sheriff's guards followed while the remaining lads took position flanking both exits.

"What is going on?" Jillian's voice quavered.

"Dinnae ken, but whatever the sheriff is about cannot be good."

Clansmen voices escalated with conjecture, sounding like a gaggle of geese. Maclay's name uttered by many. Stephen didn't like the direction of his thoughts. He had to believe the sheriff's sudden arrival had naught to do with Maclay and everything to do with Jillian and her unique origin. *Shite!*

Jillian pushed food around in circles on the trencher before them. He stilled her hand with a light touch. "Nae longer hungry?"

She shook her head. "Lost my appetite."

"They may be sequestered in Archie's study for a lengthy time. Shall we retire for the night with hopes the morrow arises a sunny day?"

"Sounds like a plan." They left the chamber to the buzz of speculation. Jillian stopped him a short distance along the passageway. "Why do you think the sheriff is here?"

Stephen shrugged, keeping his features blank. "Could be anything."

"You don't believe that any more than I do. It's about me."

"Dinnae jump to conclusions."

She rolled her eyes and pursed her lips. "I'm not."

"If 'tis about you, we will deal with what may come. Dinnae worry." He squeezed her hand and they ascended the circular stair. He protecting her back.

They reached the bedchamber, and he sought something to distract his lady. The bathing alcove's curtain hung open, and his gaze lit on the table containing a bowl, razor, and scissor. He should look his best when arriving in Jillian's future time.

"Lass, might I ask a favor?"

"Of course."

"Would you be so kind as to trim my hair and shave my beard? I could summon a *ghilllie*, but would prefer your gentle touch."

That put a smile on Jillian's lips as he intended. "I've often done the same for my brother. His hair and beard have never been quite as long as yours though."

"So you cannot handle this mess," he teased.

"I think I can manage. Sit." She shoved him onto a chair near the grooming table. He dropped the *plaide* from his shoulder and tugged off his *leine*, tossing the garment aside, his chest bared to his lady.

She arched a feminine brow. "You sure you only want a haircut?"

"Aye. And much more later." He winked.

Jillian smiled and slipped nimble fingers through his hair, kneading the scalp, sensitizing the flesh with the tips of her nails. He leaned into the sensual touch. A thrill spiraled down his spine, pooling low in his gut, making him hard. He choked on an abrupt intake of breath.

She laughed, well aware of her effect on him.

Perhaps he did want *more* sooner. He hadn't meant for her to incite his sexual desires so quickly, yet his ploy had worked. His lady's sweet chuckles lightened his heart. She nae longer seemed overcome with fearsome thoughts of the sheriff. Stephen shifted his weight on the chair. Would be hard to sit still with her so close, with her touch driving him mad, but he would make the effort to keep a rein on his urges for her sake. Besides, dragging out this moment of intimacy would make their lovemaking all the more urgent and fulfilling later.

Jillian detangled his hair then picked up the scissor. Stepping close, one leg positioned between his legs and the other to the side, her gown brushed over his thigh. He felt the warmth of her womanly mound press against him as she moved in tight and cut a lock of hair. She dropped it to the stone floor then moved in snug for another snip. Breasts at eye level, he could do naught but stare. His cock jerked, and he moistened suddenly parched lips. Her husky laugh made him harder. Needier.

Clip. Clip. Hair dropped to the floor at his feet. With each snip, she moved, rubbing against him, intimately, causing pleasure-pain, driving him to the edge of tolerance.

"Are you okay? You seem to be breathing quite hard."

"I am fine," he gritted through clenched teeth. His desire for her would be the death of him.

She trimmed his hair and then beard, taunting him with each swish of her hips. When finished, she set the scissor aside and collected the container of soap with brush. She moved behind him out of sight. Then she stepped in close and cushioned his head against those breasts he so wanted to suckle.

Later. He'd pleasure his lady later.

The lathered soap prickled bare skin and softened his whiskers. When Jillian put the blade to his throat, he inhaled sharply.

"I'll be careful. If you hold still, I won't cut you."

"I dinnae fear such. It is just…" He searched for the right words to explain his feelings, yet fell short. "You have come to mean much to me, lass. I thank you."

Jillian blushed. "And you mean much to me."

Their gazes held for a heartbeat, and then Jillian proceeded to work on his beard. The rasp of the blade, her scent, her heart beating so near, her body moving against his, left him breathless. The intimacy of the moment touched him deeply, softened his heart. Life with Jillian would be good. Days and nights filled with tender love.

When finished with the task, she handed him a cloth and set the razor on the table then stood away, appraising her handiwork. "You look like a modern man."

He shot her a grin before wiping his face and tossing the cloth aside. "Come here."

She sidled close, and Stephen wrapped his arms around her waist determined to offer gentleness this night. He guided her onto his lap. She leaned against his chest, dropping her head onto a shoulder. She remained quiet within his embrace for several heartbeats.

"I'm scared," she murmured.

"I ken. Dinnae fash yourself. We will get through this." He brushed her lips with his—a whisper-soft kiss.

A heavy knocking at the door startled them both, and

Jillian jumped away. Alarm returning to her beloved features. "Who do you think it is? Should I answer?"

"I will." Before Stephen stood, the door banged open.

Duncan strode into the chamber, face flushed, shutting the panel with a loud thud. "Sorry to disturb you, but—"

"What is going on?" Stephen demanded.

"Lady Isobell requests you and Lady Jillian join her and the sheriff in the chief's study. She said 'tis urgent and was quite adamant you hurry else I would not have barged in on your privacy."

"Why would they summon us?" Jillian asked. "It can only mean—"

"Do you have any idea what this is about, Duncan?"

The big man shook his head, lips compressed.

"Ach, well, we best find out what the sheriff wants." Stephen held Jillian's hand as Duncan escorted them through the passageway. He took the steep stairs to Archie's work chamber first, acting as a shield in case she were to stumble. Along the entire way the back of Stephen's neck itched, a likely portent of an unpleasant confrontation.

Archie's chamber was much the same as it had been when it belonged to his twin, Patrick. A work table and chair in front of the high window. Two chairs before the hearth. How many times had Stephen sat there with his cousin, Patrick, discussing clan business?

Jillian trembled and he squeezed her fingers in reassurance, but he had a bad feeling about the proceedings. He hated to imagine why the sheriff wished to meet with him and Jillian. It could only be about one thing.

Isobell sat at the desk, her facial features impassive. Aine stood behind, wringing age-spotted hands. The sheriff leaned on the hearth mantel, wearing a smug expression.

"Please be seated." He nodded to the two empty chairs.

Stephen seated Jillian and then sat beside her facing the sheriff. The man tossed the leather wrapped parcel he'd taken from one of the guards earlier onto Stephen's lap. "What do you make of this, MacEwen?"

He unwrapped the package, and his stomach plummeted. Jillian gasped, revealing more than she should. 'Twas the silver cloth from the future.

Stephen moved the cloth from side to side, light from the fire flashing on the shiny surface. "Unusual."

"Aye, 'tis. Does this belong to you, Lady Jillian?" the Sheriff's harsh voice demanded.

"I—"

"What is this about, Ninian?" Stephen wanted to direct the sheriff's attention away from Jillian.

"Ciaran of Dunadd has accused the lass of witchcraft, claiming she conjured that strange cloth to use for ill. What is the cloth for, Lady Jillian?"

So Calyn's brother had stolen the silver *plaide* from Jillian's chamber at Dunoon. How had he known it was there? Had he found it by accident?

Stephen didn't wait for Jillian to answer the sheriff's question. "You cannot believe what the lad says?"

"This cloth is not of our world," Ninian said with a stubborn jut of the chin.

"How do you ken that?"

"Just look at the fabric, MacEwen. Nae Highland weaver creates cloth such as this—"

"It is late." Isobell interrupted. She rose from her chair and stood beside Jillian, placing a comforting hand on her shoulder. "We are all tired. I will have a chamber prepared for you, Ninian."

"I am arresting Lady Jillian for practicing witchcraft." The sheriff locked gazes with the lady of the castle.

"Fine. You can post a guard outside her door." Isobell gave a quick nod to Aine, who curtsied and left the chamber, then the lady of the castle grasped Jillian by the hand. "Come. You must be exhausted from your travels."

Jillian nodded and walked to the door with their hostess. She glanced at Stephen as she passed. Worry lines marred her beloved face. Damn Ciaran! Damn Ninian!

"I am ordering several men to guard her door," the

damned man threw out, voice rising.

"Do as you wish. Just ensure the lads are quiet," Isobell serenely responded.

The women left the chamber, a couple of the sheriff's guardsmen following. Stephen nodded at Duncan, and the red-headed warrior shadowed the others.

"I can't believe you are taking this path, Ninian. You are accusing Lady Jillian of witchcraft over a piece of cloth."

"Stay out of my way or I will name you an accomplice."

"You cannot be serious."

"Heed my warning, MacEwen."

"You have nae jurisdiction here."

"I do until Archibald returns and he is far gone, chasing Maclay."

"Lady Isobell governs in his stead."

"She will not wish to gainsay me." Ninian shifted feet, his gaze wavering.

Enough of this. The man was well known as a stubborn beast. Stephen clenched his fists and vacated the chamber, leaving the idiot sheriff to contemplate his navel. He stalked the passageway, but thought better of joining Jillian in his chamber. Might complicate matters if the sheriff was reminded of his affection for the lass. Instead, he headed to the armory, intent on sharpening the blade of his claymore. A blade he was very tempted to use on the pompous arse.

The emerald in the cross section glistened in the light from many candles as he laid the sword on the work table. When they reached Jillian's future place, he'd have a matching betrothal ring commissioned for her. He had to believe they'd straighten out this trouble with the sheriff and travel together to the future. He had a sack of fine jewels—an inheritance of such from his father—he'd been hording for a time. Patrick would surely assist him in finding a quality jewelry maker. With sharpening stones and strop from a nearby rack, he sat on a stool and went to work on scratches and nicks on the blade.

Isobell sought him out as he finished and set aside the

strop. "You must take her away from here into hiding before it is too late. There are two days until the full moon and, without fae intervention, it is the only time to travel to the future."

Stephen wrapped the sword in a rough pelt to make it less noticeable as he skulked through the castle. "Must find the *bairns* then."

"I am sorry. Aine mentioned they disappeared when the sheriff arrived. I doubt you will find them within the castle or anywhere on the grounds."

Stephen frowned. Could this hell-spawned night get any worse?

He strode from the armory. Even if they could prove her innocent, he refused to see Jillian suffer the indignity of a witch trial.

Jillian paced the room, panic a breath away. She was well aware of what they did to those accused of witchcraft in this time. And if convicted…

Shivers wracked her body.

She tried the latch for the umpteenth time, but the door had been bolted from the outside. Dammit to hell! She was truly trapped. Where was Stephen?

She wanted him. Needed him.

Candlelight flickered over the muted colors of the dragon tapestry on the wall. *Secret passageway?* Duff had joined them earlier by way of a hidden corridor behind that wall hanging. Jillian grabbed a metal holder with lit taper from the mantel and lifted the corner of the tapestry, shining the light behind the textile. Nothing but gray stone. There must be an entrance. Duff had definitely come from behind the tapestry.

As she'd once seen in an historical movie, she moved a hand over the stones, digging fingertips into and around the edges, searching for a trigger. About to give up, a metallic squeal stayed her hand. Several stones rasped to the side, exposing a dark opening. *Thank you, God!*

She glanced around Stephen's room. She didn't have a

clue how this *adventure* would play out, but it would be best to be prepared. With haste, she changed into warmer clothes, tied the laces of the fur-lined boots and wrapped the fur-lined cape around her shoulders, fastening the braided frog near her throat. Prepared to escape the castle, she entered the tunnel and, gripping the candleholder, waited until her eyes adjusted to the dimness.

How to close the passage access? She ran tense fingers around the edges of the stone that had previously opened the wall and then several other stones in sequence. Nothing. Nothing but a gaping hole. Crap. She was losing precious time, but she didn't want the sheriff or anyone else, excepting Stephen, to learn how she escaped and follow. Crap. Crap. Crap. She had no way to get in touch with Stephen. How she wished they had cell phones. Jillian tugged the tapestry into place as best she could and hoped it was enough to hide her route from anyone who didn't already know about the castle's secret passages.

With her first step along the corridor, a creepy sensation whispered over her cheek. Cobwebs. Yuck. She shivered and brushed the silky strands from her face and hair. She hated tight spaces. Might there be spiders? Mice? Rats? A ghost or two? She swallowed uneasily.

Don't get all girlie, Jillian.

With one hand on the wall for balance, the other locked on the candleholder, she made slow progress along the corridor, carefully placing each foot as she plodded forward. At least, she hoped the sheriff didn't know about the hidden passageways. But really, if he had, he wouldn't have allowed her to remain in the bedchamber. Right?

A briny smell teased her nostrils as she navigated the tight space. She fought a threatening sneeze, not wanting to give her position away, in case others could hear through the stone walls. The tang became stronger and, after several more steps, the passage split into three. Shit! Which way to go? The tunnel to the right had the strongest scent of the sea. Perhaps it led to the beach and freedom.

As she stepped in the new direction, a large body shoved her sideways, pressing her against the damp wall. A hand clamped over her mouth as another tightened on the wrist holding the candle.

"Dinnae fight me and dinnae scream."

CHAPTER TWENTY-ONE

*F*ury radiated from Caitrina as she raced through the maze of hidden passageways within Castle Lachlan, her essence embedded in a blistering draft of air. Spiders and small creatures scurried to safety with her passing, hiding within cracks in the mortar, not wishing to be burned by the sizzle and spark.

She'd missed the arrival of the sheriff while taking a leisurely bath, only to learn too late of his intent. The *bairns* had gone into hiding. Jillian had disappeared from Stephen's chamber. Stephen was missing. What a mess.

And the impudence of Maclay to get in her way. He had told Ciaran of the *woman from the future*. It only took a moment of rifling through Jillian's bedchamber in Dunoon for the lad to find evidence. Why had she kept the damn space blanket with her? Dugaid's effort to protect Jillian by securing her backpack behind dark magic had been for naught.

The mere thought of the Dark Prince made Caitrina's spirit prickle with something more frightening than fear. She hated the attraction suffered in Dugaid's presence. 'Twas an intrusion into her feelings for Douglas. Her human side preferring her human lover. Her fae side—

Her growl reverberated off the stone walls. She prayed to

Danu to never again cross paths with the Prince of Darkness.

If only foolish Jillian hadn't hung onto the silver cloth from the future, they wouldn't be in this horrible mess. Flaming balls of fire! 'Twas too late to change things now. Caitrina whizzed around a corner and raced along a straight away, sparks sputtering in her wake.

As for Maclay to have inspired the impressionable Ciaran to seek out the sheriff and make accusations of witchcraft. She'd see Maclay paid dearly for the interference. Just as soon as she made things right with Jillian and Stephen. She had to win this last match against the queen. Losing was not an option.

The fault that Jillian traveled through the time gate with her backpack rested firmly on Caitrina's shoulders. She'd gotten cocky with each win. Jillian wasn't only her business partner but a friend. She'd wanted Jillian to have some sense of security upon finding herself transported to another place and time. Have some of her own things. Big mistake. Caitrina would make no more.

Hurling around another corner, her essence slammed into two human bodies, fragmented, and rushed past Jillian and her captor.

❀ ❀ ❀

"'Tis me. Stephen," he whispered close to Jillian's ear then released the hold on her wrist, easing his hand away from her mouth, praying she didn't scream. She swirled to face him, her mouth agape. "We must move fast before the sheriff learns of our attempt to escape."

When she moved her mouth to speak, he pressed a finger to her lips. "Say naught until we are clear of the castle."

She gave an abrupt nod, lips pressed tight together. They had only taken a couple of steps when an eerie howling echoed within the tunnels. An unearthly heat scorched the air.

"What the devil—" Some unseen force smashed into Stephen, pushing him back a step, forcing the breath from his lungs. Jillian seemed similarly affected.

"Hurry." He propelled her forward. Not waiting to determine the source of the unearthly occurrence, they dashed over smooth stone, then rough stone. Jillian's small candle sputtered, barely lighting the way. Finally, they came to the wooden door that opened onto the beach where the *currachs* were kept.

He pushed against the old wood. The door hesitated then creaked, exposing only a wee gap. Shoving with his shoulder, using all his might, produced snaps and pops and cracking sounds. With another heave, the door flew open amidst flying debris from overgrowth. He inhaled a welcome breath of tangy fresh air, the bay's salty savor wetting his lips.

"I guess this door isn't often used." Jillian accepted his assistance to climb through the remaining vines too tenacious to relinquish their hold.

"Nae, there has seldom been a need."

She grasped his sleeve, holding him in place. "What just happened to us in there? I felt incredible heat and pressure."

"I dinnae ken. Castle Lachlan is prone to unusual occurrences. Fae activities. I try to ignore them."

"Probably best." Her skeptical expression made him doubt the sincerity of the statement.

"We must hurry." They ran to the water's edge, and he dragged one of the *currachs* into the surf, holding it secure at the edge of the shingle for her to board.

"Where are the children?" Jillian asked as she clambered over the gunwale.

"Gone."

"We can't leave without them." She jumped back out of the craft.

"We must." Exasperation crept into his voice. "Get back in the boat."

"But—"

"Jillian, they have gone into hiding. Scooted into a hidey-hole. There is nary a chance of finding them before the full moon without being caught by the sheriff. We must leave now."

Begrudgingly, she climbed into the boat and sat on the bench, back stiff.

He joined her, secured his claymore, and took to the oars. "Dinnae be angry with me."

"I'm not. I'm angry with the sheriff." He flinched at the tears in her voice. "I promised to take them with us. I wanted Keita to…"

"I ken, but you must understand we cannot risk the time to search for them. The sheriff will…" His voice trailed off. There was no point in stating the obvious.

Jillian frowned and stared at the floorboards. A light fog settled over the still night, wrapping around them. The only sound was their heavy breathing and the lapping of oars drawn through the water.

"Shit!" Jillian cursed as they approached the mainland beach. He followed her gaze to the shore they'd just left. Shite was right. Although they couldn't see through the accumulating fog the men who carried bouncing torches marking their progression from the castle toward the beach, 'twas certain the sheriff had discovered their escape.

Stephen turned his attention to their small craft, and with one massive tug on the oars, they hit the shallows. He hopped over the side into the water and dragged the *currach* across the surface and onto the shingle. Grasping Jillian's hand, he assisted her over the side and together they raced up the hill toward the stables. Halfway there, he stopped short.

His lady bumped into his back then gasped.

A red-haired woman, richly garbed in green velvet and fur, sat a magnificent white steed with golden bridle and golden bells plaited in its mane. The beast stomped a hoof and snorted steam from flared nostrils, impatient for action. The lady murmured something in an ancient tongue and the animal calmed.

A beauty that matched this woman had been described to him enough times by Archie and Alexander Campbell for Stephen to ken the lady wasn't of this world. She was one of

162

the *Sithichean*—a faerie. Two of the fine horses the *bairns* of the wood had procured for him and Jillian—what seemed like a lifetime ago—were held by reins grasped in the gloved hand of the enigmatic woman.

"What the hell are you doing here, Caitrina?" Jillian demanded.

Stephen scrunched his eyebrows. His lady seemed acquainted with the fae woman. And more than displeased by her presence.

"There is nae time for chat. We must fly before the sheriff arrives."

She didn't truly mean *fly*, did she? He hesitated, but when Jillian hurried into action and mounted, he followed her lead, and together they shadowed the woman at a gallop across the mist-shrouded moor.

The sound of men, horses, and tack carried a distance on the humid air. Stephen urged the fleet horse to greater speed. Jillian kept pace. The fine steeds outdistanced their pursuers. At the tree line they slowed. Reining the horses onto a game trail, they rode deep into the wood.

"We need to find a hiding place to wait for the full moon," Stephen called to the fae woman.

She slowed—then halted. "There is nae need to wait. I will see you through the portal."

He and Jillian stopped beside her, Jillian guiding her horse close to the other woman. "I don't understand, Caitrina. How did you get here? What do you have to do with all of this? Did you push me into that well?"

"We dinnae have time for explanations. Let us ride for the *Sithichean Sluaigh*."

Jillian's forehead scrunched tight.

"Dinnae be dense, Jillian. The faerie knoll. The time gate. The portal to take you home."

"We can't leave without the children."

"You must."

"But—"

The sound of hooves smacking the forest floor ended the

women's debate. They encouraged the horses to a run and rode as if chased by a *banshee*—a harbinger of death.

Jillian followed Caitrina and Stephen through the thickening fog onto an unremarkable hill, but then everything changed. A fierce tingling danced across her skin. *Magic?*

"Fae magic protects you." With a wave of an arm, Caitrina made an encircling motion, defining the perimeter of the hill where they stood. "As long as you stay on this knoll, you are safe from the sheriff and his men."

Jillian twirled around. The faerie hill seemed charmed, brightly lit within a circle of thick mist. The grass at their feet was the softest spring green. The air crisp and clean. Hundreds of miniature white lights flickered around them, dazzling the senses. The lights sparkled in the grass and up high in the branches of the single tree upon the hill like dancing fireflies.

She imagined her expression matched the awe exposed on Stephen's face.

"Well, Isobell said she wanted my stay to be pleasurable." Jillian placed a palm on his chest, stepped into him and, filled with pleasant thoughts of their earlier lovemaking, kissed a pair of fine lips then smiled into his compelling eyes. "It certainly was that. And memorable? I'm afraid it will be that, too, thanks to the sheriff." She shot an angry look over his shoulder at Caitrina. A faerie? Jillian could hardly believe her business partner was a damn faerie. "Now, get us out of here, Caitrina."

"No!" her business partner shouted. "Be gone!"

Jillian and Stephen startled. Caitrina stared toward the edge of the knoll where a young woman stood holding a lantern high overhead. Her angry face eerily gleamed in the amber light.

Stephen took a step forward. "Calyn?"

"How can you leave me swollen with your *bairn*, Stephen MacEwen?" the woman cried, a protective hand splayed over an extended belly. "I ken you plan to leave. I mourned you, believing you dead on the battlefield. Grieved your death until my brother, Ciaran, returned with news you lived and traveled with another woman. With that witch." She pointed an accusing finger at Jillian.

"What the hell?" Jillian jerked her gaze to Stephen's and stepped out of his reach. "Do you know her?"

He stiffened. A mud puddle stained moisture-filled blue eyes. *Guilt.* How could she have been so misled? The pain in her chest unbearable, she wrapped trembling arms around herself in a hug of self-preservation. She'd almost rather die than be betrayed by the one she loved.

Unable to bear his visage, she glanced off in the distance and her heart thudded against her ribs. Keita and Duff were being held back by Maclay.

Abruptly, the ground fell from beneath Jillian's feet. She dropped downward. Oh shit! Everything around her spun much as it had when she fell into the well within the tunnel on the bike trail. She plummeted down...down...down into darkness.

CHAPTER TWENTY-TWO

"**N**o!" Stephen lunged for Jillian. He couldn't lose her now. Not after having found his one true love. Not with her believing the worst of him. Sudden nausea made him stagger and he couldn't grab hold of her fading form. Everything reeled. Slid sideways. When the motion stopped, she was gone.

Stephen stared at the spot where Jillian had stood moments before. Everything within him froze. She'd left him behind. She'd gone to her future place without him.

He spun on the faerie. She could help. Send him forward to Jillian. The fae woman frowned, furrowed her brow, and then her form diminished as well.

"Dinnae leave!" His plea went unheeded. The faerie vanished before he could stop her.

The knoll returned to normal. Fae magic spent. Dry amber grass replaced that of spring green. No longer did a tree stand upon the mound; no twinkling lights.

Keita and Duff broke away from Maclay, ran to Stephen, and clung to his legs. He squatted and wrapped his arms around the *bairns*. Held them tight. Fog rolled across the knoll, twirled its moist embrace around the three forlorn humans huddled together in grief. Was there any point in living without Jillian?

He should be concerned about Maclay's presence. But he couldn't shake off the despair and bother to fight the renegade outlaw. Ignoring raised voices coming from within the fog, Stephen hung his head and permitted tears to escape. The voices moved closer and became difficult to ignore. The mist thinned.

"Stephen MacEwen, you are under arrest for complicity with a practitioner of the dark arts." The sheriff stood to his right.

"You weren't supposed to arrest him. Just the witch." Calyn's annoyed tone came from the left, her lantern cutting through the dwindling haze.

The sight of her swollen belly up close jarred Stephen. He blinked, hoping she was naught but an apparition. A trick of the fae. That she would disappear.

Nae. The lass remained.

The *bairns'* small hands clutched the fabric of Stephen's *trews*. "You cannot take him. We won't let you." Duff's voice quivered yet his chin held firm as he and Keita stared at the sheriff.

"Nae worries, lad. Nary a soul is taking Stephen anywhere other than Castle Lachlan without my consent and I won't be giving such," came the voice of reason. Thank the good Lord. Archie was among those scattered about the knoll.

"MacLachlan, this is none of your affair." The sheriff's fisted hands shone in the light from Calyn's lantern.

"Says the man who, once again, allowed Maclay to evade justice. You should have taken him into custody, Ninian, rather than accuse my man and a guest of my house of something as ridiculous as witchcraft." Archie held the reins of the three horses, Stephen, Jillian, and the faerie had ridden onto the mound. "This is my land. I am lord here."

"But you saw the two women disappear," the sheriff asserted.

"Did I? Are you sure?"

"Aye. How can you doubt 'twas the work of the devil?"

"I believe the women slipped away, concealed by the fog. Dare you gainsay me?"

The sheriff threw up his hands and stomped off. Shortly thereafter, the sound of horses and men faded into the night.

Archie placed a hand on Stephen's arm. "Let us return to Castle Lachlan and talk."

Duff released Stephen's leg and climbed onto the smallest of the three horses. Stephen lifted Keita and placed her behind the lad.

"What about me? I. Am. Your. Wife." Calyn huffed.

Stephen pinned her with a frustrated glare. "*Handfasted wife.*"

"What does it matter? You are my husband." She rubbed her rounded belly. "And soon, we will have a *bairn.*"

Sadness stole over Stephen; an unwanted future with Calyn unfurled within his mind. His heavy sigh was heartfelt. Without further comment, he lifted her by the waist onto the horse he had previously ridden. She attempted to rub against him as he placed her on the animal, but he kept her at arm's length. He could barely stand to touch her. How could he have impregnated the lass?

He couldn't resign himself to the handfasting. He needed to learn what had actually happened the eve before he woke in Calyn's bed.

The clinking of tack as Archie and the other MacLachlan clansmen who'd ridden with the chief mounted their horses demanded his attention. Solemn-faced, they waited. After strapping his claymore to the saddle, Stephen mounted the white steed belonging to the beautiful faerie. A shift of weight on the leather triggered a sweet womanly scent. His nostrils flared at the unusual fragrance. He glanced around half expecting the faerie to reappear.

Disappointed when she didn't, he was thusly taken by surprise by a phantom touch of a feminine hand grazing his cheek. He unintentionally jerked on the reins. The horse reared, tossing Stephen from its back. He fell, arms flailing. Expecting to hit the hard ground, 'twas alarming to continue falling as everything around him spun wildly.

Excitement ignited his soul in a jolt of awareness that crowded out an upsurge of fear. The *Sithichean Sluaigh* was taking him also. He embraced the swirling maelstrom with joy as he fell. Down…down…down, he plunged, deeper and deeper into a void of darkness. Abruptly, bright multi-colored lights flashed, making him shut his eyes. Intense heat scorched his flesh. He sucked in a deep breath and prayed he'd survive this trial and be reunited with his only love—*Jillian*.

Jillian landed on her butt in a pile of raked autumn leaves just beyond the garden gate at *Foxgloves*. Thank God. She'd returned home. On the other side of the metal grille, freshly planted yellow, purple, and orange mums accented the flowerbeds lit by pathway lights. Had she made it to the correct time? Seemed like nothing had changed in the garden other than the addition of the mums.

Rising on trembling legs, she stumbled to the gate and clutched the cool metal for support. At the other end of the garden, lamps burned in the windows of her partner Laurie's big house. Jillian staggered over the path to the mudroom door. She didn't bother knocking. Just let herself in. Voices coming from farther within the house spurred her forward.

She stood in the kitchen doorway and stared at the normal twenty-first century family scene, feeling lost and out of place. Everything in the room was so bright and clean. Stainless steel appliances so modern. The family sat at the table in the nook beyond—Laurie and Patrick, the twins, and little Allison—eating dinner. The wholesome scene so completely normal, yet utterly strange to Jillian.

She swallowed uneasily, wondering how long she'd been gone. It seemed like an eternity. Did time pass here at the same pace as in the past?

The conundrum was more than she could handle tonight. Jillian thought to turn away and slip out of the house, but

Allison caught sight of her. The girl reached forward with both arms. "Auntie Jillian!"

Patrick swung his head in her direction and grinned. Laurie gaped then punched her husband in the arm. "How did she sneak in without you noticing?"

"I kenned she was there. Did not wish to startle or frighten her off."

The couple seemed surprised but not as shocked as Jillian would have expected.

"Come, Jillian, sit with us." Patrick stood and pulled out an empty chair. "You must be starving. Traveling through the gate makes a soul ravenous."

So they know. "I'm not hungry."

"Of course you are." He loaded a plate with pasta marinara, added garlic bread, and placed the dish in front of her along with a bowl of mixed salad. "Eat. Will make you feel better."

Nothing could make her feel better.

Young Iain handed her a container of parmesan. "It's better with cheese."

"Thank you." The boy's smile made her think of Duff. And of Keita. Her heart wrenched. She would miss them.

Iain scooted back to his seat and poked his twin brother in the ribs. "Told you Aunt Jillian would come back."

She wasn't really their aunt, though the children had always addressed her as such.

Laurie placed a glass of red wine in front of her with a wink. "It's even better with chianti."

Jillian nodded and took a long sip of wine. Several more sips smoothed the edges of her frayed nerves. Allowed her to breathe more easily. The MacLachlan children chattered amongst themselves, relieving her of a need to master conversation. Jillian felt Patrick and Laurie's expectant gazes glance her way throughout the meal. Why had she come to their house instead of slipping unnoticed into her room at the inn? Because Laurie was her best friend and Jillian needed answers only Laurie and perhaps Patrick could provide.

After some whining about wanting to stay with the adults and some bribing by said adults, the children scattered to other parts of the house. Jillian accepted another glass of wine and stared into the ruby liquid. It was question and hopefully answer time, but where to begin?

"That is a lovely burgundy gown you're wearing. If I'm not mistaken, it belongs to Isobell." Laurie broke the silence.

Jillian jerked her gaze to her friend. So much for being in control of the conversation.

"So let me guess," Laurie continued. "You've been a guest at Castle Lachlan."

"I have." Jillian nodded.

"Anything you want to tell us, hon?"

More than you can imagine. Jillian curled into herself and burst into tears.

"Oh, sweetie. It can't be that bad." Laurie squatted in front of Jillian and embraced her in a consoling hug. Patrick stood behind his wife, his expression one of concern.

"Everything is such a mess." Jillian sobbed. "Why didn't you tell me?"

"About the time travel." It wasn't a question but a statement.

"Yes." She waved an arm. "The past. Castles. Sexy Highlanders."

Laurie snorted. "Would you have believed me? Would knowing our garden gate could take you to the past have changed anything?"

"I didn't go through the gate. I fell into a well in a tunnel on the bike trail in West Virginia."

"We know. Your brother has been frantic about you. He's had the local authorities searching the trails and woods. Patrick, Finn, and Douglas went to search, too. All they found was your bike and panniers."

Jillian inhaled a loud sniffle. "Then they found my cell phone?"

"Aye. Do you want to tell us what happened to upset you so?" Patrick asked.

"Besides the fact I was accused of witchcraft?" Jillian gazed past Laurie to her husband. "I fell in love with your stupid cousin, Stephen, but the lying dog neglected to inform me of his other woman *friend*. The one who is pregnant with his *child*."

"That doesn't sound like Stephen," Patrick and Laurie said in unison.

"Well, it's the truth. I'll never forgive him. Not that I'll ever see him again."

CHAPTER TWENTY-THREE

Stephen landed hard on his arse in a wood of which he recognized naught. Winded on the strange trip through time, he sucked in great gasps of air. The unexpected prick from a blade tip in the center of his chin made him stiffen. *Shite!* He must not have made it to Jillian's future place. She'd claimed men didn't carry swords in her time. A droplet of blood slid along the curve of his neck. 'Twas definitely a Highland claymore piercing his flesh.

Even in the dark, the holder of said sword appeared taller than most men of Stephen's acquaintance—a giant of a man. A powerful warrior indeed. Stephen remained still not wanting to startle the man and get his throat slit. "You have me at a disadvantage, sir."

"Aye. That I do." The man chuckled—a dark sound prompting a shiver. "Perhaps you can enlighten me as to who you are and to why you stalk this property."

The crescent moon shed some light, but not enough to make out the man's features. From whence did he hail? His speech was that of a lord. *Who is he?*

Lacking knowledge of the lay of land, confronted by an unknown giant of a man, and without his claymore for defense, Stephen held limited options. Should he reveal his identity? The disclosure could go for him or against him.

He must still be in his own time and somewhere within the Highlands. Disappointment almost outweighed the alarm of having another's sharp blade so near one's throat. Though he was hardly defenseless. Multiple knives remained hidden on his person, as was a purse filled with jewels he could use as ransom if needed. He'd watch for an opening to extract a blade from his sleeve.

Mayhap he worried for naught. Mayhap he and the man had allies in common.

"Stephen MacEwen of Clan MacLachlan," he said, having decided to expose himself. "And you are?"

"Ah." The man nodded. "You were once Patrick of Strathlachlan's right hand. I should have guessed 'twas you stumbling through the laird's forest." The sword pricking Stephen's flesh disappeared as quickly as it appeared. "You are among friends."

Did the man jest? "'Twas hard to tell."

That dark, shiver-inducing chuckle came again. Stephen accepted the man's assistance to his feet and brushed decaying leaves from his *trews* and *plaide*. Lights burning in the near distance caught his attention, but still naught seemed familiar.

The laird's forest. Which laird?

"Dinnae fash yourself, lad. You're safe." The stranger grasped Stephen's forearm and offered a warrior's greeting. "I am Douglas MacKinnon of Clan MacKinnon friend to the MacLachlan Clan hereabouts. Welcome to the twenty-first century and Anderson Creek."

Praise the Saints! Stephen swayed and braced his weight against a large tree trunk. He'd made it to Jillian's future. And if this man kenned Patrick, he must also ken—

"Where is Jillian?" The question burst from his lips.

Startled by a loud, high-pitched sound—a horse's whinny—Stephen slipped a blade from within his *plaide* and jerked his gaze to a nearby grove of pines.

"Come out of hiding, princess." Douglas fisted hands on

hips and stared in the same direction. "The beast has given you away."

Several minutes passed before the faerie Jillian and he had traveled with stepped from the grove, lips curved in a frown, leading the magnificent white steed from the past. Thankfully, Stephen's claymore remained attached to the saddle. He returned the palmed knife to its hidden sheath.

Head held high, neck tense, and with its ears pricked forward, the horse pawed the earth. Ignoring the faerie, Douglas stepped in close and greeted the beast. Rubbed its neck. Ran a palm along the bridge of its nose. Whispered something into the animal's ear. The horse tossed its head and nickered. Douglas removed the sword from the saddle and tossed it. Thanks to a warrior's quick reflexes, Stephen caught its heft with two hands.

"You won't need your claymore for defense, but we have fun wielding our blades in mock fights and battles." Douglas grinned.

Stephen furrowed his brow, puzzling over the man's words when he noticed the fae woman's attempt to slip away.

"Not so fast, Caitrina." The other man grasped her upper arm, stopping her midstride. "You brought them here, you need to finish this."

"I plan to make things right." She scowled at Douglas. "Tomorrow. After I take a hot shower and have a wee rest."

"Wait. Where is Jillian?" Stephen asked of the woman.

"I imagine she's with Laurie and Patrick. She usually goes to them when troubled." Caitrina shrugged. "Why didn't you explain to Jillian about Calyn and the handfasting? You've added a major complication to my labors."

"I am not sure of what you are referring to by *labors*, but I demand to be taken to Jillian."

"Demand?" she screeched. "How dare you?"

Tension hummed. Douglas grasped both of her hands and held them together within the grip of one of his much larger hands. He murmured something near her ear as he had with the horse. Her shoulders relaxed. She nodded and, without acknowledging Stephen, led the steed away.

He pivoted on his heel, ready to follow. "Wait—"

"'Tis best to let her go. Safer for your manly parts." Douglas gripped Stephen's shoulder. "Come. I'll take you to Patrick."

They walked over a mound not unlike the *Sithichean Sluaigh* in the Fir Wood, and Stephen shook off a chill. A short distance farther, they came upon a hinged metal gate within a high stone wall. Douglas eased the gate open and ducked beneath the curve of the archway.

Stephen followed the man through, and another chill spread over his spine. His fingers trembled. He glanced around. Looked over a shoulder, but saw naught out of place. He inhaled a deep breath. There had been too much fae activity of late.

Continuing forward, they strode through a waning garden, larger than that of Castle Lachlan. Small lanterns dangled from what appeared to be short shepherd's hooks, lending golden illumination to a path leading to a massive wood structure with many brightly lit windows. He imagined 'twas the source of the lights seen earlier from the wood.

Douglas stopped afore the structure at a green wooden door. "Be prepared to see many new things—modern marvels—in Patrick's house."

Excitement welled. He nodded and followed Douglas through the doorway into a small chamber as bright as outside on a sunny day. The sunshine came from a fixture on the ceiling that when looked directly upon blinded. *Bairn-*sized garments hung from hooks on one wall; wee shoes and boots in a line beneath. Shelves with unusual containers hung on the opposite wall over two large chests made of white metal. Were the chests marvels?

I must learn much to live in Jillian's world.

They continued through another doorway into a larger chamber lit in a similar fashion to the first. Many cupboards and multiple-sized silver chests circled the chamber. At least, the cupboards were somewhat familiar.

Douglas squeezed Stephen's shoulder. "Dinnae worry, you'll be living like a modern man soon enough."

Stephen stood straighter. Jillian had said he looked like a *modern man* when she cut his hair. Perhaps he might adapt to this future place with time.

"I see you found our wayward man." Patrick strolled into the chamber through yet another doorway, wearing curious garments, a smirk upon his lips. Chestnut hair pulled back in a queue, his cousin looked much the same as when last seen, though lines had appeared around his eyes. The smirk broadened into a smile of greeting. "Welcome to my home."

Stephen's eyes misted. How long had it been? Numb with joy, he stumbled into the manly embrace of his cousin. Subsequent backslapping ensued.

"I have missed you." Moisture pooled in Patrick's sapphire eyes, too.

"There was nae purpose to my life after you left," Stephen said, a hitch in his voice. "I tried to follow you through the *Sithichean Sluaigh* more times than you can imagine, but the damn faeries ignored my desires and refused to let me pass."

"You are here now. And glad I am to see you."

"'Tis because of Jillian."

"Perhaps you should share the tale. She is of a mind you have done her wrong."

"On that note, I will leave you to your conversation. I have a wench of my own who needs attention." Douglas took his leave, departing the way they had entered.

"Where is Jillian?" Stephen asked, hoping she was within another chamber.

"Come. We will sit by the fire in my study and talk." Patrick showed him to another well-appointed chamber similar to the study at Castle Lachlan yet different.

Stephen collapsed into a chair afore the hearth where a small fire burned, amazed by the softness of the blue velvet cushions. He glanced about the chamber. Jillian was right. This time had wondrous comforts.

"I imagine you could use a whisky." Patrick opened an

ornately carved cupboard and withdrew a multifaceted glass flagon. After pouring the amber liquid into two matching glasses, he handed one to Stephen and sank into an adjacent chair. He lifted his glass in toast. "*Slàinte mhór.*"

"Good health to you." Stephen raised his glass then sipped the whisky, savoring the slow burn down his throat and into his gut. At his cousin's raised brow, he said by way of explanation, "I want to learn to speak in your future way."

"So you plan to stay. What of the woman you left with child in the past?"

Stephen stiffened. "Jillian told you. Where is she? I must speak with her. Explain why…" He stalled. How would he defend the flawed decisions he'd made?

"I imagine you should explain much and beg forgiveness. Howbeit, not tonight." Patrick leaned back in his chair. "Laurie has taken the lass to my parent's inn for some private *girl* time. You can speak with Jillian after you break your fast on the morrow. Now tell me what has transpired in Scotland past since Archie's last visit with us. Be sure to include *all* of your endeavors and what you plan to do about the lass with child."

CHAPTER TWENTY-FOUR

Steam and the pulse of the spray against her bare skin allowed Jillian to relax. But then her mind did a wandering walk into territory she'd rather avoid. Time travel. Had she really traveled to the past? Stephen. Had she truly fallen in love with a most inappropriate man? Again?

The image stuck to her retinas of the pregnant woman at the faerie hill in the past made Jillian curl into herself both physically and mentally. No! She shut off the flow of water.

She wouldn't dwell on Stephen's betrayal.

Jillian stepped out of the glass and tile shower enclosure and huddled within a plush bath sheet. Ah. Twenty-first century luxury. While time trotting, she'd missed all the comforts taken for granted much of her life. What a fool she'd been thinking she could stay in the past with Stephen.

Stop it! Stop it right now! No more thinking about him and the plans she'd made in her head.

"Dammit to hell!" What about poor Keita and Duff? She'd promised to take care of them.

"Are you alright in there?" Laurie called from the bedroom.

"Yes. I'll be out in a minute."

Jillian inhaled a deep breath, returned the towel to the

rack, and stepped into silky black jammy pants then pulled on a lavender cami. Topping the sleepwear with a gray fleece robe, she braced to face her friend and business partner before walking through the doorway into the bedroom.

Laurie sat on Jillian's bed, leaning against the cushioned headboard, with a remote in one hand and a bottle of beer in the other. "What do you want to watch?"

"Something mindless." It didn't matter what they watched. This was going to be the first of many long nights. She'd been through this before when she'd obsessed over wanting a relationship with Finn that never materialized. Jillian sighed and eyed the three additional bottles of wheat beer chilling in an ice bucket and the bag of double-stuffed chocolate cookies on the bedside table next to Laurie.

"They're your favorite. Right?" Laurie was trying hard to make her feel better. She truly was a good friend.

"Absolutely." Jillian smiled despite inner turmoil.

She grabbed a beer from the bucket, twisted off the cap, and dropped it into the waste basket. Then she climbed onto the bed and collapsed against the headboard, next to her best friend in the whole world.

"Oh, look. This retro station is playing *I Love Lucy* reruns without commercials. I love the one where Lucy is working in a candy factory." Laurie dropped the remote between them, scooted around, and raised her bottle in toast. "Friendship."

They tapped bottles, drank, and turned attention to the large TV screen on the wall across the room. Well, at least Laurie did. Jillian's mind stayed stuck in the past with Stephen and the children she'd left behind. When the first episode ended, she picked up the remote and muted the sound, needing to talk.

"I met Isobell and Archibald," she blurted.

"How are they?"

"Good. They're fine. However, I didn't have a chance to meet their newborn son before the sheriff came to arrest me for witchcraft and we had to run. We escaped through the hidden passageway to the beach and…" Jillian swallowed uneasily with the memory. "Anyhow, I understand the child is healthy and quite doted upon."

"Running from the sheriff must have been harrowing."

"And some." A new serge of anxiety threatened to surface. Jillian forced it down and waved a hand in dismissal.

"I'm glad to hear Isobell and Archie are doing well." Laurie smiled then grew serious. "With the rules about the time gate, we can't go back to see them and meet our new nephew."

"Why not? What rules?"

"Iain believes—" The cell phone buzzed on the nightstand and Laurie answered. "Hey, sweetie. He is? Okay. Yeah. I'll stay at the inn for the night. See you in the morning. Love you. Bye."

"What? What is it?" Jillian asked.

"It's nothing." Laurie's gaze shifted around the room settling on the duvet beneath them. She twisted the blue fabric between two fingers."

"Don't pretend nothing is wrong. What is going on?"

"Stephen is here. Or I should say, he is at my house."

"He made it through the time gate?"

"Seems so."

Jillian tensed, heat flashing her chest and face, emotions tripping through all the stages from happy excitement to anger. "I don't want to see him. Ever."

"Iain has called a clan meeting for tomorrow morning after breakfast to discuss what happened to you and what occurred while you were in the past."

"I can't. I can't face *your* family." *I can't face Stephen.*

"You know you are a member of this family—"

"If I were, you would have shared the facts about…" Jillian's voice faded to nothing. She couldn't deal with airing her dirty laundry in front of everyone. Iain and Mairi. Finn and Elspeth would probably be there. Caitrina. She glared at Laurie. "Why did you never see fit to tell me about the time travel? About Caitrina? I feel so betrayed. By everyone."

"Oh, hon." Laurie squeezed her hand. "I'm sorry. I never meant to hurt you. It just didn't seem right to burden you with all the...magic. Sometimes it is best not to know what lurks in the dark. Or what skulks in the daylight."

"Perhaps you're right. I would have freaked. Still...I can't face Stephen."

Stephen sat in a comfortable chair—upholstered someone claimed—in Iain's study at the *Whispering Pines Bed and Breakfast*, waiting for the chief to arrive. To think the once mighty chief of Clan MacLachlan had become an innkeeper and was happy about his circumstance. Stephen shook his head. Things were much different in this future place. While all sorts of such perplexing thoughts filtered through his mind, he kept a steady gaze on Jillian who perched on a similar chair across the small chamber, refusing to offer even a mere glance his way.

After what seemed like the longest time, Iain arrived dressed in the blue *trews* Patrick called jeans and a strange *leine* with buttons down the front. He crossed the chamber, stopping in front of Jillian. A gentle touch to her cheek brought a tentative smile to her face. Stephen felt that touch at his fingertips and his stomach clenched. He wanted to be the one offering comfort.

Iain took his place behind the heavy wood desk. His wife, Mairi, sat to his left with Patrick to his right. Laurie sat with Jillian, their hands clasped. Also in attendance were Iain's daughter Elspeth and her husband Finn MacIntyre, the fae Caitrina, and Douglas MacKinnon, the man who found Stephen in the wood.

"I'm sure everyone is aware why we gather this morning. Before we get into the whos and whys, I wish to provide a warning to Jillian. As I cautioned Stephen last night, before either of you make rash decisions be aware the faerie knoll is unpredictable just like the fae, and 'tis my understanding a soul may travel through the portal only once in each direction. If an additional attempt is made, no one kens where a body will travel." After a nod to Jillian and Stephen, Iain turned an intense gaze on Caitrina. "Now, lass. Tell me true. Is the Queen of the Fae responsible for Jillian's fall into that well of time on the bike trail in West Virginia?"

Douglas MacKinnon flinched, but remained silent.

Caitrina pursed thinned lips. "Nae."

"Then who?" Iain asked.

"'Twas me," Caitrina said without remorse.

"But why?" Stephen and Jillian asked at the same time.

Jillian's sad gaze fell on Stephen for a moment before she ripped it away.

"Go ahead. Tell them, Caitrina," Douglas said.

"Their mating is the last of three matches I'm required to orchestrate as required by the Fae Queen in order to win my freedom."

Jillian glanced at the unsurprised faces in the chamber then jumped from her chair and stood before the faerie. "What are you talking about?"

Stephen rose, stood behind Jillian, and placed a hand on her shoulder in an offer of support. When she didn't flinch or pull away, he breathed more easily.

"You and Stephen must mate in order for a curse placed on me by the Queen of the Fae to be lifted."

"I don't understand." Jillian's voice trembled.

"It's simple," Finn said. "Laurie and Patrick were the first. Me and Elspeth the second. We've wondered for quite a while who would be the third couple."

"We thought it might be you, Jillian, when you disappeared," Laurie said. "We weren't sure, though, because Finn and I traveled back in time through the garden gate and you went missing in West Virginia."

"You used us as some sort of pawns in a game, Caitrina?" The faerie shrugged and Jillian stiffened. "I thought you were my friend. How dare you meddle in my life."

"You will be glad of my interference when the game is ended."

Jillian spun around. "Did you know about this, Stephen?"

He held both of her shoulders and looked into her innocent brown eyes. Everyone else in the chamber faded away. 'Twas only he and the woman he loved. The woman from which he needed to beg forgiveness.

"Nae," Stephen swore. "I only kenned you were a comely lass in need of aid. I meant to only help you find your way home, but in the doing I fell in love with you."

Jillian closed her eyes then opened them. "Who was the woman at the faerie hill?"

"My handfasted wife."

"Don't touch me." Jillian pulled away. "Please, don't touch me."

Stephen glanced around the chamber. The others had left them alone. Gave him the privacy to try to make things right with Jillian.

"Believe me." He reached out a hand then dropped it to his side when she shook her head. "I never meant to dishonor you."

"Me. More the fool for not asking if you were married."

"None of this is your fault."

"Do you love her?"

Stephen lowered his gaze to the oak floor, considering how to answer the question. How much to reveal. The answer was an emphatic *no*. He had no such feelings for Calyn. Yet the matter was complicated.

He looked into Jillian's dark eyes and felt a tightening in his chest. This was the woman with whom he wanted to spend the rest of his life. If only...he hadn't agreed to the handfast. A hard lesson was learned over the years since Patrick left and reinforced that dreadful day on the battlefield with his king—you don't always get what you want.

"Will you let me explain about the handfasting?"

"Go ahead, and you better make it good."

"I wandered aimless after Patrick and Lady Laurie left. Guess you could say I was lonely." He pounded the center of his chest. "As if there was an empty space inside me needing filling. You ken?"

Jillian cleared her throat, raw emotion vivid in her eyes. "So you filled it with your wife."

"Nae, lass. I dinnae remember laying with Calyn, but when I woke naked in her bed... Ach, well..." He scraped a palm over his face. "I agreed to the handfast because..."

"You're an honorable man."

"I try to be. The answer to your question though is nae. I dinnae love her. I dinnae even like her. But I now understand I must respect the commitment made." He stepped closer to Jillian and touched her soft cheek. Moisture glistened in her eyes. "'Twas wrong of me to dismiss the pledge I made on that dreadful day and seek a life with you. 'Twas wrong of me to keep the handfasting a secret from you. 'Twas wrong of me to express my love for you and lead us both to believe we had a future together." He ground his teeth. "I wish I hadn't so easily agreed to Calyn's demands."

"Her name is Calyn. Such a pretty name."

He shrugged and frowned. "I must return to the past and set things right. If Calyn truly bears my child, which I doubt, I will stay with her and be a proper father to my *bairn*. If she lied to me, as I believe...if there is nae *bairn*, I will break the contract with the wench on the prescribed date and return to you. If you will still have me."

"You shouldn't call her a wench."

"I should call her worse for tricking me into her bed."

Jillian raised a skeptical brow. "Do you expect me to believe—"

"That is the only way it could have happened." Now that he'd unburdened his soul, his eyes were wet with tears. He didn't care if 'twas unmanly. He needed her to believe him. Believe he'd never meant to hurt her. "Can you forgive me?"

"I love you Stephen MacEwen." She stepped into him and wrapped her arms around his chest. "When will you go?"

He held her tight. Even though he'd made the decision to go back, leaving Jillian would be the hardest thing he'd done in his life. "As soon as the gate lets me through. It can be fickle."

Perhaps the fae gate would never let him return to the past and he could stay with Jillian in this future place. Caitrina didn't seem to be of a mind to aid him.

"I will see you through the time gate." Douglas MacKinnon stood in the doorway holding Stephen's sheathed sword.

"You? How?"

"Just keep it to yourself. If anyone asks, swear Munn assisted you."

Stephen inwardly sighed. 'Twas wrong of him to consider shirking his responsibilities.

They walked together to the edge of the faerie knoll just beyond the garden gate. Clouds strolled across the sun in the cerulean sky above, making the scene before them feel normal. Douglas stepped to the side, allowing Stephen a moment of privacy with Jillian.

Moisture pooled in her brown eyes. "I don't want you to go."

"I must. My honor demands such."

She leaned in to him, sobbed against his chest, anguished tears wetting his *leine*, breaking his heart. "You are a good man."

"I am sorry, so sorry, to have hurt you." He wrapped his arms around her. Hugged her tight. His heart would remain here in the future with Jillian no matter what happened in the past.

"Promise me something?" Jillian asked.

"Anything."

"Take care of Keita and Duff."

"I vow to do right by them." He held a palm over his heart.

"I will always love you, Stephen MacEwen." Jillian kissed his cheek. "Always and forever."

"And I you, *m' fhìor ghaol.*" My true love.

"Oh, Stephen."

"*Soraidh leibh,*" he murmured against her hair. Farewell to you.

But not forever. He had to believe he would return or he wouldn't be able to leave.

"'Tis time." Douglas said "We must hurry before Caitrina catches wind of what we are doing."

Stephen released Jillian from his embrace, accepted the claymore from the man, and secured the sheath to his back. He walked onto the mound as if his boots were filled with heavy weight. Turning back, he waved. Jillian's image wavered as everything spun out of control, and he remembered Iain's warning. *If you return to the past, you might not be able to travel forward through the garden gate again.*

CHAPTER TWENTY-FIVE

9 March, 1514
Dunadd Castle, Argyll Scotland

*T*he great hall held a somber hush, the clan mourning their losses six months to the day after the Battle of Flodden. Calyn sat to Stephen's side, a smile broadening her mouth as if she were a tabby cat seated before a bowl of cream. Allain served a fine board, but not that good.

What was the wench so happy about?

Stephen certainly wasn't. Since arriving at Dunadd, he'd repeatedly questioned her about how he'd come to wake in her bed on that fateful morning. She persisted with the claim he'd forced his way into her chamber, taken advantage of her affinity for him, and she succumbed to his advances. She claimed to be as surprised as he that she'd grown large with child from just that one night of carnal knowledge. A night he didn't remember.

He inhaled sharply as her hand slid up his thigh for the fifth time. He gently removed it. Her pout only lasted a moment before she smiled for those watching them.

What was her game? Why did she want an unwilling husband?

Eyes widening and upper lip curling into something ugly, she stared toward the rear passage. His eyes followed her gaze, and he understood the cause of the sneer. Munn—having willingly joined Stephen when he could have remained at Castle Lachlan with the chief—guided Keita and Duff below stairs, more than likely to the kitchens where the *bairns* would partake of the evening meal.

"Must those ragamuffins stay with us?" Calyn demanded.

Stephen cringed, still not used to the whiney quality of her voice. How could he have bedded her? He would have had to gag her first.

"As I told you before, the *bairns* stay with me. If you wish them to leave, I leave, too."

"You cannot. You are my husband."

"Handfasted husband. For but a year and a day."

"Nae matter?" She rubbed her round belly. "Soon we will have a *bairn* of our own and a committed marriage assured for our future together."

He would have sunk into despair had he not caught sight of a man he recognized. A man he remembered speaking with the night before he woke in Calyn's bed.

"Pardon me, mistress, I must—" Stephen didn't bother finishing the statement or staying to hear a litany of curses, instead he hurried across the chamber to seek out a man who might have answers he required.

Howbeit, the man was gone by the time Stephen reached the table where the man had been seated moments before. Stephen just couldn't catch a break—to use one of Jillian's future terms. When he returned to where he'd left Calyn, she'd already departed in a huff by all accounts.

He collected the *bairns* and the brownie and wandered to the cottage he'd let for his newly acquired *family*. Calyn already slept in the bed they were expected to share. That would never happen. They might be wed for the rest of their lives, but they would never again share a bed. It would be a dishonor to Jillian.

He bedded down with the *bairns*.

Sleep came slow, and when it did, Stephen tossed and turned caught within a snare of dreams. He sat at a table with faceless warriors who would travel with him to do battle for king and country. They drank rounds, toasting to future success. A buxom maid sidled close, poured ale into his cup, and propositioned him. He couldn't make out her face, but kenned he didn't want to spend the night with the lass. After another toast, he stood, wanting to find his pallet. He staggered, though he hadn't consumed enough ale to be drunk. A brawny lad offered assistance and then another. Instead they manhandled him, trying to subdue him. He attempted to throw them off, but he had no strength. He woke in a sweat.

When Calyn ventured from bed in the morning, she found him seated at the dining table glowering into a mug. He lifted his gaze and had to squash the urge to snarl at her. "Tell me true. Did I lay with you the night you conceived?"

"Of course. I have told you before." Her giggle grated on his nerves. "You ken you woke in my bed."

"Aye. But dinnae remember tupping you."

"Dinnae be vulgar." She tugged the fabric of her gown, tightening its fit, drawing attention to her large belly. "You will ken the truth of it when you gaze into the eyes of *your bairn*."

Of a sudden, she gasped, eyes widening. Clutching a hand to her belly, she stumbled. He caught her by the shoulders. Fear glinted in her eyes. "Help me to the bed then send for the midwife. Hurry! The *bairn* is coming early."

Stephen paced the yard, cold air a bracing relief from the moist heat of the cottage. Munn had taken Keita and Duff up to the castle, out of range of Calyn's screams. How long did it take to bear a child?

Finally, the screaming ended. Moments later, a good mother poked her head out of the door. "You have a strapping laddie, my lord."

Stephen strode across the icy ground and over the threshold. Within the heat of the cottage, the midwife held up the screeching *bairn*.

"His eyes are blue like mine," Stephen said, awed by the infant.

"All *bairns* have blue eyes at birth, my lord." She wrapped the lad in swaddling and handed him into Stephen's arms. He held the child awkwardly. The *bairn* was tiny. Fragile.

Still, Stephen felt no warmth toward the lad. Shouldn't he feel more for his son?

After Calyn and the wee lad had been put to bed and were soundly sleeping, Stephen approached the midwife. "I have heard *bairns* born early can be too small to live."

"You have naught to worry about with your lad." The woman patted his arm. "He wasn't born early and is as healthy as they come."

Stephen felt a fist punch to his gut. Only six months had passed since the handfasting. Calyn *had* lied about the conception.

"Are you sure the *bairn* did not come early?"

"Oh, aye. I ken what an early birth looks like." The woman smiled, displaying a missing tooth. "If you have a worry for the lad, visit the witch living near the wee loch in the wood. She can give you a charm of protection among other things."

The question now was what he should do about Calyn's deceit. Could he leave her and the *bairn* and return to Jillian in the future? That is, if Iain was mistaken and Stephen could coerce the faeries of the mound to let him travel through.

While he pondered the question and its consequences over the evening meal the next night at the castle, he again glimpsed the man who might be able to shed light on the events leading up to Stephen being compromised in Calyn's bed. Stephen hurried across the hall determined to catch the man before he left. He approached the man's table and sidled close.

"Might we have a private word, sir?" Stephen asked, keeping an eye on the man's companions. They continued to eat, paying him no mind.

The man nodded, rose, and followed Stephen into the passageway and into a curtained alcove. Although all castles had ears everywhere, Stephen thought the spot safe for a short discussion.

"My name is Stephen MacEwen. I remember drinking ale with you the night before I was forcibly handfasted and left for war."

"Aye. I ken who ye are."

"Can you tell me what happened that night?"

"Ciaran and his brother will not thank me fer talking to ye." The man's Adam's apple bobbed as he swallowed. He pulled aside the curtain and glanced both ways before pulling the fabric closed again. "'Tis hearsay. Ye ken?"

"I understand."

"Yer lass had a nasty lover. Ye ken the man we all hate? Ye ken *Maclay*?"

The shock made Stephen's stomach drop. "Aye. Go on."

"Well, they say he got her with child and her brothers needed to find someone suitable to wed her and chose you. They had yer ale tainted." The man narrowed glassy eyes. "Ye dinnae hear this from me."

Stephen handed the man a coin for his troubles, and the man slipped from the alcove.

Maclay? Stephen could hardly believe the turn of events. What had Calyn been thinking to bed such a man? Had he forced himself on the lass? 'Twas the only possible reason a lass would bed such a man.

Stephen ran a hand through his hair. Could he leave Calyn and the *bairn* unprotected, and travel to the future to be with Jillian? His conscience wouldn't allow such. Mayhap he could hunt Maclay and kill the bastard.

The midwife had said something about a witch and a protection charm. He would seek out the witch on the morrow.

At noontime, Stephen headed for the stable. When he arrived, he found Keita and Duff already mounted on a horse. Duff raised his chin. "We are coming with you."

"How do you ken where I am going?"

"Does not matter." The lad held firm. "You will not leave us behind again."

Munn strolled out from another stall with Stephen's saddled horse. The wee man shrugged. "The *bairns* are persuasive."

"Aye. They are that." Stephen shook his head and mounted the horse. Munn leapt up on the beast's rump.

Luck provided a clear sky and warmer weather than usual. They rode the better part of the afternoon, until gloaming shadows covered the ground. As they cleared the wood near the hut on the loch, the hair on Stephen's arms lifted and the air bristled with...*magic.*

"Stay here at the edge of the wood while I visit with the witch. If anything bad happens, ride like a *banshee* chases you back to the castle. You understand?"

Both children nodded, and Stephen dismounted. He handed the reins over to Munn. "Keep the *bairns* safe."

Keita grasped his sleeve. "Take a care."

He rubbed a tender spot on his chest over his heart. "I will."

With a nod from the brownie, Stephen inhaled a calming breath and approached the witch's lair. A cackle sounded from within the moss-covered structure, and he stiffened.

The heavy oak door swung open and a woman of minute stature stood on the threshold. The hunch of her back must be painful. Stringy gray hair hung over a face with creases upon creases and a hairy wart protruded from a crooked nose. Howbeit, the hag's emerald eyes were remarkable. They seemed familiar, though Stephen couldn't comprehend why.

"What brings you to my humble doorstep, Lord Stephen?"

Hardly a lord. "How do you ken who I am?"

"I saw your coming in my herbal tea leaves. Why have you come?" Her intense gaze seemed to see right through him.

Stephen shifted his weight, uneasy with her perusal. "I need a protection spell for...my newborn son."

"Ach! I ken the *bairn* of which you speak is nae of your blood, but of that of the villain Maclay."

A chill traveled over Stephen's spine. The witch had an uncanny knowledge.

"Does not matter who fathered the child."

"Heed my warning for the evil man's son can come to nae good."

"You speak nonsense. The *bairn* is my responsibility and I will see him protected."

"Hah! You have not even given him a name."

"Nae matter. What must I give you in return for a charm to safeguard the wee lad?"

She handed him a mat of woven reeds with a symbolic etched black stone at its center. "Place this talisman under the *bairn's* cradle. We will discuss your payment at a later time."

Stephen clutched the charmed mat and turned to leave.

"Not so fast."

He pivoted back to the witch. "Aye?"

"Is there not something else you need to ken?"

"I dinnae understand your meaning."

"A way through the time gate at the *Sithichean Sluaigh* perhaps?"

"What do you ken of the faerie knoll, witch? My understanding is that a body can only travel through once in each direction."

"You ken little of the ways of the fae. One faerie took you forward. Someone else brought you back. Each can take you through once again." The witch scowled. "Though I dinnae understand how a meddling brownie learned the ways of the fae royalty. Nae matter. Go to the *Sithichean Sluaigh* on the next full moon and say these words to induce the favor of the fae."

"What are the words?" Hope flared within Stephen's breast.

"*Faeries dance round me, faeries sing to me. Upon this hill I am free of strife. From this sacred place I will ascend to a new life.*"

Stephen repeated the chant so he wouldn't forget.

"If the fae look fondly upon you, they will send you to the one you seek." She swatted her hands in his direction. "Now go before a late winter storm keeps you from your journey."

He found the others where he'd left them at the edge of the wood and ordered Munn to take the *bairns* on ahead to Castle Lachlan and then to meet him on the full moon two days hence at the faerie knoll.

Unbeknownst to Calyn, and without her unwanted hysterics, Stephen placed the witch's talisman under the newborn's cradle. Relieved to have provided protection for the *bairn*, Stephen rode with haste, a bone-chilling storm on his heels as predicted by the witch.

At the Fir-wood, he found Keita and Duff waiting. "Where is Munn?"

Duff shrugged. "The brownie sent us alone."

"Then let us be about this mad business."

Moments later, Stephen stood at the center of the *Sithichean Sluaigh* holding Keita and Duff's hands securely, determined to travel to Jillian's future time. They needed the faeries to look favorably upon them.

"*Faeries dance round me, faeries sing to me. Upon this hill I am free of strife. From this sacred place I will ascend to a new life,*" he quoted the words given to him by the witch. Excitement flared. The familiar sensation of falling overcame him. Things began to spin. But then to his dismay, everything stilled too quickly.

Stephen popped his eyes wide. Maclay charged toward them, a claymore gripped within his hands, intent on striking a killing blow. Stephen pushed the *bairns* away and in one brisk move, twisted to the side, freeing his sword and dropping its sheath and his *plaide* to the ground, ready to counter the attack. He couldn't allow Maclay to travel to the future.

CHAPTER TWENTY-SIX

Anderson Creek, North Carolina

Jillian set aside the long water-wand and turned off the spigot. Water droplets dripped from hanging petunia baskets hooked on racks suspended over rows of plant benches containing a kaleidoscope of colorful bedding plants. She inhaled the mingling floral scents and savored the quiet of the greenhouse, glad the spring rush at *Foxgloves* had mellowed to a manageable pace. Tomorrow, the mid-summer gardening classes would begin and she was scheduled to teach several including her favorite, *Landscaping with Containers*.

If she gave her situation more thought than probably prudent, an emptiness within whittled away the false perception of wellbeing. She should feel better about her life. She made a good living at the garden center and enjoyed the work. Others in her position would at the least be content. More likely happy. But an anxious urgency rode Jillian daily. Inhaling a deep breath, she slipped past deserted potting benches—the staff having left early for the day—and out into the display garden where the scent of roses near to intoxicated the senses. Navigating one of the winding paths, she headed for the rear gate.

Sidestepping the pink foxgloves still blooming in the shade despite the heat, she gripped the metal of the grille with two hands and stared beyond the gate to the faerie mound, to the place where Stephen had vanished from her life months ago. He'd sacrificed so much to return to the past and make things right with Calyn, even though, as Jillian knew in her heart, he'd wanted to stay here with her. He was a good man.

They had both seen Calyn plump with child. The chances something else made the woman fat—a tumor perhaps— were slim at best, and it was wrong for Jillian to wish such a horrible thing on a person. She released a heavy sigh. When would she give up the daily pilgrimage and admit Stephen had a child with Calyn and would never return?

"Hey, sis, you need to stop torturing yourself. He's not coming back."

Jillian swung around, a palm clutched to her chest. "Kyle, you scared the bejesus out of me. What are you doing here?"

"I have a week's worth of vacation time I need to use or lose." He grinned and brushed strands of sun-bleached hair out of his not-so-innocent brown eyes. "Come on. Forget your vigil of the mound. Let's go to the inn for a beer."

"In a few minutes." She turned back and peered through the gate.

"Jillian."

"Yeah." She glanced at her brother again, surprised by his unusual tone of voice and the strange look on his face.

"I'm thinking about taking another bike trip along the Greenbrier River Trail in West Virginia. Wanna come?"

"Can't. Gardening classes start tomorrow." Not that she would want to go anyway. She didn't want to go anywhere near that old train tunnel.

Kyle tilted his head, an even odder expression scaring her.

"No," Jillian pleaded. "You can't intend to check out that time well. You just can't. I would be devastated if I lost you, too.

"It was just a thought. I'm curious about how the portal

works."

Jillian shivered and looked away from her crazy brother to stare beyond the garden gate. The setting sun cast a golden glow over the mound. Kyle was likely right; Stephen wasn't returning, but still—

Wait! She edged the grille open. There was something there, on the knoll. Someone. No. A watery image of three figures.

"Look!" She extended an arm and pointed. "Do you see them? Over there."

The golden glow turned pinkish. A trick of the sun?

"What the hell?" Kyle moved to stand beside her and cupped a hand over his eyes. "I see something. I can't make it out."

"Must be Stephen and the children." She raised a foot to step through the gate.

"No you don't!" Kyle clasped her upper arm in a tight grip, halting her momentum. "I'm not losing you to this nonsense again."

She wobbled, unsteady on her feet before catching her balance. The shimmer of color vanished, as did the image.

"There is something on the ground that wasn't there before." Her voice rose. She could hardly contain the excitement.

"Don't even think of going onto that damn faerie hill." Kyle, once again, stopped her from bolting through the gate. "I'll go see what it is."

Jillian bit her lip, waiting, eager to see what had materialized before their eyes.

When her brother returned, he held a plaid weaved by a MacLachlan craftsman. *Stephen's?*

"My. God." Jillian clutched the familiar tartan of red and green crossed with yellow against her heart. Brought it to her nose and inhaled. The wool fabric smelled of Stephen. Her mouth went dry. Had he tried to return, only to be thwarted by an unwilling gate?

A large hand settling on her shoulder made her scream.

"What is with you guys, creeping up on a girl when she least expects it?" she glared at Douglas who seemed to appear out of thin air.

He displayed no chagrin. "Where did you get Stephen's plaid?"

She pointed to the mound. "We thought we saw him there and then he was gone."

"*Shite!*" Douglas frowned. Fisted hands on hips. Strode off toward the trail for Finn and Elspeth's house.

"What was that all about?" Kyle asked.

Jillian nipped the side of her bottom lip. Might Stephen be lost somewhere in time? "I think it had something to do with Stephen. Everyone is worried about his future in the past."

"And you?"

"It is hard to put into words the many fears tightening my stomach when I think of what might be happening to Stephen."

Fir-wood, Scotland

Stephen dropped his sword to a forward position warding Maclay's cut with the flat of the blade. The resulting vibration shot up Stephen's arm, stressing already bulging muscles. He twisted his wrists and counterstruck.

The men separated. Circled. From the corner of an eye, Stephen risked a swift check on the *bairns*. Keita huddled in Munn's arms. Thanks be to the saints, the wee brownie deemed to make an appearance. Duff stood apart from the other two, straight as a rod, watching the fight with wide eyes, a heavy stick clutched in tense hands.

The distraction almost cost Stephen the fight and perhaps his life and that of the *bairns*. 'Twas only the practiced reflexes of a warrior that saved him when the next blow came. Stephen edged his hips back, avoiding a vicious slice to his gut.

"I kilt your wife, MacEwen," his opponent taunted.

Stephen couldn't allow the goading to affect him. 'Twas likely Maclay spoke false.

"And what of your son?" he retorted.

The bastard's face remained stoic. Cold. Unfeeling.

Could he have hurt Calyn and her *bairn*? Men who harmed innocents didn't deserve to live.

Stephen reached within for a warrior's calm and returned to the fight with a gruesome brutality. The clash of steel against steel echoed over the nearby hills as they each used their blades to find a weakness in the other. The metallic scent of blood rose from a slash on his arm. His strength began to wane.

Maclay tired, too. He panted. His chest heaved heavily with each breath.

Stephen needed to end this and soon. Releasing his left hand from the hilt of the sword, he struck his opponent in the throat with a fist—a move he learned from Finn several years prior. Maclay staggered backward, and Stephen plunged his blade into the man's belly. Maclay made a gurgling sound; crumpled to the ground. Duff jumped in and bashed the fallen man on the head several times.

"Easy, lad." Stephen grabbed the boy's shoulder. "The bastard is dead."

The lad dropped the stick and lunged into Stephen's arms. Stephen held him close. Patted the lad's back. Murmured words of comfort.

"Better?" Stephen asked when the lad calmed.

Duff sniffled and stepped away, cheeks flushed. Keita joined them, wrapping her little arms round one of Stephen's legs.

"Are you well, lass?" he asked, rumpling her tousled curls.

She gave an abrupt nod.

"Then let us leave this place." Stephen gripped the *bairns* hands ignoring the sting from the injury to his arm, and they walked to the top of the knoll to where Stephen had left the sheath and his *plaide*. The leather sheath was there, but not the *plaide*. No hum of magic vibrated in the air.

Munn stood off to the side, shaking his head.

"Faeries dance round me, faeries sing to me. Upon this hill I am free of strife. From this sacred place I will ascend to a new life." Stephen said the words, desperate for them to work magic.

"Too late. This gate is nae longer open to you," Munn cried, spun in a circle, and vanished.

Stephen swallowed disappointment. He'd suspected as much, but had hoped—

Keita tugged on his hand. "Did the bad man really kill Calyn and the *bairn?*"

"Dinna worry, lass. He probably just toyed with me, hoping for an advantage in the fight," he assured her, but harbored an uneasy feeling about what they would find upon returning to the cottage in Dunadd.

CHAPTER TWENTY-SEVEN

*M*unn's essence whirled over peak and glen, narrowing in on the wee loch in the wood he'd visited with Stephen and the *bairns* a couple days prior. He landed on his butt on the hard ground in front of the weathered wooden door of the witch's dilapidated hut. A biting wind whipped his face.

"Witch, my arse," he grumbled. "More likely a charlatan."

The feminine giggle of a young woman came from within the structure. Huh? Odd. Yet he sensed the *witch* was alone.

Munn stood, straightened his garments, and pushed into the hut without knocking. He didn't fear the old hag even if she had the ability to mimic another. What was a mortal witch to a seasoned brownie? To a brownie who'd survived the wrath of the Fae Queen? To a brownie who'd traveled to the future? Munn's chest expanded with pride.

The old woman continued to giggle like a much younger lass. Like a female faerie...

"Should have guessed 'twas you," Munn groused.

The hunched body before him stretched and thinned. Coarse gray hair lengthened and took on an auburn sheen. A smooth pert nose replaced a malformed one. The only thing the woman standing before him retained of the hag was the distinguishing emerald eyes. He should have recognized

Caitrina sooner.

The mingling scents of peony and freesia and sandalwood wafted from her exquisitely garbed form. How had she concealed that cloying fae perfume while in the form of the hag so he hadn't suspected 'twas she the previous time they visited? He should have smelled her from a great distance and certainly from the edge of the woods where he'd waited for Stephen with Keita and Duff.

"What are you doing here, wee man?" Caitrina stretched slender arms over her head—a gauzy, emerald silk gown molded to pert breasts—as if trying to grow accustomed to her true form.

With a frown, Munn adjusted his *trews*, not that he was attracted to the faerie or anything about her. Nor any other female. Definitely not.

"I came to seek help from the hag." His voice came out higher pitched than usual.

"For what, pray tell?"

"The spell she…*you* gave to Stephen. It only sent his *plaide* forward through time."

"Flaming balls of hell!" Her fingertips sparked. "How could you let that happen?"

"'Twas not my fault. Maclay arrived filled with blood lust. He claimed to have kilt Calyn. Stephen kilt him."

"And Maclay's *bairn*?"

Munn shrugged with a shake of the head. He didn't ken what happened to the *bairn*. Nor did he care. The evil man's son could come to no good.

"Grrr!" Caitrina paced to and fro.

Munn edged toward the door. There would be no help for him here. Caitrina's glare stopped him with his hand only halfway to the latch.

Hands fisted on hips, her eyes narrowed. "How is it a wee brownie learned to sift time?"

Munn wrinkled his brow. "Nary a one amongst my kind kens the ways of the mound."

"Yet you guided Stephen back through the time gate, away

from Jillian."

"Nae." Munn opened the door, ready to spin out into the yard and to vanish.

Anger distorted Caitrina's features. "Then who?"

He gulped. Her tone of voice was more frightening than that of the Queen of the Fae when having a temper tantrum. He shook his head. He didn't ken who had interfered. He'd thought Caitrina had brought Stephen back through time.

"Never mind." Her facial muscles relaxed as quickly as they'd soured. "'Tis only a matter of time before I learn who keeps thwarting me." She rubbed her chin, shoulders relaxed. "There is another way to reunite Stephen and Jillian in the future. Take him to the spot in the forest where Jillian arrived and met the *bairns* of the wood. Push him into the time well, and I will see him through the portal to West Virginia."

"Ach, aye." Munn should have thought of the other time gate himself. He didn't care for Caitrina bringing its existence to his attention. Not one bit. She would gloat over him for years. He kicked the dirt floor.

"Dinnae make this into more of a disaster," she warned and disappeared into the nether.

Damn faerie always had to have the last word. Munn would show her; he'd see Stephen to the future and maybe he'd stay there himself. He liked the place when he visited with Archie.

Uh-oh! He didn't actually ken where to find the time well. Shite! Munn spun in a circle, dissolved into specks of dust, and rode a bitter wind in search of Stephen.

Snowflakes dusted the ground as the two horses neared the village outside Dunadd Castle. Stephen signaled Duff to halt. "Stay hidden in these trees until we learn the truth of Maclay's claims."

The lad nodded, and Stephen handed over his reins. 'Twould be better for him to travel the remainder of the way to the cottage on foot. Keeping to the shadows, he darted from structure to structure, his extra *plaide* wrapped around his upper body and over his head both to ward off the cold and to hide his identity.

The door of the cottage hung open. Stephen crept close. No one seemed to be about. He slipped across the threshold. An acrid stench fouled his breath, leaving no doubt as to what he would find. The place showed signs of violence. Tables and benches were overturned. A chair had been smashed against a wall, leaving a hole in the surface and shards of wood on the floor amongst pieces of broken crockery.

With unease, he stepped behind the curtain separating one of the sleeping quarters from the living area. The bed where Calyn slept remained unmade. The cradle empty. The foul smell strengthened and he covered his nose with the wool of his plaide. He rounded the wood frame of the bed, stopping short of the battered body on the bloody rush mat. Maclay had obviously tortured the lass before dispensing the final death blow.

A sour taste rose in Stephen's throat, but he didn't turn away. He tugged a sheet free of the bed and covered the poor lass. She might have lied to him and wrongly forced him into a handfasting, but nary a soul deserved to die in such a violent manner.

He wished he could kill Maclay again. Slowly and with as much pain as the lass had suffered. Or perhaps more. Payment for the man's many sins.

Stephen shook off the bloodlust. Maclay's punishment would come from the hand of God.

Where was Maclay's bairn? Stephen lifted covers and sheets and pillows, but found naught.

Grinding his teeth, concerned he wouldn't find the wee *bairn*, he strode into the main living area of the cottage. With hands on hips, he surveyed the carnage. A whimpering came from the second curtained off sleeping quarter. The one Stephen shared with Keita and Duff. He dashed across the chamber and shoved aside the hanging cloth. Naught had been touched within.

Silence. Nary a sound indicated the presence of the *bairn*. Stephen could have sworn he'd heard—

A murmur of a cry had him crossing to the wooden chest covered with one of his *plaides*. When he pulled the wool fabric away, he found a basket containing the *bairn* hidden behind.

Thank the good Lord, Maclay hadn't harmed the *bairn*.

Pale blue eyes stared at Stephen before the wee *bairn* let loose a high-pitched wail.

Stephen wrapped the lad in the *plaide* and cradled him in his arms. He'd take the *bairn* to the castle and hand the lad over to Calyn's family. Then Stephen would compel the faerie mound to hurl him, Keita, and Duff to Jillian in the future.

The clatter of someone rummaging through the debris in the outer chamber made Stephen twist his body in a manner to protect the *bairn*. Calyn's da tore open the curtain. Her two brothers stood behind their da, blocking the threshold—the only way out of the cottage except for the bolt hole under the floorboards. If there was trouble, Stephen would have to push past them while protecting the infant in his arms.

"So you learnt the brat was Maclay's and kilt the wench." Calyn's da spit the words.

"Maclay killed your daughter." Stephen spoke calmly, refusing to be goaded by the older man. He hoped to get out of the cottage without a fight.

"Says you?" Ciaran joined his da. "The sheriff may see it differently."

Stephen ignored the veiled threat and held the *bairn* out to his grandfather.

The man stared at the wee lad with disgust. "I dinnae want Maclay's bastard. I dinnae want anything born of the slut."

How could the man be so cold? "So you admit Calyn was with child before the handfasting."

"Said nae such thing. She was your wife, the *bairn* is your problem." The older man cursed under his breath. "More than likely 'tis a changeling."

"You cannot mean to abandon the wee lad."

Calyn's da shoved his sons aside and hurried from the cottage, a hobble to his gait.

"We will seek reprisal for Calyn's death." Ciaran raised a fist in the air. "I swear it. We will see you destroyed, MacEwen."

"Not now. The man is too well-loved by the chief." The other brother tugged on Ciaran's arm. "Come. Let us be away from here before we are blamed for any of this."

Ciaran tossed off the grip and stormed from the cottage, his brother at his heels.

Now what was Stephen to do with the *bairn*? He glanced at the innocent within his arms. Could he take him to the future too? Would Jillian accept the lad?

She had such a kind heart. A love for *bairns*. She wouldn't want the wee one to be deserted in the wood. Nae. But if Jillian refused to accept the lad, Stephen would need raise the child alone. Could he manage?

What if Iain and Patrick cast them out when he arrived with Maclay's spawn? Nae matter. Stephen would convince Jillian they should raise the *bairn* as their own, with or without the clan's approval. That was, if he figured out how to get the lot of them to the future.

Determined the lad shouldn't pay for the means of his birth, Stephen bundled the *bairn* for warmth and placed him in the basket then strode out into the cold night air. A waxing moon lit the yard, and he bounded for the darkened area provided by a nearby structure. Once again sticking to the shadows, he stole into the trees where Keita and Duff waited.

Before he secured the *bairn* to his horse, a large man of tall stature stepped from the gloom cast by a dense fir grove. Stephen froze. The inability to reach for a weapon with the basket in his arms left him at a disadvantage.

"'Tis the man who gave us the pretty garments for Jillian to wear to Castle Lachlan," Keita blurted.

If he helped them before, perhaps...

The stranger wore black leather and a dark mask covered

most of his face. He approached at an unhurried pace, arms hanging loosely at his sides. He might pose a threat. Why wear a mask, if he did not?

"I mean you and the *bairns* nae harm." The man stopped a short distance away.

No visible weapons draped the man, but that didn't mean a blade or thrice weren't hidden within his garments. The stature of the man seemed familiar, though Stephen couldn't offer a guess as to why, or from where he recognized him. Maintaining a cautious guard might prove best.

He made quick work of lashing the basket containing the *bairn* to the horse, keeping the stranger in view while working the hemp.

"Come with me," the man offered when Stephen finished. "I shall see you and the *bairns* safely to the future."

Caitrina emerged into substance at the well a half-day's trek from the Caves of the Gray Women. The very spot where Jillian arrived in the past. Excitement surged within Caitrina's fae breast. Naught remained to stop her from winning the queen's challenge. Soon, her freedom would be won.

She spun in a circle of bliss. To finally realize her heart's desire. To once again frolic amongst other faeries in *Tir-nan-Og*. To enjoy the royal status of a Princess of the Fae.

An unexpected ache over her heart slowed the rotation of joy to a stop. Douglas, her human lover, could never join her in the faerie paradise. She wiped a teardrop from a moist cheek.

She couldn't think about the loss of her love now. She needed to see Stephen and the *bairns* through the portal to the future and ensure he and Jillian conceived a child of their own.

Where was Munn anyway? Stephen's wee party should have arrived here by now.

As if she'd conjured the brownie, he appeared in a whirl of snowflakes, spinning and spinning until the frenzy petered out.

"What took you so long?"

"Not my fault. Took time." He lowered his gaze, nudged a toe into the mud. "Needed to find the well."

"And where are the others?" she demanded. "If you have screwed this up on me, I will see you banished to the Sands of Time forever."

"Gone. Disappeared."

"Impossible."

A violent shudder shifting the forest floor forced Caitrina and Munn to collapse to their knees. The ground quaked and split. Smoke fouled the air.

Within the smoldering haze materialized three fae horses carrying Stephen and the *bairns* and… *Dugaid.* Oonagh's son. The Prince of Darkness.

"Danu be damned!" Caitrina rubbed tired eyes, wishing her vision mistaken.

She rose to her feet as the Dark Prince strode forward, his face still masked. He grasped a lock of her hair, twirling the curl around a finger before she had the thought to pull away. The rogue leaned in close and murmured, "Be careful who you curse, princess. The goddess is always watching. As am I. Remember that."

"You are the one thwarting me." She pretended to ignore the thrill from his breath teasing her flesh. The ache at her core. "You want me to fail."

"Nae, lass. I am your champion. Always." Impassive amber eyes held her gaze for a second. For a minute. For a lifetime. She forgot to breathe and wavered.

A grin displaying perfect white teeth burst onto his face as he supported her weight. She wanted to scratch away that masculine arrogance, but didn't dare.

Without uttering another word, he released the hold on her hair, set her aright, and turned on a heel, leaving her bereft. The air buzzed with dark magic, the tone shrill to those sensitive to such sounds. She and Munn slammed palms over their ears. With a wave of the prince's muscular arms, the others traveled forward through the time gate, leaving Caitrina alone with the damn brownie, cursing the prince.

CHAPTER TWENTY-EIGHT

Anderson Creek, North Carolina

Jillian strolled through the product displays in Foxglove's gift shop, searching for a perfect ornament for the garden she planned to install behind the inn for Mairi. She selected a birdhouse from a table containing avian gifts. Holding the wooden structure in her hands, she smiled. Crimson hollyhocks graced a lime green exterior. It would create quite the picture in a bed of summer blooms.

The crunch of a vehicle's wheels on gravel grabbed her attention and drew her to the open doorway. Kyle's yellow Jeep careened into the parking lot. What on earth—

A blond-haired man wearing sunglasses, black jeans, and a black t-shirt slipped out of the truck's passenger seat, pushed forward the back of the seat, and retrieved...a baby from an infant carrier. When he turned around, she gasped. My God, it was Stephen. And Keita and Duff leaned out from the backseat and waved. They wore twenty-first century clothing, too. How had Kyle found them? Why hadn't he called to say they were here?

She dropped the birdhouse on the counter, ran through the doorway and across the crushed stone, ready to leap on

Stephen, but his hands were full—the baby.

Jillian stopped short, unsure what to think, trying to keep the dismay—inner turmoil—from showing on her face. She attempted to peer into the backseat without appearing too obvious. *Had he brought Calyn?* "You brought your child. Did you also bring your wife?"

Stephen flinched. "I have much to explain."

I just bet you do. Before she could offer the retort, Keita and Duff ran from the other side of the Jeep, rocketing for her, faces bright with exuberance. Jillian threw open her arms to catch them in a three-way hug fest.

"I've missed you so much," she murmured for their ears only.

"'Tis so warm here. 'Twas snowing when we left. Kyle *purchased* new garments for us so we will *fit in* and took us to a barn for *ice cream...*" Keita prattled. "*Chocolate* ice cream with *fudge* on top. He said it is your *favorite.* He said we are going to live in a big house with you and Stephen and we can have ice cream whenever we want."

Stephen stepped forward and tilted his head to the side, seeming wary, perhaps unsure of his reception. Meanwhile, Kyle sauntered around the front of the Jeep as if he hadn't just blown Jillian's world apart with one of those smart bombs. Her brother could have, at the least, warned her about the baby.

"I found them wandering, lost, near the train tunnel on the bike trail," Kyle said. "Figured they belonged to you. Took them shopping. They cleaned up real nice, don't you think?" He grinned and *Groucho Marxed* his brows. "By the way, the hole you fell into is gone. Disappeared. Why do so many weird things happen around you and your friends?"

Jillian snorted. She couldn't help it. Weird was an understatement. She glanced into Stephen's eyes and fell into two compelling pools of blue. Lost herself. Why had he returned if he fathered a child with Calyn and couldn't stay?

"I hope you are happy to see us," he said, his voice rough.

"Of course. I've missed the children and..." Her throat

went dry and her voice sounded as gravelly as Stephen's had. "Thank you for bringing them to me."

"I ken I owe you explanations. Might we find a quiet place to speak? Just the two of us?" He turned to her brother and held out the baby.

"No way. Not me." Kyle threw up his hands, palms forward, and backed away.

Duff frowned and rolled his eyes to the side with a tilt to the head. He accepted the child from Stephen and cradled *him* in the crook of an arm as if he'd done the same many times before. *Stephen had a son.*

"Keita and I will watch wee Malcolm." Duff cooed softly to the infant.

"Malcolm," Jillian repeated. So that was the child's name.

Stephen winced. "'Tis a long story."

"Perhaps we all should hear the tale," Iain said. "A clan meeting in my private chamber in one hour, where you will explain yourself."

She hadn't heard Iain's approach or that of Mairi, Patrick, and Laurie as they joined the gathering in the parking lot. Stephen pursed his lips before giving Iain an abrupt nod.

"Come, Jillian. Let us go to the inn now so we can get these *bairns* settled and have tea," Mairi suggested.

"I think whisky may be required this night before the telling is done." Patrick clapped Stephen on the back. "Glad you managed to return to us, cousin."

"You may not feel the same after you hear what I have to say."

Jillian chewed the edge of her lip. What had Stephen done?

Stephen regrouped with the others in the chamber outside Iain's study at the inn after putting Keita and Malcolm to bed. Though still young, Duff had become a man during the fight with Maclay and deserved to participate in the clan meeting.

Jillian sat on the other side of the chamber with Laurie and Mairi. Stephen understood her attempts to avoid him—she wouldn't even look his way—but it had to stop, and before Iain arrived and called the meeting to order. He needed to explain things to her privately before sharing the sordid details with the rest of the clan members present.

"Do you think you can lure Jillian away from the others?" he whispered to the lad leaning against the wall beside him.

With a grin, seemingly pleased to be part of a conspiracy, Duff sauntered across the chamber to Jillian. He said something that Stephen couldn't hear and the two of them disappeared into the passageway.

Stephen waited a moment then signaled to Patrick his intent to step out of the chamber. With a soft stride, he followed after two of the four people who meant the most to him. He prayed he could keep them in his life after he shared what needed to be said.

Halfway along the passageway, Jillian had stopped and stood alone in front of a closed door. She spun toward him, palm pressed to her breast upon his approach. "You startled me."

"I did not mean to cause discomfort. Where is the lad?"

She blushed. "He needed to use the um…you know…loo."

"And I need to speak to you privately. Duff can find his way back to Iain's study." He grasped her elbow. Thankfully, she gave a quick nod instead of pulling away and allowed him to escort her to the front of the inn where they found an empty chamber.

Several of those upholstered chairs and wee tables were scattered about the interior. He seated her on a wide chair covered in a pale blue velvet, and knelt before her. When he gazed into her brown eyes, he became mired in his thoughts. How would he explain all that had transpired since they parted?

"I dinnae ken where to begin," he said.

"The beginning is usually best."

"I think I would rather tell you the most important thing first. Tell you what is in my heart." He held one of her delicate hands within both of his palms. "I love you. I wish for you to wed with me."

"But—"

"The *bairn* is not mine. Calyn was with child before the forced handfasting. Her father and brothers tricked me. I have never had carnal knowledge of the lass."

Jillian's brows scrunched tight. "But the baby. Why then do you have the child?"

"'Tis a long story, as I told Iain. The short of the tale is both parents are dead and Calyn's family refused to care for the wee lad. They wanted him dropped in the wood as were Keita and Duff. They claim he is a changeling. I am hoping you will accept the *bairn* and raise him with me as our own."

Jillian's face brightened with a tentative smile. "I think I would like that."

Stephen relaxed back on his heels. He prayed the last bit of the tale wouldn't change her mind. "There is one other thing you must ken before you agree. Maclay is wee Malcolm's father—thus the name."

"I don't care. I love you, Stephen. I have room enough in my heart for all three children and any others we are fortunate enough to bring into this world."

He lunged over Jillian, and the chair groaned beneath his added weight. They both laughed. Kissed. Slid to the floor, laughing and kissing and holding each other in a loving embrace filled with hope for the future.

Still, she hadn't quite agreed to wed with him. "You will be my bride, aye?"

The kiss she planted on his lips and then took deeper was answer enough.

When they realized they'd been gone too long, they rose, and Stephen wrapped an arm around her shoulders as they strolled back along the passageway. He stopped Jillian short of returning to the others. "There is something more, sweetling. Some of the others may not want Maclay's *bairn*

215

living amongst them."

"Don't be ridiculous, they can't blame the child for the father's sins."

"I hope you are right. If you are not, will you consider making a new life with me somewhere else?"

"I will. I love you, Stephen. But let's pray it doesn't come to that."

Stephen gave her a loving squeeze and they entered Iain's study to find the chief seated behind the large desk with Mairi at his side. Patrick stood in back of a wide chair where Laurie sat next to Duff. Douglas, Finn, and Elspeth had joined the group.

Jillian dropped next to Duff on the wide chair and Stephen took the spot next to Patrick behind his future wife and son. God willing.

"Since everyone is here except Caitrina, who I doubt will join us, let us begin." Iain inclined his head to Stephen.

"Maclay is dead." He stated the detail that would be of the most significance to those gathered.

"Are you sure?" Finn slid forward in his chair. "I had thought I killed him, but still he lived and continued to harass our people, reiving cattle and plundering villages."

"My claymore pierced the man's belly." Stephen placed a palm on Duff's shoulder. "And our lad here dealt the final death blow to the head. The bastard will nae longer trouble Clan MacLachlan."

Everyone started talking at once. Patrick kissed the top of Laurie's head. He thanked Duff for his part and welcomed the lad to the clan.

When the voices quieted, Iain pinned Stephen with a questioning stare. "We are all relieved to hear of Maclay's demise, but what of your handfasting to Calyn and your return to us with a *bairn*?"

Jillian glanced over a shoulder, giving him a reassuring smile.

"Calyn's *bairn* came too early to be mine, proving her family's deception and nulling the handfasting."

"Then why do you have the *bairn?*"

"The wee lad's father and mother are both dead. Maclay killed the lass before coming after me at the faerie hill."

A collective gasp sounded in the chamber.

"Why didn't you leave Maclay's spawn with Calyn's family?"

Stephen raised a brow. "How do you ken the lad is Maclay's son?"

"Why else would you have named the child Malcolm?"

"Ach, well, Calyn's father accused the *bairn* of being a changeling and wanted him dropped in the wood. I could not allow such a loathsome thing to occur." Stephen swallowed hard hoping he didn't have to take Jillian away. "Jillian has agreed to wed me, and we will raise wee Malcolm as our own. We understand you may not want him raised amongst your family and we will leave if that is your command."

"Dinnae be foolish," Mairi said, rising. "The child is naught but an innocent."

"Do you agree, Iain?" Stephen asked.

"Aye." He looked at his son. "Patrick?"

Patrick shared a glance with his wife, and then they both nodded agreement.

"There is nae need for you to leave. You and the *bairns* are welcome to remain with the clan in Anderson Creek."

Stephen released the breath he hadn't realized he'd held, grasped Jillian's hand and squeezed when she rose, stepping back to stand beside him.

"You will need an occupation," Patrick said. "You can work with me, building log homes. We will start with one for you and Jillian. The two of you and the *bairns* cannot stay at the inn forever."

Laurie kissed Jillian on the cheek. "Congratulations. We'll have such fun planning the wedding."

CHAPTER TWENTY-NINE

*J*illian gazed into the antique cheval mirror in her bedroom at the inn, her bewildered image reflected in the beveled oval. Had she fallen through the looking glass into Wonderland? Goodness. She was dressed in a very modern Irish lace wedding gown and would marry a sixteenth century Highlander in less than an hour. Who would have thought such a thing possible when she'd moved to Anderson Creek a few years ago to join in the garden center business with Laurie and Caitrina?

"Is that really me?" Jillian pointed to her reflection, eyes bright and hair piled atop her head in a soft bun adorned with a tiara of faux diamonds.

Laurie chuckled. "You look beautiful."

"Thank you." Jillian swirled in a circle. She adored the princess cut of the ivory gown and the row of covered buttons extending down the length of its back. "It's my dream wedding dress."

"Stephen will love it."

"You think?"

"How could he not? Now, hold still so I can put this on you." Laurie draped a silk sash of MacLachlan tartan over Jillian's shoulder and clasped it at the hip. "Perfect."

After a soft knock, the door swung open and Keita rushed into the room, dancing about, showing-off her forest green dress that matched Laurie's matron of honor gown. Keita stopped next to Jillian. "You look like the princess in the storybook Mairi gave me. So pretty."

"You look lovely too, sweet pea." Jillian blew the girl a kiss.

The darling child preened.

Kyle entered the room next looking handsome in a kilt, waistcoat, and jacket, matching those worn by Stephen and Patrick, carrying a velvet jewelry case. "I have something for you."

Jillian accepted the box. "What is this?"

"Mother's pearls," he said, all nonchalant as if it wasn't a big deal. "She gave them to me, but you should have them."

Jillian tensed. *Mother didn't want me to have them.* "She meant them for your future wife."

"They're mine to do with as I please and I want you to wear them today. Consider them a wedding gift." He slew her with his famous pleading gaze—a look that always got him what he wanted. "Please."

"Okay. I'll return them after the wedding reception."

"No." He shook his head. "I mean for you to keep them. They're yours to give to your daughter at her wedding."

"Thank you. I'll cherish them always. Not because they belonged to our mother. But because you gave them to me." Jillian's eyes misted and her hand shook as she removed the short strand from the satin-lined case and handed the pearl necklace to Laurie. "Would you put this on for me?"

"Of course, hon." Laurie stepped in behind Jillian, slipped the string under the tartan sash and around Jillian's neck and then secured the silver clasp. "They're perfect with your gown."

Lovelier than the faux pearls she'd intended to wear. Jillian put the matching dangle earrings on and took one more glance in the mirror. "Okay, I'm ready."

The skirl of a bagpipe in the distance sent a chill across

Jillian's bare shoulders as she exited the rear of the inn with the others. The glint of the sun from a cloudless blue sky bore witness to a perfect September day. Had it truly been a year ago her journey began? The weird inconsistency in the flow of time from one century to the next while hopping through the time gate made the passage of real time, here in the current century, feel surreal.

"Shall we?" Kyle held out an arm, and she leaned on him as they strolled through the formal garden and beyond to the edge of the grand lawn.

The inn's gazebo sat in the center of the immense swath of meticulously groomed grass. Chairs covered in white linen fabric with forest green bows at the back had been placed to either side of a red cloth running the length to the white Victorian structure. Garlands of white roses, heather, and ivy twined the wooden pillars. And the semi-circular flowerbeds to either side were planted with Montauk daisies in full bloom. The effect was storybook quality.

Many of the townspeople from the Village of Anderson Creek were seated in the chairs. As Jillian approached the gathering, she felt like pinching herself to prove the reality of the day. They stopped upon nearing the back row.

Laurie kissed Jillian's cheek and squeezed her fingers. "Everything will be fine."

Then why were her insides doing an Irish jig? "I know. I thought Caitrina would be here. I'm not mad at her anymore."

"She would be if she could." Laurie handed Jillian the bridal bouquet of white heather tied with green velvet then did the slow, one-step-stop, one-step-stop, wedding march along the center aisle past those gathered to witness the nuptials. When she reached the halfway mark, Jillian urged Keita to follow Laurie down the aisle. The child dropped white rose petals on the red runner from a white wicker basket beribboned in green to match her and Laurie's dresses as she'd practiced the previous afternoon. She joined Mairi and Iain in the front row while Laurie climbed the one step to the gazebo and stood with Patrick, Stephen, and Duff facing the minister.

The piper, in full Highland dress, had moved closer to the gathering and began to play the wedding processional. All heads swiveled toward Jillian and Kyle.

Jillian's pulse quickened as she slowly paraded along the aisle on Kyle's arm. He gave a brotherly hug and kissed her cheek then moved to the side, joining Keita. Jillian inhaled a nervous breath, stepped up onto the wooden floor, and took her place beside her future husband.

Stephen looked so damn sexy in his kilt, waistcoat, and jacket. The thrill throbbing at her core had Jillian curling bare toes against the oak floorboards. Yeah. She was barefoot beneath her gown. And why not? Her Highlander was barefoot beneath his kilt. Other parts—more manly—were probably also bare. Heat radiated up from her chest, flushing her face, and she glanced sideways at Stephen. She could hardly wait for the wedding festivities to end so she could be alone with him.

He smirked, as if he knew the direction of her thoughts. Duff grinned. He'd better not have an inkling of what Jillian had been thinking. The boy wore a plaid kilt the same as the men in the bridal party, but with an ivory tunic. He held a matching tartan pillow upon which satin ties secured two gold rings etched with Celtic designs.

Once Laurie and Patrick were in position, they all faced the minister.

The minister cleared his throat. "Is there any among those gathered today with reason this couple should not wed?"

No one spoke, but a commotion from behind made Jillian spin around. One of the guests righted a fallen chair and assisted an elderly woman Jillian didn't recognize though thought familiar, to another seat. A chill passed over Jillian's bare shoulders and she glanced at Stephen. He shrugged and they once again faced the minister who seemed unfazed by the disturbance.

"Please, join hands." The minister clasped Jillian's right hand, gave her fingers a gentle squeeze, and placed her hand in Stephen's left palm then wrapped their hands together with a strip of MacLachlan tartan, tying a knot, binding their love together.

Jillian gazed into Stephen's eyes and felt the special connection they shared.

"We are gathered here today to…" The minister's voice droned. Stephen paid it little heed, too obsessed with the woman standing beside him. His chest swelled with pride. His Jillian was the comeliest creature he'd ever seen. And she looked delicious in that scandalous gown. Stephen ground his teeth. 'Twas difficult to become accustomed to the way modern people dressed. How much flesh they revealed.

He loved the sight of Jillian's skin, but he didn't care for the fact other men could also see her delicate, bare shoulders. Why hadn't she worn a shawl over the damn gown?

Jillian shot him a startled look and Patrick snickered. Had Stephen just growled?

The minister's lips twitched as if the man fought a smile. He cleared his throat and continued preaching about the significance of the vows they were about to exchange. Stephen didn't need a reminder. He understood, and was humbled by, the duties he would perform in his marriage with Jillian. He loved her and would always set her needs above his own.

"Stephen MacEwen of Anderson Creek, previously of Strathlachlan, Scotland, will you have this woman as your wedded wife?"

"I will." Stephen gazed at Jillian. "I pledge thee my troth."

"And you, Jillian O'Donnell of Anderson Creek, will you have this man as your wedded husband?"

"I will." She beamed at Stephen. "I pledge thee my troth, as you have to me."

"The rings?" The minister glanced at Patrick. Patrick removed the rings from the pillow Duff held forward and handed them to the minister. One held in each hand, the minister raised the gold bands for all to see, but spoke to

Stephen and Jillian. "Let these rings become a symbol of the love within your marriage—as a ring has no beginning and no end, so too will the love between you have no beginning and no end."

He released their bound hands and offered Stephen the smaller ring. Stephen withdrew a second ring from his sporran turned to his beloved and slid the ring with the emerald stone upon her delicate finger and then the gold wedding band. "I place these rings upon your third finger, Jillian, where the vein runs directly to your heart, so you shall always feel my love. And with this gold ring I do vow to thee the first cut of my meat, the first sip of my wine, and from this day only your name shall I cry out in the night and only into your eyes shall I smile each morning. I will be a shield for your back as you are for mine. Above and beyond this, I will cherish and honor you through this life and into the next."

Her eyes had widened at the sight of the emerald ring, but she quickly regained composure. "Wow. Thank you," Jillian whispered for his ears only. "By the way, nice vows."

She accepted the larger ring from the minister and gazed at Stephen. "With this ring, I take you into my heart at the rising of the moon and the setting of the stars. I will love you and be your forever partner through thick and thin. I will love you through all that may come our way in this time and in any other to which we may inadvertently travel."

The minister's brows furrowed then he shook his head as if shaking off confusion from Jillian's obscure vow. "I pronounce you man and wife," he said. "You may kiss the bride."

Stephen didn't need encouragement. He wrapped his arms around Jillian, pulled her close, and kissed her deep. The guests hooted.

"The bride and groom will receive guests in the front hall at the inn. Cocktails and hors d'oeuvres will be served shortly thereafter by the staff of *Le Petit Café* on the veranda," the minister announced.

A piper played a celebratory tune. Stephen grasped Jillian's hand and together they walked past those seated to where two additional pipers joined the first, then they, the bridal party, and all the guests followed the piping trio across the lawn, through the garden maze and formal gardens to the inn. In the front hall, the pipers headed for the bar, and Stephen stood beside his new wife—the love of his heart—to receive their guests along with Laurie, Patrick, Duff, and Keita.

"This is so much fun," Jillian enthused later, after dinner had been served and consumed and the tables removed for dancing.

Stephen whisked her around the floor, having quickly learned the modern way of dancing. "I am glad you are happy, sweetling."

As they passed the table displaying the wedding cake, one of the pipers, a hearty lad, stopped them. "It's time to cut the cake."

He played a short tune on his pipes. When finished, a dirk appeared in his hand. He handed it to Jillian. "It is custom here and about to cut the cake with a Scottish blade."

As she sliced the first piece, Stephen reached out and guided her hand. When their gazes met, his chest tightened. "'Tis ancient tradition."

"Of course." She smiled. "Our modern tradition is for you to feed me a piece and then I feed you one. Be careful not to get any on my gown. Please."

He placed a small piece of cake into her mouth. When she licked a crumb from her lip, his blood raged, and he grew hard. The consummation of their vows couldn't come soon enough.

The sight from the corner of his eye of an emerald-eyed, aged woman standing in the doorway made him whip his head to the side for a better view. *It couldn't be.* The cake Jillian meant for his mouth smashed into his cheek. Those in attendance roared with laughter. He chuckled, too, while Jillian cleaned his face with a damp cloth and gave him a chaste kiss on the lips.

"What made you glance away?" she asked.

"I thought I saw someone...familiar. Someone from the past." He scanned the chamber for the old woman, but she had vanished.

CHAPTER THIRTY

"What do you mean by someone from the past?" Jillian asked in a hushed tone. "Who?"

"Do you remember the Gray Women of the caves? I thought I saw the one with the emerald eyes standing by the doorway a moment ago." Stephen shook his head. "Ach. I must be mistaken."

"Perhaps it was the elder woman who arrived late to the ceremony," Jillian mused aloud. "I couldn't discern the color of her eyes, but she seemed eerily familiar."

"If 'twas the woman I am thinking of, she was the one that gifted you the fae blades."

"How would she have gotten here? Why would she have come?"

"The same way as us, I would venture. But the why?" Stephen flipped both hands palm up. "I cannot offer a reason."

"Do you think she wants the blades returned? They are museum quality and probably worth a mint. I never expected to keep them."

"What are you two plotting?" Laurie joined them. "I hope you're not planning your escape from the celebration. At least, not yet."

"Nae need to worry about *the bedding* ritual in this time period." Patrick winked at Jillian, offering his hand. "They are playing a slow song. How about dancing with the best man?"

"Of course." She allowed him to swirl her into the wake of other dancers and gave up the speculation about the emerald-eyed woman.

Stephen and Laurie also took to the dance floor. Shortly afterward, Jillian stood to the side with Brigit, the owner of the *Le Petit Café*, and Elspeth. "I want to thank you both for the wonderful job you did catering the cocktail hour and dinner. Everything was delicious."

Brigit beamed. "You're welcome."

Elspeth squeezed Jillian's hand. "We wanted to make your day special, so we took extra care with the menu."

Stephen danced past with Keita mounted on the tops of his feet. The child laughed and grinned—a lopsided, deformed smile, but one of joy. Jillian's chest filled with warmth, her love for Keita only second to that which she felt for Stephen.

"He is good with the *bairns*," Elspeth said. "He will make a terrific father."

"I believe so," Jillian agreed. "Though I'm nervous about the adoptive proceedings since he—"

"You will both do fine." Elspeth tilted her head toward Brigit in warning, reminding Jillian the French woman didn't know about the oddities of those living in her community.

Around ten o'clock, Mairi escorted the yawning Keita and Duff upstairs to bed. It was two hours past the bedtime Jillian had mandated upon their arrival in Anderson Creek, but an exception had been made for this one day. Jillian and Stephen were to stay in one of the guest cottages for their wedding night. From experience, Jillian knew the celebration would last far into the wee hours of the next morning with much whisky being consumed.

"Do I see a glimmer in your eye, sweetling?" Stephen asked. "Are you ready to become my wife in truth?"

"Absolutely. Let's sneak away."

At the cottage door, Stephen picked Jillian up and cradled her in strong arms. She gave him a questioning look. "'Tis believed evil spirits inhabit the thresholds of doors, you ken?"

"You don't believe that. Do you?"

"Nae, but it gives me a reason to hold you in my arms. Not that I need an excuse." He strode through the living room and into the bedroom and gently laid her on their wedding bed, which had been strewn with all sorts of flower petals.

Jillian sneezed. "I think someone must have accidently included ragweed with the other blooms." She scrunched her nose to hold back another sneeze. "But I have an idea. Since everyone will be partying at the inn until the wee hours, how about we take a blanket out into the garden and enjoy the waxing moon?"

Pillow in hand, and with nothing but a tartan blanket clasped by Stephen's emerald brooch wrapped around her, Jillian strolled hand-in-hand with him to a grassy spot within the garden surrounded by evergreen shrubs.

"The perfect place for a tryst with one's wife," he said, a suggestive grin curving his lips.

He placed another tartan on the grassy padding and Jillian added the pillow then sat. She carefully removed the brooch holding the wool in place. "By the way, thank you for my beautiful emerald ring."

"You are welcome." Stephen grinned. "I was pleased to learn the wee gems I brought with me from the past are of great value in this time. You are wed to a wealthy man."

"I love you despite the fault."

Stephen's lips pursed. "Fault?"

To make up for the dig, she slowly unwrapped the fabric, first revealing one breast, then the other. She felt awkward playing the vamp, but when she exposed the cleft between her legs, Stephen's quick inhale of breath made the striptease worth the rush of nervous heat flushing her neck and face.

"Ach, lass, you are beautiful in the moonlight." His voice was gravelly with desire…

For her. She preened at the sexy sound. Nipples pebbled and aching, she arched her back, giving him a better view.

Stephen wasn't one to neglect the offering Jillian set before him. He quickly stripped and knelt beside the nymph he married. Certainly, she was a forest sprite of ancient times sent to seduce him.

"Thank you for becoming my wife."

Jillian blushed and stretched her arms out to him. He slipped into the embrace and held her close, kissing her hair, her face, her lips. Stephen took the kiss deeper, loving the rasp of their tongues performing a mating dance.

"I love you," Jillian whispered near his ear after their lips parted and he pressed a kiss to the base of her throat.

He slid lower to lave a pert breast, sucking the pebbled nipple into his mouth. Jillian arched into him, and he growled. The wet nipple popped out of his mouth and she giggled. Had the nerve to laugh at him.

She brushed fingertips over his hair as if to tame him. "I need to ask you something, I should have asked you before we got married."

Unease crept across the back of his neck. "What is it?"

"Will you be disappointed if we don't have a child of our own? If for some reason I can't have a baby?"

Disappoint him? So that was what she feared. "Nae, sweetling. Childbearing is risky. I lost my mother to the fever. And then my wee brother also passed. I would understand completely if you are unwilling to go through birthing a *bairn.*"

"It's not that I don't want to have a child. Having a baby is much less dangerous in this time than it was in the past. It's just that there is a chance… Well, some women are unable to have babies. What if I am one of those?"

"Nae worries, lass." He squeezed and released her fingers.

"But isn't having a son important to you?"

"Creating a son—or a wee lass—with you would give me great joy. Whether that happens or nae, I am happy to call

Keita daughter and Duff and Malcolm sons."

Jillian lunged for him, rolled him over, and kissed him with a frenzy that left Stephen breathless and more than ready to perform his husbandly duty. He placed a palm on each side of her head and kissed her hard. She slid onto his erection, and he bucked. The exquisite pleasure near to pain. He needed…

She didn't leave him wanting. She rode him to a world full of light. Love mingling with the pleasure pulsing along his cock. They reached the pinnacle simultaneously and plunged over the edge with their lips fused, Stephen's seed pumping deep into Jillian's womb.

He lingered within the bliss for a spell, satiated, limbs entwined with his love's, her breath against his chest. Then it occurred to him that he gripped her too tightly, but he couldn't seem to let her go. He loosened his hold. "Are you all right, sweetling?"

"Heavenly."

He kissed her and rolled to the side, giving her space to breathe. They lay hip against hip, holding hands, enjoying the evening sky, a slight breeze cooling their skin.

Suddenly, Jillian stiffened beside him. Sat bolt upright.

"What's wrong?" He rose to a sitting position, too.

"Was that a giggle?" Her gaze scanned the shadows. "I feel as if someone watches us."

"I dinnae think anyone is there, sweetling."

"*My God! Emerald eyes.* Of course. Why hadn't I thought of it sooner?" She gripped his arm. "You saw Caitrina. She must have posed as the hag in the past and the elderly woman at the reception and possibly at the ceremony."

Caitrina didn't allow the glamour of invisibility to falter as she peered through the shrubs at Jillian and Stephen. She hadn't meant to make the silly sound, to give herself away. The giggle had slipped from smirking lips. And how could she have avoided the utterance?

She won! She shot her arms in the air and swiveled her hips, performing a victory dance.

Besides, the excitement of witnessing Stephen and Jillian conceive a new life made her giddy. She'd be like an aunt to the child. That is, if she were to stay on earth. But alas, the challenge was now complete, and she was free to return to *Tir-nan-Og* as a royal princess.

Her greatest desire fulfilled.

Then why did sadness overcome her as she faded into the vanishing, leaving Jillian and Stephen alone to enjoy the remainder of their wedding night?

CHAPTER THIRTY-ONE

*C*aitrina emerged into substance in the courtyard behind *The Celtic Image* shop. Douglas had outfitted the space like a medieval list. 'Twas where he trained wealthy men who wanted to pretend they were sixteenth century warriors. They participated in tournaments on weekends, calling themselves reenactors. Men hadn't changed much throughout time.

She sensed Douglas watching from the shadows.

"Why did you leave the reception?" she asked.

"Why should I have stayed?" His voice slid over her, triggering desire and other emotions better left hushed. "I offered best wishes to the bride and groom."

"I was there."

He stepped into the beam of light shining down from the brass fixture hanging on the wall beside the shop's door. He'd been working out and wore naught but a pair of snug fitness shorts and a moist sheen on his tanned skin. "As yourself or someone else, princess?"

She ignored the taunt and insinuation in his tone. "I wanted—"

He grabbed her by the shoulders, pulled her close and covered her mouth with the softest, sensual lips she'd had the pleasure to kiss. Wet and deep, his kiss was all-consuming, his tongue exploring the moist recesses of her mouth. She became liquid within his arms. Wanting and needing what only he could provide. When he leaned away, he left her panting, wet and needy.

"Marry me." His sword hand encircled her wrist, thumb over her frantically beating pulse. "I feel your love for me."

In an attempt to harness wayward emotions, Caitrina twirled her fingers in the hair on his chest, stalling for time. She gazed into amber eyes. In return, he searched her gaze, seeking the answer she couldn't give. "I cannot wed you."

His lips thinned as expected. Annoyance darkening his eyes. "One of these days you'll give me the right answer." He jerked away and leaned against the shop door, arms crossed over a broad chest.

Regret seared the human portion of her halfling heart. Saying goodbye to him would surely be the hardest thing she'd ever need do. There was no place for him in *Tir-nan-Og*. She could never wed a mortal man.

Then her thoughts brightened. She now had the freedom to come and go as she pleased. She could visit him on occasion. Then a thought as chilling as a winter frost froze her blood. Caitrina remembered how he seemed to fancy a certain red-headed singer from a Scottish tribal band that frequented the Highland Gathering at Grandfather Mountain every July.

Would Douglas follow the singer from gig to gig, or find someone else to mate with while Caitrina enjoyed the pleasures of Faerie paradise? Would he give up on their love? Abandon their bond? Marry another?

She stepped into him, hoping he would embrace her, send her away with his taste on her lips.

"Nae worries, love. I'll keep asking until you agree." He rubbed gentle fingers over the furrow in her brow. "What has you vexed? Surely not my desire for us to spend the rest of our lives together?"

"I need to go away for a time."

"You mustn't." He roughly gripped her upper arms and

shook. "The queen will never let you return to earth. You will become her pet, kept in a luxuriously decadent cage."

"What ken you of the queen or my future?" Caitrina raised her chin. *How could he ken anything about the queen? Or her eternal life? He was naught but a mere mortal.*

"More than I can share at this time." He dropped his hands, curling them into fists at his sides.

The lure of *Tir-nan-Og* called to her. She needed to leave Douglas before she made a regrettable mistake and agreed to marry the damn man and became rooted to earth.

"Caitrina..." Her name seemed torn from him. His voice and amber gaze pleaded for her to remain.

She hesitated, fae and human halves warring. She couldn't stay. Unable to deal with the onslaught of emotion, Caitrina faded. He reached for her. Before his touch could change her mind, she vanished.

"Damn your foolishness! The queen won't let you return." His bitter words sent a burst of fear through her veins as she traveled on the breeze. Would his warning ring true?

She reemerged just beyond the garden gate on the faerie mound.

"Bravo! Bravo!" The queen clapped. "Such a touching scene.

The fine hairs at the back of Caitrina's neck bristled. "You have been watching."

"Always, *princess*. I suppose I must call you *that* now. You may have won the challenge and the right to return to *Tir-nan-Og* as royalty, howbeit..." The queen held up a pampered hand to stop the retort ready on Caitrina's tongue. "You will never have what you truly desire."

"And what would that be, pray tell?"

"Love eternal."

"Ha! I dinnae want any such thing. I have nae time for such drivel." Caitrina laughed although it sounded forced even to her ear. Her fae half found the queen's declaration humorous. Faeries, as everyone kens, are incapable of love. But she was also half human and in love with a human.

Totally and completely in love with Douglas.

"Then you will not mind that your father has betrothed you to my son."

A bolt of fear—*excitement*—pierced Caitrina's belly. "That cannot be."

"'Tis true. Dugaid signed the contract with Prince Torgil in fae blood. Your fate is irreversibly sealed."

"Nae! 'Tis impossible. My father wouldn't do that to me."

"Oh, but he did." The queen smiled like the Cheshire cat. "I am sure the Dark Prince will give you a wee amount of time to adjust to the happy tidings. Have no fear though, he will come for you if you refuse to go to him."

The queen's smile dripped vengeance and, with a flash of silver light, she vanished into the nether.

Caitrina stumbled to the garden and leaned against the gate for support. What a fool she'd been. This was not how things were supposed to go. She was to have lived the rest of eternity free of all encumbrances in *Tir-nan-Og*. Not become the chattel of an overindulged, domineering fae prince. 'Twould have been better to remain on earth as she'd been— in service to Mairi MacLachlan and free to lovingly spar with Douglas.

Five months later
Charlotte, North Carolina

"Let's go see our little girl." Jillian opened the door and they entered Keita's hospital room. Jillian kissed the child's forehead and took a seat in the chair next to the bed. Stephen and Duff chose to stand.

"Hey, sweet pea," she murmured to the imp lying so quiet on the mattress.

Mossy green eyes, a tad glassy, glanced her way. The poor dear appeared so tiny amidst the white sheets of the hospital bed. And with the white cap on her head and the bandages covering the better part of her face, all Jillian could see were those sweet, compelling eyes and pert nose.

An abrupt knock on the door preceded the entrance of Jasmine, the pediatric nurse assigned to Keita for the morning shift. "How is our patient doing?"

"We hoped you would tell us," Stephen said.

Jasmine smiled and went about examining the child.

"Her vitals are good." The nurse added a small glass bottle of clear liquid to one of the ports lower on the intravenous tubing in addition to a new fluids bag. "This should help with pain. She's been advised not to try to talk. I hope you will keep that in mind while you visit with her today."

"Of course. We understand." Jillian clasped Keita's hand and received a faint squeeze in return. The child comforting her. Her eyes misted.

"Please keep your stay short so she can rest. I'll be back later to check on her." Jasmine gripped the doorknob. "If you have any questions, feel free to stop by the nurse's station." She opened the door and departed.

"Well, sweet pea, we'll talk and you can listen. How's that?"

"Stephen said we can get a puppy when you come home," Duff blurted.

Stephen shot the lad a warning glance.

"Well, you did say you would think about us getting a dog."

"And I will. Think about it." Stephen chuckled.

Jillian was truly amazed at how easily Stephen and the children had adapted to modern life. The transition wasn't always smooth, but amazing just the same.

"So, Keita. I thought we would celebrate your birthday after you're completely healed," Jillian said, wanting the child to have something special to look forward to while recovering from her surgery.

"We are changelings," Duff said. "No one kens when we were born."

"You are not changelings," Stephen said. "You are our *bairns* as is Malcolm."

Jillian sniffled to keep tears at bay. Both she and Stephen loved the children. She rubbed her rounded belly with her free hand. The children would be raised as brothers and sister to the child she would birth in another four months. "As soon as Keita is well, we will see a man who will make the adoption official."

"Then I want to have a birthday, too." The boy's grin was contagious.

"So you will." She smiled at Stephen and he returned her admiration. "When Keita comes home from the hospital, you can both pick days from the calendar to claim as your birthdate."

Stephen clasped Keita's other hand and both he and Jillian grasped Duff's hands, creating a circle of love.

EPILOGUE

Five years later
Whispering Pines Inn, Anderson Creek, North Carolina

*J*illian swayed with the music as Keita swirled past, dancing with Duff. Stephen came up from behind and wrapped strong arms around her waist.

"Let us slip away." His breath teased the fine hairs at the back of her neck.

"We can't leave our daughter's birthday *ceilidh*. She'll only be eleven once."

"She will understand."

"No she won't. She's too young."

"Thank the good Lord. I dinnae ken what I will do when she starts dating. I shudder at the thought. She is too comely by far, and I have seen what the other fathers in the reenactment group go through with their *teenage* daughters."

"Promise you won't challenge the fellow Keita selects to a sword fight."

"Pfff! 'Tis a thought, but I would most likely first need to teach the lad which end of the blade is pointed and sharp."

Jillian turned within his arms and planted a sweet kiss on his lips. He took it deeper.

"Ahem." Patrick interrupted.

Laurie joined them. "'Tis time to cut the cake."

As they approached the table, five-year old Malcolm burst into the room, circled the dessert table, and skidded to a stop at a stern look from Stephen. Four-year-old Tevin followed in hot pursuit, tripped over Malcolm's outstretched leg, and banged into the table. A pedestal plate of cookies fell over, some of the cookies landing on the cake. Malcolm smirked and Tevin looked mortified.

Oh dear. A grim frown curved the lips Jillian had just been kissing. Stephen would scold the boys. There would be feigned tears on Malcolm's part. Real tears from Tevin.

"Sorry, Da," Malcolm said in a rush.

Keita hurried over and squatted in front of Tevin, offering *sisterly love* as she often did when Malcolm got the better of his younger brother. She grasped Tevin's rounded shoulders. "It's okay. You didn't do anything wrong." She reached up to the table, grabbed a cookie, swiped it through the cake icing, and took a bite. "See, Tev. Tastes great."

Malcolm followed her example and popped an iced-cookie in his mouth. "Yummy."

Tevin's eyes widened, and Keita handed him a coated cookie. He shyly accepted her offering and bit into the sugary treat. He smiled adoringly at his big sister.

Jillian bit back a chuckle, and waved her hands at the boys. "Off with the two of you, but stay close."

"Let's play warrior and slay dragons in the garden," Malcolm suggested.

Tevin nodded and the boys trotted out of the room. All previous offences forgotten.

Laurie burst out laughing. "You have your hands full, Jillian."

Duff sailed past with three wooden swords tucked under an arm. "I'll watch after them."

"Keep them away from the garden gate and faerie mound," Stephen warned, as if Duff wasn't aware of the dangers.

Jillian glanced at Stephen and they shared a loving smile. They adored their four children.

On the morning after the party, at home, Jillian woke half-sprawled across Stephen's chest, a hard-on poking her hip. She shifted her weight, and received a deep-throated growl in return.

She laughed and extended a leg over his waist, rising up, making ready to ride him. "I think you like it."

"Oh, Aye. Good morrow to you, lass." His blue gaze burned before he captured her lips, tongue delving deep for a tantalizing kiss.

"Mmm. I love waking like this every morning. Have you been awake long?"

"Long enough to be mesmerized by your beauty."

Perhaps they would conceive another child. They had room in their hearts for more than four. She wrapped a hand around his cock and guided him to the entrance of her womb. With a soft chuckle, she slid over his flesh, and together they soared around the universe.

As they always would.

STORY NOTE

Smoo Cave in Durness, Scotland provided partial inspiration for the caves of the Gray Women. Geothermal hot springs exist in England and Wales, but not in Scotland to the knowledge of the author. If you know of hot springs located in Scotland, Dawn Marie would love to hear about them.

author@DawnMarieHamilton.com

Just Within a Highland Mist

A Highland Gardens Novella
The 5th tale in the series.

Coming Soon
from
Dawn Marie Hamilton

Turn the page for a sneak peek…

CHAPTER ONE

Present day
North Carolina

*M*ist snaked over the hills and vales of the Blue Ridge Mountains settling on the Village of Anderson Creek and surrounding woods like a shroud. Emily stumbled through ever-thickening fog, trying to avoid the slap of tree branches obscured by vaporous wisps, fear pressing against a constricted chest. How had she lost the boys?

Malcolm was too bold for a seven-year-old and the year younger Tevin followed his adopted brother into every unfortunate escapade. She'd only turned away for a moment to check her smart phone for a signal—a nonexistent signal—and the boys jumped upon the opportunity to bolt through the woods away from her, brandishing wooden swords more than likely against the beast they claimed to track—an orange dragon.

"Life or death!" The Clan MacLachlan battle cry spat in the distance from the children's lips hung heavy on the humid air.

Emily raced in the direction she believed the bellow came from and tripped over an aboveground root, losing balance.

"Dammit to hell." She slipped on decaying leaves and banged an elbow on the trunk of an old oak; the jolt of shock lit up her nervous system. "Ouch, ouch, ouch!" She danced around and shook out her tingling arm, then taking a moment to regain composure, leaned her forehead against the rough bark of an old oak and inhaled a deep calming breath. "Please let me find the boys."

Jillian and Stephen MacEwen would never forgive her if anything bad happened to their sons while she babysat them. The sharp snap of a twig sent her off in an altogether different direction. How had the walk from the inn to the MacEwen's log cabin become such a nightmare? Normally, Emily knew the way through the woods to and from the MacLachlan and MacEwen homes, *Foxgloves* garden center, and the *Whispering Pines Inn*, but the fog made everything appear different—menacing.

Stepping away from the tree, she scanned the immediate surroundings. Unable to discern a path, she chewed on a chapped lip, feeling turned around, unsure of her whereabouts in relation to that of the boys or to the places of safety. To where had the boys run?

"Malcolm! Tev! Where are you?" she called into the fog.

Tevin's little boy shriek made her heart jam into her throat. She sprinted in the direction of the frightening screech, ignoring the sting of branches grazing her face as she darted past haunting tree after tree.

She slid to a stop at the base of the forbidden mound just beyond the garden gate of *Foxglove's* display garden. Like with the eye of a storm, no mist encroached upon the knoll. Malcolm stood at the far edge, feet apart, wooden sword held forward in two firm hands, tip pointed toward Tevin, whose feet were planted on the hilltop in a wide stance, sword held in a similar manner although *his* hands trembled. Emily had been warned numerous times by Iain MacLachlan, chief of the local branch of Clan MacLachlan and her boss at the inn, to never, ever, not under any circumstance, step foot onto the mound. And certainly she wasn't to permit any of the

MacLachlan or MacEwen children in her care to go there. She'd never understood why. Never asked why. Had thought the warning silly.

Dread stole her breath and she inhaled sharply. "Tevin, come here."

"I don't want to go away and fight the dragon alone," he groused.

"It's okay, Tev. You don't have to fight dragons. Come with me. We'll cut through the garden to Laurie and Patrick's house. I bet your cousins have hot chocolate."

Tevin didn't move, didn't say anything, didn't look at her. He kept a level stare on his brother.

"Malcolm, tell him to come to me."

"No. He's on a quest to kill a dragon."

"Oh, for pity sake. Enough of this." She'd just drag him off. Patience gone, Emily stepped toward the mound and into some sort of barrier. She pressed a finger into it and released. *Snap.* The obstruction seemed to be made of clear…plastic wrap? She moved to the right and then to the left, but the barrier remained. She couldn't get through it, as if the mound was encased in a clear plastic bubble. None of this made sense.

She glanced over a shoulder. Through the garden, lights brightened the windows of the MacLachlan family's house on one end and the garden center's gift shop at the other, but neither building was close enough that anyone inside would hear a call for help. She glanced at her phone. Halleluiah! She had a signal. Without removing her gaze from Tevin, she rang the house phone. The phone rang and rang. No answer.

Hu…hu-hooooo. The eerie call of a barred owl unnerved Emily even more.

"Please, Tev, please come here," she pleaded. He ignored her. There must be a way to get him through the barrier.

Perhaps his mother was still at the garden center even though it should have closed an hour ago. Emily rang the number for the gift shop. "Oh, thank God. Jillian, I'm with the boys in the woods near the mound. We got lost. The fog is so thick. I lost the boys. Then I found them. I can't get Tevin to come to me. He's on the mound just beyond the garden gate. Some sort of…oh, I don't know…barrier is keeping me from going to him. I don't know what to do." *Dammit. I'm rambling.*

The, "Oh, shit," coming from the phone's tinny speaker confirmed her fears.

"Tev, your mom's on the phone. Come talk to her. Pah-lease."

He touched her with his gaze, shook his head, blue eyes solemn, damp blond curls stuck to cherub cheeks.

Suddenly, tiny sparkling lights flashed about, darting to and fro, settling high in the branches of the one tree on the mound—a beautiful sight. Tevin looked up. His eyes widened in amazement. And…and the little boy vanished.

August, 1521
Fir-wood, Scottish Highlands

A snagged thread in the fabric of time sent a ripple through the earth realm felt only by those sensitive to such things. Munn stopped in his tracks and perked a pointed ear. Did he hear the murmuring of a new changeling in the wood?

He desperately wished to ignore the woeful sound, but something unbeknownst to him drew him to the *bairn*. He whirled onto the *Sithichean Sluaigh*, the knoll of the Fae, spinning in circles, sucking last year's fallen leaves into the whirlwind propelling him until he slowed to a stop.

This wee male was different than the other *bairns* of the wood. Dressed different. Cleaner. Munn scratched a whiskered chin. He should flee. Not get involved.

The blond lad stood. Stared with narrowed eyes. "Munn?"

"How do you ken my name?" He'd never seen this lad afore.

The *bairn* sniffled and wiped his nose on the sleeve of his tunic. "My cousin Allison tells stories about you. You're the Clan MacLachlan brownie. Your duty is to watch over the clan."

Munn puffed out his chest. *I am legendary.*

"You look just like Allison said." The lad canted his head to the side. "You've pointy green boots, pointed ears, and a pointed green cap. You even have a scrunched brown face with whiskers."

"Humph." Munn frowned. "What be your name, lad? Who be your father?"

"Tevin." The *bairn* raised his chin. His gaze direct for one so wee. "My name is Tevin. My father is Stephen. Stephen MacEwen. He wouldn't want you to hurt me."

"Stephen's son?" *For Danu's sake.*

The wee time traveler nodded.

"Nary a one will harm you be you in my care." Munn tried to reassure the lad. "Where is your father?"

"I'm alone." Tevin squatted and picked up a wooden practice sword perhaps dropped upon arrival. He sliced the blade through the air. "Is this ancient Scotland? I'm on a quest to slay a dragon."

"Ach. A dragon you say?" Munn dithered. Should he impart the *bairn's* whereabouts? Might frighten the lad to ken he'd traveled through time. What should Munn do with the lad? Stephen would want him to protect his son. 'Twas obvious the *Sithichean* were involved in this mischief. But why would the Fae guide a *bairn* from the future to the past? "You are in Scotland, but not ancient Scotland. There are nae dragons here. By the bye, how did you get here?"

"My brother, Malcolm, pushed me onto the faerie hill and I traveled back through time." The *bairn* pursed his lips. "I guess not far enough."

Maclay? Damn that villain and his spawn. Even in death, Maclay was a boil upon Clan MacLachlan. Munn kenned the man's *bairn* would come to nae good. Stephen should never have championed the lad after his father's death and raised him as his own. Still…one of the Fae must be involved for the magic of the faerie hill to thrust a being through time. Especially such a wee being.

"Are you sure there aren't any dragons? He's orange," Tevin persisted.

Munn jerked his gaze to the *bairn*, annoyed by the interruption to his deliberation. He hated the need to think, but he must figure out what to do about the lad. "Who's orange?"

"The dragon. The one I'm destined to slay."

"I told you. There are nae dragons here."

"But Allison and Malcolm said—"

Munn held up a hand. "You best forget about dragons and come with me to Castle Lachlan. The chief will ken what to do with you. And I dinnae want to hear any more about the winged beasts."

Tevin fell into step behind Munn. "What about the little faeries that brought me here? They have wings."

Munn stopped short, and the *bairn* slammed into his back. He spun around and righted the lad. "What faeries?"

"I thought they were dragonflies at first, but they're really cool. They're girls with wings. They brought me here. There was one with green wings and another with purple and—"

"Whist! Needs be I think."

Pixies? Why were pixies sifting time? What mischief did the ebony-haired Marcail and her pesky clan ponder?"

Present Day
Anderson Creek, NC

Emily gaped at the empty mound. "Where did Tevin go?"

"Don't know." Malcolm's darting gaze made her stomach drop to her knees. She hurried around the edge of the knoll to where he stood, a smirk on his face. He knew more than he'd admit.

"Yes you do. Your mom is on the way. She'll want to

know where Tevin went. Tell me where your brother is hiding before she gets here. Once we find him, we can go home."

"No!" He slammed two palms against her chest and shoved hard.

She propelled backward through the barrier as if it was nothing more than a bubble of soap. The cell phone flew from her hand, and she landed on her butt, the moist grass of the mound seeping through her leggings. "You little brat!"

Wow. He'd always been a handful, but she'd never called Malcolm a brat before. *Shit.* He seemed hostile—dark. The look in his eyes almost maniacal.

She pushed her palms against the ground to rise, but hesitated. Those little sparkling lights flitted about her. Like lighting bugs. No—

Larger. Dragonflies? Perhaps—

Tee teehee hee. Tee teehee hee. Tee teehee hee. Feminine voices surrounded her with tinkling giggles.

"Who's there?" Emily's voice cracked. She leapt to her feet and whirled about, but didn't see anyone other than the gloating Malcolm.

Then everything went crazy. Spun. Or was she spinning?

She placed a hand on her stomach as if it was possible to hold nausea at bay. The ground fell out from beneath her. A scream caught in a suddenly parched throat. She plummeted downward into nothingness. Down...down...down, she dropped. What the—

A sonic boom made her head throb. She slapped her hands over ringing ears.

Something pulled her horizontally toward a bright white light. What was there? *Who* was there? She wished she could backpedal. The light burst like fireworks into bright colors. Red, orange, yellow, green, blue, indigo and violet—the colors of the rainbow.

Her vision dulled to gray then went black.

Just Beyond the Garden Gate
A Highland Gardens Novel
Highland Gardens Series #1

by Dawn Marie Hamilton

Time Travel Fantasy Romance

Determined to regain her royal status, a banished faerie princess accepts a challenge from the High-Queen of the Fae to unite an unlikely couple while the clan brownie attempts to thwart her.

Passion ignites when a faerie-shove propels burned-out business consultant Laurie Bernard through the garden gate, back through time, and into the embrace of Patrick MacLachlan. The arrogant clan chief doesn't know what to make of the lass in his arms, especially when he recognizes the brooch she wears as the one his stepmother wore when she and his father disappeared.

With the fae interfering at every opportunity, the couple must learn to trust one another while they battle an enemy clan, expose a traitor within their midst and discover the true fate of the missing parents. Can they learn the most important truth—love transcends time?

Journey from the lush gardens of the Blue Ridge Mountains of North Carolina to the Scottish Highlands of 1509 with *Just Beyond the Garden Gate*.

Just Once in a Verra Blue Moon
A Highland Gardens Novel
Highland Gardens Series #2

by Dawn Marie Hamilton

Time Travel Fantasy Romance

What happens when a twenty-first century business executive is expected to fulfill a prophecy given at the birth of a sixteenth-century seer? Of course, he must raise his sword in her defense.

Believing women only want him for his wealth, Finn MacIntyre doesn't trust any woman to love him. When, during Scottish Highland games, faerie magic sends him back in time to avenge the brutal abduction of his time-traveling cousin, he learns he's the subject of a fae prophecy.

Elspeth MacLachlan, the beloved clan seer, is betrothed to a man she dislikes and dreams of the man prophesized at her birth, only to find him in the most unexpected place— facedown in the mud.

With the help of fae allies, they must overcome the treachery set to destroy them to claim a love that transcends time.

Journey from the lush gardens of the Blue Ridge Mountains of North Carolina to the Scottish Highlands of 1511 with *Just Once in a Verra Blue Moon.*

Just in Time for a Highland Christmas
A Highland Gardens Novella
Highland Gardens Series #3

by Dawn Marie Hamilton

Time Travel Fantasy Romance

Can a determined brownie craft a perfect match?

When the Chief of Clan MacLachlan travels to the stronghold of his feuding neighbors to fetch his betrothed, she is gone. A year later, she is still missing. Making life more vexing, a band of reivers are stealing clan cattle, leaving behind destruction. Archibald MacLachlan determines to capture them and administer harsh punishment.

Though once in love with the man, Isobell Lamont refuses to wed her clan's enemy. After running away she joins the band of reivers set on revenge.

Can Archibald forgive the raven-haired beauty? Will a journey through time bring them together for a Highland Christmas?

Journey from the Scottish Highlands of 1511 to the Blue Ridge Mountains of North Carolina with *Just in Time for a Highland Christmas.*

Twelvetide
Twelve Nights of Highland Magic
An Enchanted Highlands Holiday Novella

by Dawn Marie Hamilton

Time Travel Romance

He has twelve nights to gain her love.
She has twelve nights to save his soul.

Fulfilling a childhood promise, Ashley Dumont returns to an ancient Druid garden in the Black Hills of Scotland on the eve of the winter solstice—a time when magic hums and the veil between realms thins and tears, allowing all manner of supernatural creatures through. Will the ghost who claimed to be her destiny still be there?

Caelan Innes awaits her arrival. Unjustly murdered in the sixteenth century, a second chance at life depends on this woman. The Druids grant them the twelve nights of Yule to find love and save Cael's soul. Will a trip through time and the treachery of enemies make the sacrifice too dear?

Sea Panther
A Crimson Storm Series Novel

by Dawn Marie Hamilton

Paranormal Romance

2013 Golden Heart® finalist for Best Paranormal Romance

Can love mend a fractured soul?

After evading arrest for Jacobite activities, Scottish nobleman Robert MacLachlan turns privateer. A Caribbean Voodoo priestess curses him to an eternal existence as a vampire shifter torn between the dual natures of a Florida panther and an immortal blood-thirsting man. For centuries, he seeks to reverse the black magic whilst maintaining his honor. Cruising the twenty-first century Atlantic, he becomes shorthanded to sail his 90-foot yacht, *Sea Panther*. The last thing he wants is a female crewmember and the call of her blood.

Although she swore never to sail again after her father died in a sailing accident, Kimberly Scot answers the captain's crew wanted ad to escape a hit man. She's lost everything, her fiancé, her job, and most of her money, along with money belonging to her ex-clients. A taste of Kimberly's blood convinces Robert she is the one woman who can claim the panther's heart. To break the curse, they travel back in time to where it all began—Jamaica 1715.

Future Works:

Time Travel Fantasy Romance

Just Within a Highland Mist
Highland Gardens Series Novella

Just His Fae Kiss
Highland Gardens Series Novel

Paranormal Romance

Raven's Revenge
Crimson Storm Series Novel

Dear Readers,

Thank you for reading *Just Wait For Me!* I hope you enjoyed Jillian and Stephen's tale.

If you love time travel romance, consider joining the **Hearts Trough Time** closed Facebook group and/or Website where myself and several other time travel romance authors gather with readers to discuss our favorite genre—time travel romance.

Join the discussions at:

Facebook: www.facebook.com/groups/heartsthroughtime
Website: www.heartsthroughtime.com

Hope to greet you there.

~Dawn Marie

ABOUT THE AUTHOR

Dawn Marie Hamilton dares you to dream. She is a 2013 RWA® Golden Heart® Finalist who pens Scottish-inspired fantasy and paranormal romance. Some of her tales are rife with mischief-making faeries, brownies, and other fae creatures. More tormented souls—shape shifters, vampires, and maybe a zombie or two—stalk across the pages of other stories. When not writing, she's cooking, gardening, or paddling the local creeks with her husband.

Visit Dawn Marie on the web at:
dawnmariehamilton.blogspot.com
facebook.com/authorDawnMarieHamilton

www.ingramcontent.com/pod-product-compliance
Lightning Source LLC
Chambersburg PA
CBHW020553180626
46810CB00007B/2489